utche

ron cha

approached the window w

curtain aside.

There, sitting on the external sill, was a large black bird.

Bansi's first feeling was one of relief, but very quickly caution overtook her. She opened the window just a fraction, not enough to let the bird squeeze through.

'Is that you?' she asked quietly.

The raven tilted its head to one side and stared at her. It blinked slowly, once.

'No, it's someone who *isn't* me,' it said, sarcasm dripping from its beak. ''*Course* it's bloomin' me. Who'd you think it was . . . ?'

Also by John Dougherty, and published by Random House Children's Books:

In Young Corgi Yearling Books for junior readers:

BANSI O'HARA AND THE BLOODLINE PROPHECY

'A highly entertaining read with plenty of comic relief to the book's darker moments' *Carousel*

'A romping good read' *INIS*

In Young Corgi Books for primary readers:

ZEUS ON THE LOOSE!

'Energetic and page-turning' *INK magazine*

SHORTLISTED FOR THE BRANFORD BOASE AWARD

ZEUS TO THE RESCUE!

'Instantly involving, constantly hilarious . . . Zeus is a superb character'

Andy Stanton (author of *Mr Gum*), *Junior Education Magazine*

ZEUS SORTS IT OUT

Coming soon in Young Corgi!

NITERACY HOUR

'Unique . . . a great example of the quirky humour that younger readers enjoy'

Children's Books in Ireland

SHORTLISTED FOR THE NOTTINGHAM CHILDREN'S BOOK AWARD

JACK SLATER, MONSTER INVESTIGATOR

'A clever story, cleverly told' *Carousel*

SHORTLISTED FOR THE OTTAKER'S CHILDREN'S BOOK PRIZE

JACK SLATER AND THE WHISPER OF DOOM

'A rollicking adventure . . . plot by the bucketload, an interesting world to investigate, scary monsters, a snivelling rival, quirky humour, lessons to be learned, and everyone's home again in time for breakfast' *Bookbag*

For more information about John Dougherty:

www.visitingauthor.com

Bansi O'Hara
and the Edges of Hallowe'en

John Dougherty

CORGI YEARLING BOOKS

BANSI O'HARA AND THE EDGES OF HALLOWE'EN
A CORGI YEARLING BOOK 978 0 440 86792 0

Published in Great Britain by Corgi Yearling,
an imprint of Random House Children's Books
A Random House Group Company

This edition published 2011

1 3 5 7 9 10 8 6 4 2

The Random House Group Limited supports the Forest Stewardship Council® (FSC®), the leading international forest certification organization. All our titles that are printed on Greenpeace approved FSC® certified paper carry the FSC® logo. Our paper procurement policy can be found at www.randomhouse.co.uk/environment.

Set in Palatino by Falcon Oast Graphic Art Ltd.

Corgi Yearling Books are published by Random House Children's Books,
61–63 Uxbridge Road, London W5 5SA

www.**kidsatrandomhouse**.co.uk
www.**totallyrandombooks**.co.uk
www.**randomhouse**.co.uk

Addresses for companies within The Random House Group Limited
can be found at: www.randomhouse.co.uk/offices.htm

THE RANDOM HOUSE GROUP Limited Reg. No. 954009

A CIP catalogue record for this book is available from the British Library.

Printed and bound in Great Britain by
Printed in the UK by CPI Bookmarque, Croydon, CR0 4TD

All my love and grateful thanks, as before and as ever, to Kate, Noah and Cara.

Big thanks to the fabulous Jane Taylor for lending Bansi such a beautiful song. You can find out more about Jane, and hear *I Will Get There,* at www.janetaylor.co.uk.

Thank you to Dr Sue Pouncey for ensuring that no-one was accidentally poisoned during the story!

Thanks also to my wonderful agent Sarah Molloy at AM Heath & Co, and to everyone at Random House who has believed in Bansi and helped to get her second adventure into print, not least my editor Lauren Buckland – always a pleasure to work with – and Annie Eaton. And of course to Sue Cook, without whom . . .

And thanks to you for reading.

Chapter One

It was already growing dark as Bansi O'Hara and her mother emerged from the tube station. Scraps of litter, caught in a wild and sudden gust of wind, danced and swirled around their feet. There was a sharp, almost gritty taste to the cold October air, as if the weathered shops and the cars that crawled impatiently past them were somehow bleeding dirt into the twilight sky.

'Brrr!' Asha O'Hara pulled her coat tight around her. 'It's getting chilly. Still a bit early for all that, though,' she added, with a glance at a huge shop window. 'Hallowe'en's not for weeks yet.'

Bansi stopped to look, her strikingly grey-green eyes taking in the garish scene before her. The window was full of cobwebs and witches, skulls and skeletons and glowing pumpkins, all cheap plastic and coloured nylon. It wouldn't have scared a five-year-old. Bansi was twice that age and, more to the point, she knew what real evil looked like. She'd met it; faced it; beaten it.

So it made no sense that, as she looked at this cheap parody of dark magic, she shuddered.

'Cold, love?' her mum asked. 'Come on, let's get home and put the heating on. We should probably get the winter clothes down from the loft, too.'

Bansi only half heard her mother. Unwelcome memories were surging back into her mind: memories of how just a few months earlier she had been captured by the Lord of the Dark Sidhe, a malignant faery who had done his best to take her life in pursuit of the power promised by an ancient prophecy. Against the odds Bansi had beaten him, fulfilling the prophecy herself and unleashing the promised power against the Dark Lord; but the confrontation had been terrifying, and she still had nightmares about it.

Now, however, she was wide awake; and yet she felt the same sense of approaching danger with which the bad dreams always began. She scanned the window, searching for some clue as to why she might suddenly feel this way.

The plastic masks leered unconvincingly back at her. Between them her own face – elfin yet strong – showed in faint reflection as if looking at her from another world.

'Come *on*, Bansi,' her mother said, stamping her feet. 'My toes are freezing!'

Uneasily Bansi stepped back from the window. She put her arm through her mother's, and they turned towards the pedestrian crossing that would lead them home. The signal was against them, the rush-hour traffic creeping sullenly and obstinately past, so they paused at the kerb and waited for the lights to change.

That was when she saw him: a tall, graceful figure wearing a shapely top hat, weaving easily towards the crossing through the shuffling pedestrians on the opposite pavement. The footpath was crowded with jostling, bumping shoppers; yet none jostled him, for he seemed to know just where to find the few empty spaces between the bustling bodies. Indeed, it almost looked as if the others on the pavement were, all unknowingly, stepping out of his way to let him pass. It was most strange.

Now he had almost reached the crossing, and even in the gathering dusk Bansi could see that both his top hat and his long, elegant coat were shimmering curiously, peacock-blue and sea-green against the dull and drab October tones around him. He made a truly arresting sight, yet oddly he seemed to be attracting no attention at all: not a single inquisitive glance.

Without a pause, the man stepped off the pavement; and even the sluggish traffic seemed to allow for his presence, slowing or accelerating just a little, as if to ease his lightly dancing passage over the road.

Then he was safely across; for almost without knowing it Bansi herself had stepped back to allow him onto the pavement in front of her. She looked up at him, intrigued and wary, and he looked down at her with – she thought – just a hint of surprise on his merrily handsome face. One eyebrow arched itself in an amused and quizzical manner; his head inclined in an ironic little bow.

A moment later, as his gaze shifted to Bansi's mother, his haughtily amused expression transformed into one of delighted surprise. His eyes sparkled, fixing on Asha O'Hara, and he swept his hat from his head and bowed once more – this time a deep and courtly gesture. Then, giving Bansi scarcely a second glance, he was gone, stepping nimbly through the evening crowds towards the tube station.

Bansi stared after him, her feeling of disquiet growing stronger. 'Do you *know* that man, Mum?' she asked.

'What man, darling?' her mother answered distractedly.

'*That* one, of course,' Bansi said impatiently, just as the man disappeared from view. 'In the top hat.'

'Top hat?' Asha O'Hara repeated, her voice tinged with a faraway quality, a not-entirely-here tone that was quite unlike her. 'I didn't see anyone in a top hat.'

The uneasy feeling in Bansi's stomach suddenly chilled. There was no way her mother could have failed to see the strange and elegant man who had bowed right in front of her.

Or rather, she realized, there was only *one* way. Faery magic.

Bansi looked up sharply. Her mother was gazing into the distance, the hint of a blush fading from her cheeks. There was something not quite present about her expression: something dreamy and otherworldly; something enchanted.

Automatically Bansi's hand dipped into her pocket and clutched her key ring. It was special, a present from her grandmother in Ireland. Her parents teased her about it – 'What did your granny send you that ugly old thing for?' her dad had said when she'd unwrapped it and seen for the first time the decorative charm, a small misshapen lump of metal that dangled from the steel ring. She'd smiled to herself, knowing exactly why Granny had sent it to her: it was made of iron, the best defence against the magic of the faery people.

She slipped the ring over her middle finger and palmed the charm. Then, drawing it from her pocket, she took her mother's hand.

'Ow!' her mum said, the dreamy look vanishing from her face. 'What's that you're holding?'

'Just my key ring.'

Asha O'Hara laughed, suddenly sounding like herself again. 'You're funny about that key ring. Put it back in your pocket; it scratches.'

She tried to disengage her hand, but Bansi tightened her grip, a teasing expression on her face. 'When we get home,' she said. 'Till then, it's keeping us safe.'

'Keeping us safe from what, you daft thing?'

Bansi nodded back towards the shop window, towards the plastic jack-o'-lanterns of the unimpressive Hallowe'en display. 'Dark enchantments,' she said in a mock-spooky voice. 'It's a magic charm, Mum. Made of iron. It'll keep the goblins away.'

And then the lights changed at last and, still pressing the charm against her mother's palm, Bansi O'Hara led the way across the road and turned for home.

If you had been there on that chilly October evening, and if just at that moment you had happened to look up, you would have seen something strange. On the roof of the tube station a shape bloomed and blossomed out of nothingness, resolving into the form of a large black bird – a raven. It shook its wings, stretching them out wide and making a ragged silhouette against the darkening twilight-grey sky. Then it folded itself small, as if hiding from something.

'Oh, bloomin' 'eck!' the raven muttered. 'What *now*?'

Chapter Two

A few hundred miles away and a few minutes earlier, in a house on the edge of the sleepy village of Ballyfey, Bansi O'Hara's grandmother had been staring out of an upstairs window into the deepening dusk and whispering anxiously into a telephone.

'I'm telling you, Nora, there's someone out there! I think there might be more than one of them!'

The elderly voice on the other end of the line was brusque. 'Well, don't call me, then, you daft old haddock – hang up and dial nine-nine-nine! What do you expect *me* to do about burglars?'

'I don't think it *is* burglars,' Granny hissed, eyes scouring the garden. 'I think it might be . . . some of the Good People.'

'Good People?' Nora Mullarkey barked a scornful laugh. 'Are you telling me, Eileen O'Hara, that you're scared of the f-a-e-r-i-e-s?'

'You just stop that at once, Nora! You know as well as I do how dangerous—'

'I know how many years I spent trying to warn

you about them, Eileen, only to have you telling me that it's all nonsense! Not only that,' Mrs Mullarkey added pointedly, 'I remember a time when you'd quite happily say the word rather than spelling it out or calling them the Good People, taking no notice of me and not believing you'd attract their attention and bring all manner of bad luck down on us; and how you even went as far as inviting them all into your house despite my warnings, and you know how *that* ended up!'

'Nora, I've already admitted that your crazy notions *happened* to be right – except for your ideas about brownies, of course, which were completely wrong and just go to show that you were guessing about all the rest and had no more idea than I did – so if you'd just stop arguing and help me to deal with these f-a-e-r-i-e-s at the bottom of my garden . . .'

'Ah, now, hold on, Eileen – you're getting nervous in your old age. It can't really be them. How would they have got here? You know as well as I do that the gateway into the Other Realm doesn't just open up any old time.'

'Be that as it may, Nora, there's someone – or some*thing* – in my garden, and it . . . it *feels* like it did on Midsummer's Eve . . .'

'But it's *not* Midsummer's Eve, nor Midwinter's neither. If it was, I'd be round to your house straight away with my old iron saucepan and a box full of horseshoes, but since it's not, you'll forgive me if I don't just drop everything and drive over. I'm off to call on someone at the moment.'

'Nora! You've spent all these years telling me to be wary of . . . of *them*, and now you're telling me I'm imagining things?'

'Well, now, I didn't exactly say that . . .'

'But that's what you meant!'

'All right, Eileen, if you must be like that: yes, I think you're imagining things. Or maybe it's burglars, come to steal your underwear. Look, call the Gardai if you're worried. Or else go and make a cup of tea. I'll come over to your place later and make sure you're all right.'

'Oh, *later*, is it, Nora Maura Margaret mysterious-other-name Mullarkey? And what if I'm kidnapped and on my way to the land of Tir na n'Óg by then? Well?'

For a moment, there was no answer, and Granny was struck by the ridiculous – and faintly worrying – notion that she might have won an argument with her friend outright.

'Nora!' she repeated. 'Would you at least have the good manners to answer me?'

Still there was no reply.

'Nora!' Granny said, suddenly as worried for her

friend as for herself. 'Nora, is something happening? Can you hear me? Nora, what's going on there?'

Nora Mullarkey's voice came again, but this time it was a distant shout, as if she had taken her mobile phone away from her ear and begun to yell. There was a sound of rapid footsteps, and then the signal suddenly cut out. The phone went dead.

'Nora?' Granny said urgently. 'Nora! Are you there?'

There was no answer but a soft click, and the endless unmusical held note of a broken connection.

Granny O'Hara hung up the phone and felt her heart thumping in the sudden silence. She stared out of the window again; her garden had taken on a strange, otherworldly appearance in the gathering twilight. Down by the gorse bush, something moved.

Nora Mullarkey felt no less uneasy than her old friend did. While she was talking to Eileen O'Hara on her mobile, she had been carefully making her way down a nearby hillside, following a grassy track from the car park to the place where the slope levelled out somewhat.

This was the site of Ballyfey's single tourist attraction – a ring of ancient standing stones on the side of Slieve Donnan, the hill that overlooked the village. To the average visitor, the stones were of interest because they were so old; to one or two students of legend they were worth a footnote or two in papers about local folklore; but to Nora Mullarkey they were much more than just interesting. They were dangerous.

The stones marked the location of the only gateway between the mortal realm and the mythical Tir na n'Óg – the Other Realm, the Land of Faery. A few months previously, on Midsummer's Eve, the gateway had opened and a number of creatures of Faery had passed through, setting in motion a train of events which had quickly raced out of control. Nora and Eileen O'Hara had had to pass through the gate themselves in order to rescue Eileen's granddaughter Bansi from the Lord of the Dark Sidhe and stop him from spilling her blood in fulfilment of an ancient prophecy, and as far as Mrs Mullarkey was concerned they had been lucky to escape with their lives. Privately, she doubted that they would ever have done so had Bansi O'Hara not been such an exceptionally brave and resourceful child; but she would never have admitted as much to Granny, who was fiercely proud of her granddaughter and would have crowed over such an admission for months.

As she spoke to her friend on the phone, Mrs Mullarkey pushed all thoughts of their adventure from her mind. That had all taken place at

Midsummer, and the gateway was closed now; it opened, she knew, only at what Pogo – a cantankerous brownie who had shared their danger – called 'the border times': the times when the world of Faery and the mortal world were closest to one another, and the veil that separated them was at its thinnest. It was safe enough, she told herself, being up here now, with both of those border times, Midsummer and Midwinter, months away. It was certainly safe enough down in the village; although it was true that she'd spent much of her life warning her friend of the dangers of the faeries, Nora Mullarkey now knew that they could only pass through to the mortal realm when the gate was open.

It was for this reason that she was being so dismissive of her friend's fears. *You've been startled by a fox or something, most like, you silly old fool*, she very nearly said to her friend; but she didn't. Instead, she said, 'But it's *not* Midsummer's Eve, nor Midwinter's, neither. If it was, I'd be round to your house straight away with my old iron saucepan and a box full of horseshoes, but since it's not, you'll forgive me if I don't just drop everything and drive over. I'm off to call on someone at the moment.'

And it was true; she was going to visit someone – someone she could see now as she neared the standing stones: someone else who had shared their adventures and played an important part in them. The raven was perched on a low branch of the ancient oak that stood in the centre of the stone circle. She hadn't told her friend that she'd taken to visiting the bird – Eileen O'Hara would have mocked her mercilessly for showing any hint of concern for a creature of Faery. But since those strange events of Midsummer, never a week had gone by without her bringing it something good to eat.

She made these visits at twilight, when she knew the bird would be there. It was under a curse, doomed to remain in raven's form for five hundred years, and if it was not in the tree in the stone circle throughout every twilight of dawn and dusk, the five hundred years would begin again – as, much to its irritation and distress, had happened during the events of Midsummer.

Mrs Mullarkey stepped forward, one hand reaching into her bag for the leftover slices of roast beef she'd wrapped up after lunch, the other hand still holding her mobile to her ear. Eileen O'Hara was protesting at the other end of the line. 'Well, now,' she told her, still moving towards the stone circle, eyes fixed on the bird, 'I didn't exactly say that . . .'

The raven turned and saw her; fluffed up its wing-feathers and feigned nonchalance, as always. She affected a similarly casual attitude herself – as if she happened to be passing and had only just noticed the raven – and continued listening. 'All right, Eileen, if you must be like that: yes, I think you're imagining things. Or maybe it's burglars, come to steal your underwear. Look, call the Gardai if you're worried. Or else go and make a cup of tea. I'll come over to your place later and make sure you're all right.'

Eileen O'Hara began speaking again; and Mrs Mullarkey drew breath to reply. But before she had the chance, something dreadful happened.

The raven, clearly visible as a silhouette against the twilight sky, folded up and disappeared.

Mrs Mullarkey's jaw dropped open. The bird had just vanished as if by magic. No, never mind *as if*; it had to *be* magic. *Faery* magic.

'Are you there?' she shouted, stepping forward, the phone forgotten in her hand. 'Where are you? Can you hear me?' She hurried forward towards the stone circle.

Before she reached it the stones, too, vanished.

Or rather, *almost* vanished. The landscape around her flickered; the stones, the ancient oak and the village far below all began to waver in and out of existence; trees and people and cars suddenly strobed all around her so rapidly it was impossible to tell if she was passing through four different places or standing in all four at once. She seemed to be on the hillside; by a small clearing in a forest; inside some kind of underground station; above a busy city street. A pair of yellow eyes peered at her from a nearby thicket; commuters and shoppers bustled past her on their way to and from the escalator; vague shapes of birds swooped around her. The air smelled different; felt different. She knew she hadn't entered the circle, and yet she was certain that at least some of what she was seeing was a scene in Tir na n'Óg. A glance at her mobile phone confirmed there was no signal. Eyes alert and keeping watch, she slid the roast beef back into her handbag and drew out an iron horseshoe. The worlds blurred around her, faster and faster.

Then there was a man – a tall, elegant man in a top hat and long coat that shimmered shades of peacock-blue and sea-green – skipping merrily through the station. No – the clearing. Or was it the stone circle? He was in all three at once; like her, he was simultaneously in the mortal world and the realm of Faery. As he passed her he laughed merrily but soundlessly and tipped his hat.

On he danced, down the escalator, into the forest, and disappeared among the trees and into the tunnels.

Consumed with curiosity, Mrs Mullarkey moved after him . . .

. . . but she had hardly taken more than a few

steps when the trees and station and rooftops around her somehow folded in on themselves, and she was back on the hillside facing the standing stones.

'*Their* magic!' she muttered. 'That's for certain. But how? It's nowhere near Midwinter yet.'

That was when two disturbing thoughts occurred to her at once. Eileen might be in danger. And worse – much worse, almost unthinkably, horribly worse – Eileen had been right, and she, Nora Mullarkey, had been wrong.

She checked her phone. The signal was at full strength. Quickly she auto-dialled her friend's number; it was answered almost immediately.

'Eileen! Are you all right?'

'Yes, but—'

'Right! Arm yourself with iron! I'll be there in a minute!'

'Oh, so you believe me now, do you, Nora?'

Mrs Mullarkey was not in the mood for an argument. She disconnected the call as she hurried towards her car.

It was barely a minute later that a knock came on Granny O'Hara's front door, followed almost immediately by another one.

'All right, all right!' Granny muttered, hastening to the door. 'Keep your hair on, you barmy old haddock.' Hurriedly she drew back the iron bolts, turned the key and pulled the door open. 'You were quick getting here, if nothing— Oh!'

She broke off; for it was not Nora Mullarkey on the doorstep. Rather, it was a little man, hardly tall enough to reach her chin and dressed all in scarlet. He nodded his wee round head, as if a bow would be too much trouble, and gave her a cheery grin that ran from apple-cheek to apple-cheek but somehow never quite reached his eyes.

'Good evening to you, Eileen O'Hara, and a lovely night it is, too. You won't mind if come in.' It was not a question.

'Indeed I will mind!' Granny stepped back from the door and tried to shut it, but the little man made a gesture with one hand and the door refused to move.

'Well now, Eileen O'Hara,' the little man said, his voice charming but his eyes speaking another message entirely. 'It's disappointed I am with your lack of hospitality. Didn't you once say that all the people of Tir na n'Óg would be welcome in your home?'

'Maybe I did,' Granny admitted frostily. 'But that would've been before some of the people of that place kidnapped my granddaughter and tried to kill her.'

The little man shook his head in mock sadness. 'Ah, but Mrs O'Hara, such an invitation cannot be withdrawn, however much it may be regretted later. So stand aside, please, and let me in. You have something that does not belong to you, and I am here to reclaim it for its owner.'

With that, the little man stepped forward as if to enter. But no sooner had his foot crossed the threshold than he let out a howl of agony. His face twisted into a mask of anger as he hopped backwards, clutching his leg. 'What? But—'

'You don't enter this house, Mister Hobgoblin or whatever you may be, and that's an end to it,' Granny said fiercely, but keeping back from the door, for despite Mrs Mullarkey's warning she had not got as far as fetching her iron skillet. Fortunately her house had other defences.

'But . . . but *how*?' the little man howled, his former dignity gone.

'Think I'm going to tell you? Think again.' Granny tugged on the door, but still it would not move.

'You have something that does not belong to you, old woman,' the faery hissed again, 'and its owner *will* have it back. It'll be the worse for you if—'

'Ah, take your old threats and stick them up your trouser leg,' Granny snapped.

'I *warn* you . . .' the wee man said, his face now as

scarlet as his coat. But he got no further, for just at that moment there was the roar of an engine, headlights swept the hedge, and then Mrs Mullarkey's tyres were kicking up the gravel of Granny's drive. The little man hissed fury once more, and then he turned round on the spot and vanished into thin air. Seconds later, the dark green Morris Minor Traveller screeched to a halt by the front door and Mrs Mullarkey, waving her horseshoe, leaped from the driver's seat.

'Eileen!' she said. 'Get yourself indoors at once! Don't you know there are Good People abroad tonight?'

'You don't say, Nora,' Granny answered, her hand absently stroking the steel wire that ringed the inside of the door-frame, held in place by dozens of iron nails. It was warm to the touch. 'I might just have a story to tell you about that.'

'And I,' Mrs Mullarkey said darkly, 'have a story and a *half* to tell *you*.'

Chapter Three

Bansi's dreams were cloudy that night. She had an odd sense of eyes staring from the darkness, although it was unclear to her what or whom they were watching. At one point she thought she heard hoofbeats in the street outside, and it seemed to her in her sleep that she went to the window to look for the rider, but could see nothing except a pale mist.

It was still dark outside when she began to wake, disturbed by a noise in the room. Someone was bending over her. Startled, she reached for her weapon, her iron key ring, on the bedside table; but as her sleepy fingers found it, a strong hand closed over them. Strong – but gentle. She relaxed as she realized who it was.

'Easy, sweetheart,' her dad whispered. 'Sorry – didn't mean to wake you. Just wanted to kiss you goodbye before I go.'

Bansi yawned. The confusion of the night's dreams still weighed in on her. 'Where are you going?' she asked, her voice sleepy.

Fintan O'Hara sat down on the bed beside his daughter and stroked her hair gently. Bansi smiled up at him through half-closed eyes. Her dad was the most reassuring person she could imagine; she always felt safe when he was around. Even in the darkness, she could see the twinkle in his eye as he smiled back, warmly and lovingly.

'I'm off to my conference, remember? Just for a few days; I'll be back Sunday.' He kissed her forehead gently.

Bansi reached up and ruffled her father's already tousled hair. 'Have a good time, Dad.'

'I will, Bansi. I'm looking forward to it.' He kissed her once more, and stood. 'I'll miss you, though. Enjoy the rest of the week, love.'

Bansi nodded, stifling a yawn. 'I will. See you Sunday. Love you.'

'I love you too, darling. You settle back down, now, till it's time to wake up.'

Bansi closed her eyes again. 'Bye, Dad.'

'Bye, sweetheart. Take care of your mum for me, won't you?'

Then he was gone, and Bansi felt herself drifting off. But at the edge of her consciousness something flickered, like a warning flag fluttering on the periphery of her vision. Her dad's last sentence was bothering her. *Take care of your mum for me, won't you?*

It was the sort of thing he always said when he went away; they both knew it didn't mean anything, and yet this time she felt . . . oddly . . .

A warm blanket of sleep smothered her thoughts, and Bansi sank silently back into her restless, cloudy dreams.

When next she woke it was starting to grow light outside, and someone was tapping on her window. The sound had entered her dreams, growing louder and more persistent until it pulled her from her slumbers and she was awake. She listened; the noise was definitely coming from her window, and it certainly sounded like someone was doing it deliberately – tapping, then pausing and waiting for a response, before tapping more loudly and impatiently.

Yet her bedroom was on the first floor.

She sat up and clutched her key ring. Then, holding the misshapen iron charm for protection, she approached the window warily and twitched the curtain aside.

There, sitting on the external sill, was a large black bird.

Bansi's first feeling was one of relief, but very quickly caution overtook her. She opened the window just a fraction, not enough to let the bird squeeze through.

'Is that you?' she asked quietly.

The raven tilted its head to one side and stared at her. It blinked slowly, once.

'No, it's someone who *isn't* me,' it said, sarcasm dripping from its beak. ''*Course* it's bloomin' me. Who'd you think it was?'

It certainly sounded like the raven who'd helped her that summer, when she had faced the Dark Lord in the land of Tir na n'Óg. But Bansi had seen too much of the faery people to accept what she saw at face value.

'How do I know it's you?' she asked. 'I mean – no offence, but, well, you could be a . . . you know, something else, disguised as a raven.'

'*A* raven?' The bird was clearly offended. '*A* raven? I'm not just any old raven! I'm me! And I might remind you, I'm not supposed to be a raven at all – at least, I wouldn't be one if I wasn't under a curse. Which, as you well know,' it continued with more than a touch of bitterness, 'has recently been extended for another four hundred and ninety-three years, thanks to your granny and her daft old pal. And that wouldn't have happened if they hadn't been coming to rescue *you*. And *that* wouldn't have happened if you hadn't gone off to Tir na n'Óg on the back of a *real* shape-changer. And *that* wouldn't have happened if—'

'All right,' Bansi interrupted, 'but the point is, you could be someone else – or some*thing* else – disguised as you, couldn't you?'

The raven thought about this. 'Not likely,' it concluded after a moment. 'Anyway, I'm not. I'm me.'

'But how do I know that?' Bansi persisted. 'I mean – I think it's you. You look like you, and you certainly sound like you. But you might not *be* you.'

The raven sighed dramatically. 'Look, it's bloomin' cold out here, and all these car fumes and stuff are making me dizzy. Couldn't I come inside?'

Bansi shook her head. 'Sorry. I'm not inviting you inside until I know for certain it's you.'

'Oh, bloomin' 'eck!' the bird retorted, ruffling its feathers bad-temperedly. It smoothed them out again, calming itself. 'No, got to be cautious, haven't you? Considering you've already had a whole bunch of faeries turning into wolves and leaping out of bushes and carrying you off, not to mention trying to kill you.' Then it paused. 'Hang on, I've got it. Why don't you just open the window a bit more?'

'Why should I do that?' Bansi asked, her eyes narrowing suspiciously.

'Because,' the raven said, making a big show of being patient, 'if I was one of them powerful big faeries that can change shape, I wouldn't be able to come in unless you invited me, would I? That's how it works. So you can open the window as wide as you like and no harm done.'

Bansi had to concede the bird had a point. 'I'm not inviting you in, you know,' she said as she slid the window open.

The raven hopped through the window and fluttered down onto the carpet in front of her. 'Ahahaha!' it cackled. 'Now I have you in my power, foolish mortal! No, only joking, it's me. Close the window, would you, it's draughty.'

Bansi pulled the sash down again and sat on her bed. 'So . . . what are you doing here?' she asked.

'Oh, that's nice,' the raven said grumpily. 'No "hello", then? No "nice to see you again"? No "sorry I doubted you and thought you were an evil shape-changing faery out to kill me even after you did me all those good turns"?'

Bansi smiled in spite of herself. 'All right. Hello, nice to see you again, sorry I thought you *might* be an evil shape-changing . . . f-a-e-r-y out to kill me even after you did me all those good turns. What are you doing here?'

Shrugging their shoulders is not something that comes naturally to ravens, but this one had a go at it. 'Search me. One minute I'm sitting in my tree, minding my own business and thinking about how to pass the next five hundred years' – here it paused, and gave Bansi a meaningfully miserable stare – 'the next, I'm up on top of some kind of railway station in the middle of London! Tube station, it was, though I didn't know that – I didn't even know it was London straight away; had to do a bit of exploring to find that out. But as to how I got there: no idea. It was like . . . well, you know how it was when the gateway opened up?'

It looked at Bansi, as if to check that she was following. She nodded, remembering. Bansi was one of only a handful of people alive who had passed through the gateway in the stone circle.

'But it's the wrong time of year for the gateway to open,' she said. 'And it would have taken you to Tir na n'Óg, not London!'

It was the raven's turn to nod. 'Yeah, I know. Anyway, as long as I'm up in the tree, I'm safe. I stay where I am. I don't see how it can have been the gate.'

'But it's some kind of magic. It has to be.' Bansi stared out of the window, searching her imagination for a possible answer. None came. 'OK – let's just assume that somehow the gate opened, even though it's the wrong time of year, and caught you, even though you were up in the tree, and brought you here, even though it should have taken you to Tir na n'Óg . . . or that something else happened . . . Anyway, how did you know where I live?'

'I didn't,' the raven admitted. 'Had no idea you lived anywhere near here. After I'd done a bit of scouting around and worked out where I was, I went back to the tube station; but there were a couple of jackdaws there, up late and giving me the evil eye, so I thought I'd just go and sit on the building opposite. Had to scare off a couple of pigeons that seemed to think I was muscling in on their territory. Anyway, I'm sitting up there, and it's getting dark, and I'm wondering what to do next, and how to get back to my tree. Then' – and here the raven leaned towards her, at least as far as a raven can be said to lean, and lowered its voice conspiratorially – 'just as the last glimmers of twilight are fading into the darkness of night – here, that's good, isn't it? Quite poetic? Anyway, just as the sun's finishing setting, I get this odd feeling, like something's about to happen. So I wait, all my senses tingling. Ever had all your senses tingle? Not pleasant. Makes you want to sneeze. And then – well, that's when it happened.'

The raven lowered its voice still further, as if frightened of being overheard, and now it was Bansi's turn to lean in, for fear of missing anything. The chill feeling in her stomach had crept back, all unnoticed, like a premonition of evil, and now it had hold of her.

'Suddenly,' continued the bird, 'this huge white

horse gallops out of the tube station, going full pelt. There's something scary about it – it doesn't *feel* like a real horse, mortal or faery. It's like it's something else, *pretending* to be a horse. And though it's white – a pure, bright white – it's not a *clean* white. It's a ghostly white; the colour of sun-bleached bone.' The raven shuddered. 'As for its rider . . .'

It fell silent, as if lost in thought.

'Go on,' Bansi urged.

The raven swallowed audibly. 'Couldn't see his face. He was dressed all in fine clothes that shone like blood-red rubies, with a hooded cloak of midnight blue, and . . . well, you know how the Lord of the Dark Sidhe gave you the creeps?'

Bansi nodded. She would never forget.

'That was nothing, compared to this bloke. It was like, the moment he appeared, the air smelled suddenly poisonous. Horrible, it was.' It shuddered again, and ruffled its dark feathers. 'Out he gallops, but it's clear none of the mortal folk can see anything. They just move out of his way, like it's their own idea. Except this one woman doesn't move fast enough, and the horse clips her as it gallops out. Next thing, she's on the ground screaming, leg broken or something. The rider just gallops on, across the road. This looks bad, I think, but I reckon I'm beneath his notice, so I follow at a distance, doing my best to look like an ordinary dumb bird. And that's how I found you.'

'What do you mean, that's how you found me?' The chill was growing colder inside Bansi, gnawing at her stomach. 'This can't be anything to do with me. The prophecy's been fulfilled! The blood of the Morning Stars was returned to the sacred earth of Tir na n'Óg! It's over!'

The raven shook its head. 'That's as may be,' it said, 'but the thing is: this blood-red rider . . . he's a faery all right. One of the bad ones. Powerful, too, I'd say – worse than the Lord of the Dark Sidhe. Much worse, if that's possible.

'And he's been outside your house all night.'

Chapter Four

Bansi shuddered. Wrapping her duvet around her shoulders and curling her feet up beneath her, as if trying to comfort herself, she thought about what the raven had said: a powerful faery – probably more powerful than the Lord of the Dark Sidhe, and almost certainly as evil – was watching her house.

Once again, it seemed, her parents were in danger because of her.

'Is he still there?' she asked.

The raven shook itself. 'Naw,' it said. 'Think I'd've drawn attention to myself by tapping on your window if he was? Not likely. He galloped off before the sun came up – his sort don't tend to hang around and wait for the morning. They like it nice and dark. I dare say he'll be back tonight, though.'

It was as if a cold wind was blowing through Bansi's mind, chilling her thoughts and emotions. Something a little like despair settled over her; with an effort, she shook it off.

'What are we going to do?' she asked.

'*We?!*' the raven exclaimed, a sudden startled explosion of feathers and fright. 'You don't expect me to hang around, do you? Sorry, no offence, but I ain't tangling with . . . with *him*, whoever he is. Not a chance. You're on your own here, kid.' It began to groom itself, smoothing its anxious plumage back down. 'I've come here and warned you; that's risky enough for me. It's bad enough being a raven; I don't even want to *think* about what that bloke might do to me if he knew I'd warned you about him.' It shivered, making itself small. 'Come to that, strikes me he wouldn't need a reason to turn me into, I dunno, a squashed toad or something; I reckon he's the sort that'd do it just for fun. Gave me the willies, he did.'

Not for the first time since the summer's adventure, Bansi found herself missing Pogo. The little brownie might have been grumpy and pessimistic, but he was also loyal and wise, and she felt sure he would have known what to do.

'So – what are you going to do next?' Bansi asked.

'Dunno. S'pose I'll just have to fly back to Ballyfey— Aw, *no*!' The bird's head dropped in sudden anguish.

'What is it?'

'The enchantment,' the raven said bleakly, hardly lifting its head to look at her. 'I'm supposed to be up in my tree every sunset . . . and every sunrise, too.'

Bansi understood immediately. 'You've just missed sunrise, haven't you?' she said sympathetically. 'You poor thing! That means—'

'Yeah,' the bird cut in. 'That means I'm back to square one. Except that I'll never get back to my tree by sunset, and I can't go flying about in the dark. Could be a couple of days before I can even start the five hundred years all over again. I'll *never* get back to my own shape at this rate! Unless . . .' The bird's beady eyes lit up with sudden hope as it looked at Bansi. 'I don't suppose . . . you haven't learned to use them magic powers of yours, have you?'

Bansi shook her head. She had discovered during her adventures that she was descended on both sides from powerful and noble faeries of an ancient royal line, and her companions – the raven included – were certain she had inherited the fantastical abilities of her faery ancestors. Bansi was not so sure. She had apparently performed some great magic in Tir na n'Óg, it was true; but it had almost felt to her as if some force – perhaps those same ancestors, reaching out somehow across countless generations – had worked the magic through her, and the more time went on, the less she was convinced that it had really had anything to do with her at all.

'Sorry,' she said. 'I really am. But Midsummer was

the only time anything like that's ever happened to me. I really don't think it was me at all, you know.'

''Course it was!' the raven said, clearly trying to appear cheerier than it felt. 'No doubt about it. You just wait. One day you'll be able to do all kinds of magic, you'll see.'

Bansi smiled. 'Well, if you're right, then changing you back'll be top of my to-do list.'

The bird perked right up. 'Really? Top of the list? Even before marrying a handsome prince and turning your granny's daft old friend into a toad? Even before getting yourself a big bag of faery gold?'

'Even before those,' Bansi promised.

'Well, that's more like it,' the raven declared. 'At that rate, I might get turned back before the original five hundred years is up! Maybe even by Christmas – you never can tell with faery magic!' It hopped up onto the windowsill. 'I ought to get back to my tree, mind you; just in case – but you know where to find me once you've learned how to undo spells. Here,' it added as Bansi opened the window, 'watch yourself – especially with the blood-red rider. I can't promise to come to the rescue like last time, not if you get tangled up with that one.' With a shudder, it launched itself from the window, wings spread wide to catch the wind. Within moments, it was no more than a small black dot in the sky. Bansi watched it go, a small sadness tugging at her heart, and wished once more that Pogo was there.

As it disappeared from view, there came a knock on the front door.

There was something oddly familiar about the handsome young man who stood on the doorstep, dressed in expensive jeans and a flamboyant shirt. It was a familiarity she felt, rather than saw.

'Good morning, young lady,' he smiled, all charm and good manners. 'I have a message for the lady of the house.'

Bansi made no reply, but continued to stare at him. The face was not one she recognized, and yet she knew that she had seen the man before. She concentrated; and as she did so something stirred inside her, and she knew who it was.

'Not wearing your top hat today?' she enquired coldly.

The man started, surprised. Just for a moment he let his guard drop and Bansi saw him as he really was, still wearing his long shimmering coat. Then he snapped his fingers as if realizing something, and the disguise slipped firmly back into place.

'Aha!' he said. 'The changeling child. Delighted to renew our acquaintance.'

'I'm not a changeling,' Bansi told him flatly.

The man waved this away with a light laugh. 'As you wish,' he said, drawing an envelope from his pocket. It looked old, even antique, with something written on it in a wonderfully flowing script: *For the lady of the house.* He held the envelope out towards Bansi.

She refused to take it. 'You're not welcome here,' she said.

If the man was at all perturbed by the coolness of his reception, he did not show it. 'Now why all the mistrust?' He smiled with what almost looked like genuine warmth. 'I mean no harm to the lady – or to you, either. Quite the opposite, in fact. We should be friends, you and I. Tell me your name.'

Bansi glared at him. 'So you can bewitch me? No thanks. Why don't you tell me *your* name?'

The man threw back his head and laughed merrily. Then his fingers touched his forehead, and for just a moment his hat was almost visible as he swept it from his head and bowed before her. 'Hob Under-the-Hill, at your service. And you are . . . ?'

'I am . . . closing the door now,' Bansi said. 'Goodbye, Hob Under-the-Hill.'

She just had time to see the disbelief on his face, and a flash of what could have been anger, before the catch clicked shut.

* * *

Bansi had not quite reached her bedroom when the door to her parents' room opened and her mother stumbled out, yawning and tying a towelling robe around her.

'Morning, sweetheart,' she mumbled. 'Did you sleep well?'

Bansi forced a smile. 'Better than you, it looks like.'

Asha O'Hara rubbed her eyes and yawned again. 'Glad to hear it,' she said. 'I feel like I've been tossing and turning for hours. You weren't calling out for me in the night, were you?' Bansi shook her head. 'Must have dreamed it, then. I kept thinking someone was calling me, but I couldn't quite wake up. Who was that at the door just now, by the way?'

'Oh, um . . . just some trick-or-treaters,' Bansi invented quickly. 'Not even dressed up or anything. I told them to come back next week.'

Bansi's mother sighed. 'This is getting silly. Before you know it, they'll be starting Hallowe'en in July. And trick-or-treating in the morning, too!' She glanced down the landing to the clock in the bathroom, and her eyes widened with alarm. 'Bansi! Look at the time! You'll be late for school!'

Several minutes later Bansi O'Hara, pulling on her coat, left the house at a run with her mother following moments behind.

'This is so embarrassing!' Asha O'Hara pretended to complain as she caught up. 'I look like I've just got out of bed!'

'You *have* just got out of bed!' Bansi pointed out, settling into a steady jog, book-bag bouncing at her hip. 'Anyway, you look fine!'

In fact, her mother looked better than fine. Wild waves of black hair flowed out behind her as she ran; her round, pretty face looked if anything even prettier as her cheeks grew pink with exercise. Her brown, almond-shaped eyes looked somehow both mysterious and mischievous. Even without make-up Asha O'Hara was, Bansi thought to herself – and not for the first time – miles better-looking than any of the other mums at school.

As they ran along the road to school, neither one noticed a tall, elegant, top-hatted figure skipping along the rooftops above them.

Chapter Five

Miles away in Ballyfey, Bansi's grandmother was finishing breakfast. And so was her house-guest, for unusually – having refused to let her friend be alone in the house, following the appearance of a threat-uttering faery on her doorstep – Mrs Mullarkey had spent the night in one of Granny's two guest rooms.

Much less unusually, the two were squabbling.

'And I have told *you*, Nora Maura Margaret whatever-it-is Mullarkey, that there is no *way* I'll be getting in a car with you if you don't even know where it is you're going!'

Mrs Mullarkey rolled her eyes and shook her head in the way she did when she felt Granny was being at her most exasperating. 'Really, Eileen, you do make a fuss. When have we ever got lost while I've been doing the driving, I ask you?'

'When have we not? What about that time last year when we went to Roscommon?'

'What about it?'

'We were *wanting* to go to Sligo!' Granny pointed out.

'There's nothing wrong with Roscommon!' Mrs Mullarkey said, aggrieved. 'My dear old mother, God rest her soul, is buried in Roscommon!'

'Aye, I know,' said Granny unsympathetically. 'You meant to bury her in Cavan, only you couldn't find it.'

Nora Mullarkey folded her arms and pursed her lips. 'Load of old nonsense, Eileen, and you know it! Anyhow, the only time we've ever got lost is when I've been relying on *you* to read the maps!'

Granny was scandalized. 'What! Sure, didn't I read the map all the way there the time we *did* get our day out in Sligo?'

'You did, Eileen. Only *that* time, if you recall, we were aiming to get to Dundalk.'

Now it was Granny's turn to fold her arms and glare. 'Is that so, Nora? Well, then – who was it who got us all the way to the ferry when we went to pick up Fintan and Asha and Bansi in the summer?'

Mrs Mullarkey tutted. 'Lady Luck, Eileen; that's who. With a bit of help from me, seeing as I happened to remember the way in any case, regardless of where your navigation would have taken us. Anyway, talking of young Bansi – shouldn't we be doing something, instead of just sitting here?'

Granny snapped her fingers. 'We should,' she said, 'and I know what. If you'll just tell me the name of the place we're looking for, I'll download some directions from the Internet . . .'

'Ach, no need to go to all that sort of trouble,' Mrs Mullarkey interjected. 'If you're that worried about getting lost, we'll use the wee talky box thing.'

'Wee talky box thing? Nora, what are you on about now?'

'Och, did I not tell you, Eileen? Our Michael bought me one of those sit-nav contraptions. It came in the post yesterday.'

'Sit . . . ? You mean *sat*-nav, Nora.'

'Sit, sat, what's the difference? The point is, Eileen, it'll get us where we're going without any need for me to tell you when you're holding the map upside down. Now, how about it?'

Granny still looked unconvinced. 'So how did you find out about this place you want to take us to, then?'

'You're not the only one who knows how to sofa the web,' Mrs Mullarkey told her.

'You mean *surf* the web, Nora; not *sofa*.'

'I know what I mean, Eileen, and I mean sofa the web. I have one of those laptops, and I like to sit in comfort on my sofa while I use it. Now, are we going or not?'

* * *

By mid-afternoon, Granny was sure they were well and truly lost.

'Well,' she commented tartly, 'if only you'd let me navigate, maybe we wouldn't be in this pickle now.'

'If I'd let you navigate, we'd be lucky to be in the right county,' said Nora Mullarkey. 'If you ask me, this place we're looking for has got some kind of enchantment on it. That'll be why it's so difficult to find.'

'*After two hundred metres, turn left*,' the sat-nav said, sounding like a slightly computerized newsreader.

'Or perhaps it's because you keep ignoring the wee talky box thing,' Granny suggested as the dark green Morris Minor Traveller roared straight past the turning.

'Can't possibly have been that road, Eileen,' Mrs Mullarkey said. 'I think it's just making it up.'

'And how would you know better than it does? You've never been here before!'

'Well – neither has the wee talky box thing!'

'*Recalculating*,' said the sat-nav. '*In one point two kilometres, turn left*.' On its screen, the road in front of a little blue car icon changed colour to indicate the turning.

'Yes, Nora, but it's been programmed with all the maps, hasn't it?'

'Aye,' said Mrs Mullarkey dryly, 'and it's probably holding them upside down, just like you. Trust me, Eileen, I know where I'm going. I can read the signs.'

'Didn't you tell me already there are no signs pointing to this place?'

Mrs Mullarkey sighed dramatically. 'Not road signs,' she said. 'Just signs. Like . . . well, you know.' She waved her hand vaguely in the air, as if to indicate something too obvious and yet too complicated to be put into words.

'I do know, Nora,' Granny observed. 'I know you well enough to know you're just bluffing, because you can't stand to think anyone might know better than you!'

'After five hundred metres, turn left,' the sat-nav said. *'Recalculating,'* it added moments later as Mrs Mullarkey sent the car shooting down a narrow turning, thick with trees, half a kilometre early.

'Nora!' Granny scolded. 'What *are* you doing?'

'Just trust me, Eileen,' her friend said smugly. 'Nearly there!'

'Make a U-turn when possible,' the sat-nav said, its on-screen map showing a bent-back arrow on the road in front of the little blue car.

'Ah, be quiet,' Mrs Mullarkey muttered. 'Now . . . look, Eileen! What did I tell you! That'll be it, there!'

Granny looked. Some distance ahead, through the trees, she could just make out what looked like a small and unimposing hill.

'*Make a U-turn when possible*,' repeated the sat-nav.

The car was juddering now as the surface of the narrow lane roughened.

'Don't you think you ought to slow down?' Granny asked.

'And why would you think I should do that?'

'Because if you don't we're going to go right into that river up ahead.'

There was a screech of brakes and a rather satisfying skid, which brought the Morris Minor Traveller to a halt a surprisingly safe distance from where the lane – by now no more than a dirt-track – ended suddenly with a sheer drop into the water. Granny smiled smugly at her friend, who scowled at the river as if it was *its* fault for being in the wrong place.

The silence was broken by the politely measured voice of the sat-nav. '*Make a U-turn when possible*,' it said for the third time.

'Perhaps you'd better make a U-turn, Nora,' Granny suggested helpfully. 'When possible, of course.'

'No need,' Mrs Mullarkey said stubbornly. 'We can walk from here. There's a wee footbridge – see?'

'Call that a footbridge, Nora? It's barely more than a branch lying across the river!'

'Sorry, Eileen,' Mrs Mullarkey said pointedly. 'I forgot how frail you are these days. We can go round the long way if it's easier on your legs. And of course your sense of balance isn't as good as it once was.'

'Frail!' Granny exploded. 'Oh, I'll show you frail, Nora Mullarkey!'

Moments later the two of them were determinedly making their way over the roughly carved fallen tree-trunk that served as a bridge over the stream. In competitive silence, they bustled through the undergrowth among the narrow strip of trees on the far bank, hacking thorny brambles out of the way with their walking sticks. As they emerged on the other side, they found themselves in a wide field, dominated by the hill they had seen from the lane.

'So, is that it?' Granny asked as they huffed and puffed their way towards the mound. It was not large – maybe three times Granny's height at its peak – but what was peculiar was that it was perfectly regular, as if someone had built a shallow dome there and then covered it with grass.

'Aye,' Nora Mullarkey said smugly. 'The Knoll of Aphrodite.'

Granny sighed. 'So you've brought us here to

have a look at an old hill that's named after a Roman goddess, for some reason.'

'Greek,' Mrs Mullarkey said scornfully. 'Aphrodite was the Greek goddess of love. The Romans called her Venus.'

'Well, thank you for the history lesson, Nora. But it still doesn't explain what we're doing here.'

'I just thought there might be some clues up here to help us work out what happened last night, that's all.'

There was a long pause.

'All right, Nora, I'm sure you're dying to tell me what clever piece of detective-work you've been doing. Go on, then.'

Mrs Mullarkey allowed herself the smallest hint of a smile. They had reached the knoll now, and she began to lead her friend in a gentle stroll round its perimeter.

'Well, Eileen, I was just sofaing the web a couple of weeks back when I came upon a website all about this place, and there was a page on it called *The Knoll of Aphrodite and the Wee Folk*. It had all kinds of legends to do with the Good People and this place here; and all kinds of stuff about the knoll being special to them; and then it had a bit where people can leave comments, and some young lad had written that he was up here just before sunrise one morning when he saw a strange glow around the mound.'

'So? I'll bet he was drunk!'

'I might have thought the same myself, except that then I noticed the date he was saying this had happened. It was Midsummer's Day. Do you see, Eileen? Just before daybreak on Midsummer morning. Now, that *might* be coincidence . . .'

Granny nodded, beginning to see what her friend was driving at. 'But considering it was Midsummer morning when the ancient prophecy was fulfilled and the magic happened and we all came back from the Other Realm . . .' she said.

'Exactly,' said Mrs Mullarkey approvingly. 'So I thought I'd just keep a virtual eye on this place and see if anything else happened. And when I got up this morning, I had another wee look on your computer, and blow me down if the same fellow hadn't posted a message to say he'd seen some strange figures dancing around up here last night.'

Granny O'Hara drew in her breath sharply. 'Last night,' she said, 'when I had Good People appearing and disappearing on my doorstep and messing about in my vegetable patch!'

'Exactly.'

'All right, Nora; it certainly sounds like you've done your homework. But what could be so special about this place that it would have *them* cavorting about here?'

Mrs Mullarkey's smile was more than just a hint now. She was clearly very pleased with herself.

'I was wondering that myself,' she said. 'And to tell you the truth, it's only now I think I've worked it out.' She paused, collecting her thoughts. 'I started thinking about something it said on the website, about the name: the Knoll of Aphrodite. The history professors reckon it was once named after some queen from ancient times, but at some point in the Dark Ages scholars and monks and what-not somehow got this queen mixed up with the Greek goddess of love. So, slowly across the centuries, it started to be called after Aphrodite instead and the old name died out. Only what none of the eggheads and wise men can work out is: why did this great queen get mixed up with a classical goddess in the first place?

'And I have to confess, Eileen, I've been puzzling the same thing out myself; and it's only when you called her a Roman goddess that it hit me. For like I said, Aphrodite is the same as Venus. And the planet Venus, when it rises, has another name, too.

'It's called the Morning Star.'

There was a pause as Granny thought about this.

'So,' she said, 'you think this place might originally have been named after . . .'

Mrs Mullarkey nodded. 'Caer, Warrior Queen of Donegal – one of the Morning Stars of Tir na n'Óg.'

'And my ancestor, don't let's forget,' said Granny, her voice tinged with pride.

'As if I could,' Mrs Mullarkey said dryly. 'You go on about it often enough. Like it makes you special or something.'

'And do you blame me?' Granny asked indignantly. 'It's my Fintan being descended from Caer, and his lovely Asha being descended from Caer's brother Avalloc, that makes Bansi the child of the Blood of the Morning Stars. And if it wasn't for that, she wouldn't have been kidnapped by that Dark Lord villain and nearly had her throat cut and her blood spilled out all over their blessed sacred earth. Nor, for that matter, would she have done some kind of mysterious magic and saved us all, or practically got herself crowned queen of a whole tribe of brownies; and if all that doesn't make her a bit special I don't know what does. And if this place *is* named after Caer, then it's named after a royal and illustrious member of my family, so it is, and don't you forget it. Mind you,' she added, 'even if it *was* named after her, that wouldn't necessarily mean anything.'

'Oh, but I think it does.'

Their path around the hill had led them almost to

its other side, and now Granny could see that its circumference wasn't entirely regular after all. They were approaching some kind of depression in its surface. As they drew near to it, Granny could see that it was in fact an opening in the hillside, framed by three stones set into the turf like a doorway. Inside was a narrow passageway which quickly faded into darkness.

'You see, Eileen, this hill isn't a natural thing at all,' Mrs Mullarkey said. 'It was made by the ancients. If I'm right, this hill isn't just named after Caer.

'It's her grave.'

Granny felt a sudden sense of reverence fall upon her. She drew close to the doorway and laid her hand gently on one of the stone uprights, as if by doing so she could somehow connect with her distant ancestor. 'Her grave?' she repeated softly.

Mrs Mullarkey nodded. 'Which would explain, perhaps, why it was – why it *is* – a special place to the Good People, maybe even a place of power. And perhaps,' she went on, suddenly businesslike, 'there'll be some kind of clue around here to tell us what happened to the raven, and who that man in the top hat was that I saw, and what that wee red man of yours was looking for last night.'

Just then, there was a sound. A dark, scuffling

noise, like an animal being disturbed in the blackness of the tomb. Granny, startled, stepped back from the stone doorway.

Like a hunting dog, the little scarlet-clad man sprang out from the dark passageway and seized Granny by both wrists, gripping hard. She cried out in pain; the little man showed no emotion.

'Now, Mrs O'Hara,' he said. 'Now I have you, and you'll not be getting away. And I can tell you true, I won't be letting go of you till you've given me what I'm after.'

Chapter Six

'Take your hands off her!' Mrs Mullarkey snapped, stepping forward.

'Ah,' said the little man slyly, 'you'll be Mrs Mullarkey, will you? Well now, Mrs Mullarkey, I'll let your friend go just as soon as she returns what she took. She has something that isn't hers; it belongs to a friend of mine.'

'I'm warning you, little man, let her go right now!'

'Or you'll do what?' the faery taunted. 'Hit me with your handbag? I see your hand twitching there, Mrs Mullarkey, and if you're wanting to swing your bag at me then go right ahead; it'll do me no harm at all. I'll hardly even feel— OOOOFFFFFF!'

The force of the blow lifted him clear off his feet and sent him crashing into the stone frame of the doorway.

'Run, Eileen!' Mrs Mullarkey shouted, helping her friend to her feet; and they ran.

'Back to the car!' agreed Granny breathlessly. Mrs Mullarkey made no reply but a single grunt, and on they hastened, not daring to look back.

Behind them, the little man stirred and groaned. He forced himself into a sitting position, rubbing his head, and looked hazily first one way and then another, but it was not until he struggled to his feet and limped round the knoll to the other side that he spotted the two elderly ladies hurrying through the trees. Shaking his head as if to clear it, he raised a horn to his mouth and blew. A high, strident, piercing note sounded.

Hearing it, Granny and Mrs Mullarkey pressed ahead. To each of them the note sounded like a signal, and neither wanted to find out who or what it was that the signal was meant for. Through the trees they pushed, to the river bank, and across the makeshift bridge towards the car. From far behind them a wild thundering rang across the field: the clattering rhythm of hoofbeats, echoing from deep inside the tomb.

As Mrs Mullarkey fumbled in her handbag for the car key, Granny looked anxiously towards the Knoll of Aphrodite. She could see something moving at speed around the rim of the mound and across the field towards them – some kind of animal. No – animals, for there were at least two of them.

'Quickly, Nora!'

'Ah, keep your hair on, you daft old bat,' Mrs

Mullarkey muttered, finding the key at last and wrestling it into the lock. Into the car she clambered and unlocked the passenger door.

Granny swung herself inside and locked it again, buckling her seat belt hastily as Nora Mullarkey twisted the ignition key. She could see the shapes moving through the trees now; caught glimpses of white and red and moving shadows. The engine fired into life and Nora Mullarkey slammed it into reverse; with a whine the car shot backwards, juddering up the narrow lane.

And then the shapes burst from the trees, splashing across the stream towards them.

'Nora!' Granny exclaimed.

'I'm looking at the road behind us,' Mrs Mullarkey reminded her tersely. 'What kind of beings are they?

'More wee men in red,' Granny said. 'Three of them. On wee white horses with red ears.'

'Och, is that all? I thought it would be something scary.'

'Take a look at them and then say that. They look scary enough from where I'm sitting.'

'Aye, well, they can't do us much harm while they're out there and we're in here. And at this speed they couldn't get in even if the car *wasn't* made of steel.'

As if in answer, something hailed against the windscreen; cobweb cracks appeared across its surface.

'They're firing at us!'

'Make a U-turn when possible,' the sat-nav suggested politely. *'Recalculating.'*

'Well, now, that changes things,' Mrs Mullarkey said grimly. 'Hang onto your hat, Eileen; this could get bumpy!'

'With you driving, Nora? You don't say!'

The car accelerated backwards, the little horsemen in wild pursuit. Their faces spoke of fury and the joy of the hunt; their horses, savage as carnivores, pounded the track with thunderous hooves. An arm whirled; again the windscreen crackled, thin fractures starbursting across it. The car reached the top of the lane; not slowing, Mrs Mullarkey shot backwards into the road, twisting the steering wheel madly so that they slewed round; there was a grinding of gears and they leaped forward again. The pursuing horsemen erupted from the lane in front of them; there was a moment of chaos as the riders scattered to avoid the oncoming car. Mrs Mullarkey stamped on the pedal and ploughed through. The little horses wheeled; slings spun in their riders' hands, peppering the fleeing car with something hard and sharp.

'Go, Nora, go!' Granny exclaimed.

'Make a U-turn when possible,' the sat-nav added helpfully.

'Eileen,' Mrs Mullarkey said through gritted teeth as another volley of shots rattled against the rear doors, 'see if you can get that thing to tell us the way home, will you?'

Granny leaned forward and fumbled with the screen. Another burst sprayed the car; but this one seemed lighter, as if perhaps by just a tiny fraction they were pulling away.

'They're not gaining on us, at least,' Nora Mullarkey remarked with grim satisfaction.

'No, but we're not likely to lose them, either,' Granny pointed out. 'They're fast, those wee horses. And I'll bet they don't get tired like mortal horses do.'

'Lose them or not, they know where you live, Eileen,' Mrs Mullarkey reminded her. 'If we can shake them off, we'll head back to mine – they may not know where that is. But if not, then we'll try to beat them to yours by a good length. We'll be safe enough indoors until . . .'

She tailed off. There was a silence, broken only by the roar of the engine, the occasional patter of faery sling-shot on the rear door and, after a short while, the calm, measured voice of the sat-nav: *'After one point five kilometres, turn right.'*

'Aye, Nora, until what?' Granny asked eventually. 'We've no idea if they'll ever have to go back to the Other Realm, and we've no one to come and help us. And we don't know what it is they want, either.'

'Aye, there's a thing,' Mrs Mullarkey agreed. 'What was it that wee red man said? That you have something that belongs to a friend of his? What could that be, now?'

Granny stared at her, an idea dawning. 'You know, Nora, I hadn't even thought about that! There's only one thing it could be, too – do you remember?'

It took only a second or two for Mrs Mullarkey to cast her mind back. 'The wolf-skin,' she said slowly. 'The magic cloak that wee hoodlum – what's-his-name, the Dark Lord's henchman – put on to change himself into a wolf.'

Granny nodded. 'But I thought that young fellow was . . . gone.'

'As did we all, Eileen. And maybe he is, and those wee red fellows are spinning us a yarn. But if he's still in the land of the living, then maybe so is the Dark Lord, too.'

A single *crack* came from the rear. Granny looked round to see that the riders had fallen further behind – not yet far enough to make her breathe a sigh of relief, but enough to put them almost out of range for now.

'Well, you mustn't let him have it, Eileen. That young hallion's caused enough mischief with it already!'

Granny gasped, one wrinkled hand going in horror to her mouth.

'Now what's wrong?' Mrs Mullarkey asked impatiently. 'You haven't left it out in your shed or somewhere daft like that, have you?'

'No, Nora, it's not that! Do you not recall? I gave it to Bansi!'

Mrs Mullarkey took one hand off the wheel and stroked her chin thoughtfully, hardly noticing the car swerve towards the centre of the road. 'So you did, Eileen. That's not good, now, is it?'

'It is not!' her friend agreed. 'If they think of that . . . Nora! Suppose they work out a way of getting to London! She could be in terrible danger!'

'*After two hundred metres, turn right,*' the sat-nav said.

'You'd better call her,' Mrs Mullarkey said. 'My mobile's in my handbag there.'

Granny reached the handbag from the back. Mrs Mullarkey jerked on the wheel, sending them suddenly skidding round a sharp corner.

'*Continue for nine kilometres,*' the sat-nav advised.

'That was some clout you gave that fellow with this,' Granny observed, undoing the clasps.

'Aye, well, it's some handbag. Customized it

myself. See those silvery-looking studs all over the side? Stainless steel, every one.'

'And here I thought they were just for decoration,' Granny said, undoing the clasps. 'Was that the trick, then?'

'Half the trick. Have a feel inside the lining there. All the studs on each side are welded through the leather to an iron plate.'

'Ah,' Granny said.

There was something about the tone that prickled Mrs Mullarkey. 'What do you mean, "Ah", Eileen O'Hara? I should patent that handbag. Very useful for elderly ladies who have daft old friends who get themselves caught by the Good People at unexpected moments.'

'Oh, aye, it certainly got me out of a jam, there's no denying that. It's just that if you're going to belt somebody with two solid iron plates . . . it's probably best not to put your mobile phone in between them first.'

She held up the ruined remains of the device. It was smeared with what looked like mashed lipstick, and dusted with some kind of dark brown powder.

'Ah,' said Mrs Mullarkey.

'Exactly what I said,' Granny pointed out.

'Well, if only you'd got a mobile of your own . . .'

'Aye, well, I haven't. We'll just have to call her as

soon as we get back to Ballyfey,' Granny added worriedly, 'and hope she's all right till then.'

'I'm sure she'll be fine, Eileen. Sure, if they knew she had it, they wouldn't be after you and me.'

Granny brightened. 'You have a point there, Nora.' She brushed her hands together absently and then looked down at them. 'What on earth is this powder? It's all over the inside of your handbag, and now it's all over my hands, too.'

Mrs Mullarkey glanced at her warily. 'No idea,' she said.

Granny rummaged around inside the bag. 'It's your pills,' she said a moment later, producing a silvery blister-pack, the foil hanging loose at one end. 'Looks like your tablets are all crushed up, and a couple of them've got out.'

'They're not my tablets,' said Mrs Mullarkey curtly. 'There's nothing wrong with *me*. I picked them up from the chemist for old Mary Donnelly.'

'Aye, well, you'll have to get her a new packet,' Granny said, returning the blister-pack to a very crushed and crumpled cardboard box. 'These are nothing but crumbs and powder now.'

'Hmmph. I dare say it'll do her no harm to put the powder in a glass of water and take it that way.'

'Och, now, Nora, you have to be careful with medicines not to take too much . . .'

'Well, sure, isn't it the same amount whether it's powder or pill? And aren't they still most of them sealed up in their wee plastic bubbles?'

Granny shrugged. 'I suppose so. Still, no point in letting them get ground up any further.' She turned and tossed the box of ground tablets onto the back seat. 'Here,' she added, peering through the rear window, 'we haven't seen them wee red fellows in a few minutes. Where've they got to, do you think?'

Mrs Mullarkey glanced in her mirrors. 'I think maybe we've lost them—'

There was a sudden hail of shot against the driver's side; glass cracked and crackled. A blur of movement; two of the riders broke from the trees that bordered the road on its right, almost level with the car. The third suddenly appeared just ahead of them, charging straight at them, aiming to force them off the road. Another burst of stones peppered the windscreen.

Mrs Mullarkey didn't hesitate. She slipped down a gear and accelerated straight at the little horseman. For a moment it was uncertain whose nerve would break first; then the faery steed gave a sudden neigh of fright and vaulted high over the roof of the car. At the same moment, Mrs Mullarkey yanked the wheel hard left and the car spun off down a side road.

'*Recalculating*,' announced the sat-nav.

'Can you see anything at all through this windshield, Nora?' Granny asked anxiously. The windscreen was hopelessly fissured and cracked by now; here and there what appeared to be sharp triangular stones were buried in the glass, the points of some of them protruding inside. Granny reached out curiously to stroke one.

'Don't touch that!' Mrs Mullarkey told her. 'They look like elf-shot. It's said they carry disease. Mind you, it's said they're arrowheads, too, so who knows.'

'You never answered my question, Nora,' Granny said, withdrawing her hand quickly. 'Can you see all right through this glass?'

'Och, don't worry, Eileen. I know where I'm going. And there's always the wee talky box thing to point out the turnings, too.'

'*After five hundred metres, turn right, then turn left,*' the sat-nav said.

'Right,' Mrs Mullarkey added. 'Home as quickly as possible, keeping ahead of these wee hallions, so you can phone Bansi.'

'Oh, I hope she's all right,' Granny fretted.

'She'll be fine, Eileen, don't worry. Like I said, it's us the Good People are after this time. She'll still be at school now; and when she gets home I doubt she'll have anything to worry about but her homework. I'll bet you anything you like there are no Good People on the loose over in London.'

Another volley of elf-shot peppered the rear doors. Mrs Mullarkey checked the rear-view mirror and squeezed another burst of speed from the old and increasingly battered car.

Chapter Seven

How she knew, she had no idea; but Bansi sensed something was wrong the moment she returned to the house. Instinctively her hand went to her pocket.

That was when she realized that, in her hurry to leave the house that morning, she'd forgotten to take her key ring with her. As quickly and quietly as she could, she climbed the stairs and slipped into her bedroom. Heart thumping, she closed the door – and stopped in bewilderment at the sight that met her eyes.

The room was in turmoil. Her bedclothes were heaped on the floor; toys, games and clothes spilled randomly out of the cupboards and drawers.

Her key ring was nowhere to be seen.

Urgently she hunted through the tangled bed-clothes and searched the uncupboarded piles, but there was no sign of it. Nor was there any sign of the other little iron trinkets she'd taken to hoarding.

And then, with a start, she realized that the magnetic notice board that usually hung on the wall was also missing; it, and all the magnets that held the notices and reminders in place. Letters from school and party invitations lay scattered across her homework desk.

There was without doubt a pattern emerging. But what to do? How to arm herself? She cast around for inspiration; and for some reason her attention was drawn to a box that was mostly hidden in a jumble of clothes. It was the chemistry set she'd been given at Christmas by an uncle who didn't know her well enough to choose something she wanted. She'd never even opened the box – for almost a year it had lain forgotten – but now she realized she might be glad of it after all. Quickly she tipped the contents onto the floor; a moment's searching was enough to find the small glass vial she'd hoped might be in there.

Moments later, she tiptoed cautiously downstairs. Her senses were all alert, and as she reached the ground floor of the house, she heard a noise. She stilled, and listened harder as it came again.

It was laughter. Her mother's laughter, pure and true, coming from the kitchen. Relieved, Bansi almost ran to the door, and pushed it open. There was her mother, cheerful and relaxed, standing by the kettle.

And sitting at the kitchen table was Hob Under-the-Hill.

Bansi clenched the glass vial in her fist, her thumb

pressing angrily against the rubber stopper. 'What are *you* doing in here?' she demanded.

'Bansi!' her mother said sharply. It was her *I'm-surprised-at-you* voice, but Bansi was too angry to care. She glared fury at Hob.

Hob smiled pleasantly. 'Ah, the pretty changeling child! Yes, I know, I know,' he went on before Bansi had a chance to challenge him, 'you're not a changeling. But then, you said I wasn't welcome here, and you seem to be wrong about that, too.' He glanced at Asha O'Hara, who was now casting puzzled looks from him to her daughter and back again. 'You're not ready for this conversation yet, mortal lady,' he said, waving his hand vaguely in her direction. 'Take no notice.'

Asha O'Hara smiled hazily and turned back to the kettle as it came to the boil.

Bansi felt a fresh tangle of anger and fear rise within her. 'Mum?' she said; but there was no reply. Her mother began serenely to make the tea.

'She can't hear you,' Hob said pleasantly. 'Not really. There'll be a nice sort of blah-blah-blah sound going on in her head, and she'll maybe catch bits and pieces, but she's off in a bit of a day-dream. So we can bargain and deal, and she'll hear nothing.'

Bansi could feel herself trembling with anger.

'We've got nothing to talk about. Take that enchantment off my mum and go.'

Hob Under-the-Hill threw his head back and laughed. 'Ah, now, you'll be a hard one to haggle with, I can tell. But—'

'We're not going to haggle about anything!' Bansi said. 'You're going to take your enchantment off my mum, and you're going to leave!'

Hob's grin was infuriating. 'Well, firstly, pretty changeling, she's not really your mother, is she?'

Heedless of any danger, Bansi leaned in close, eyes blazing. 'She *is* my mother. I am *not* a changeling. And you have no right to be here.'

Hob just went on smiling. 'The lady of the house invited me in; so I have every right to be here. And it may please you to pretend to be a mortal; but you and I both know the truth. You have the smell of Tir na n'Óg all over you. And how would a mere mortal have known me as you did this morning, or seen me good and clear as you did last night? So let's end the pretence, and strike a bargain.' He leaned in closer, almost nose-to-nose with her, clearly amused by her angry refusal to retreat. 'What do you want? Anything my master can give you, little changeling, it'll be yours – in exchange for your help.'

'I'm not helping you do anything.' Her fists were clenching in fury now, one thumb still unconsciously working away at the rubber stopper. 'And all I want is for you and your kind to leave me and my family alone.'

''Scuse me, love,' said Bansi's mother vaguely, reaching past her with a steaming mug of tea and a plate of biscuits. 'There you are, Bob. Sugar?'

'Yes please, Asha, sweetheart,' Hob replied, with a wink that was mostly for Bansi's benefit. 'That'd be grand.' Taking the proffered bowl, he spooned in four or five heaps and, ignoring the fact that the drink was scalding, took a great and appreciative swallow. 'Ah,' he said, reaching for the biscuits, 'that's the stuff! Thanks, Asha. Now, young changeling, you can be our friend, or our enemy, but really – what are these mortals to you?'

Bansi had learned long ago that there are some people with whom it's not worth arguing. She folded her arms and glared at him, one hidden thumb still worrying away at the glass vial's stopper.

'So,' Hob continued, 'what'll it be? Riches? Power? Maybe immortality, if you want to stay here in the mortal realm – though I should tell you that Tir na n'Óg's a brighter place now than it's been in a long time.' He smiled winningly. 'You might want to come back with me – maybe to join my master's court? There'd be a great reward in it for you if you helped him.'

Bansi continued to stare. 'Are you going to take the enchantment off my mum now?' she asked coldly.

Hob rolled his eyes good-humouredly. 'You know as well as I do that she's not your real ma, girl. Your real mother's one of – how did you put it? – *my people*. Just like you, however you choose to deny it. Now, come on; what'll it take to gain your help?' He stood, stretching luxuriously so that Bansi had to step back, and flung his arms wide, indicating the room around him. 'The mortal world's fine for a bit,' he said. 'You can have fun here, sure enough. But for a changeling child, all alone, that's about as good as it gets. Now on the other hand,' he went on, and his smile grew wider and sharper, 'just think of the fun you could have, and the power you could wield, and the sheer mayhem you could create, if my master's favour fell upon you.'

It was the third time he had mentioned his master, and Bansi suddenly felt it was important she should know more.

'And who is this mighty master, then?' she challenged.

There was something predatory in Hob's smile now. He had the air of a hunter, luring his quarry into a snare. 'My master,' he confided, leaning closer like a false friend, 'is the Dread Cruach, Sovereign of the Red Court and Monarch of the Nightlands – a great and mighty faery lord. Help him, little changeling, and he will not be slow to show his gratitude.'

Just the name gave Bansi the shivers. *Not the Lord of the Dark Sidhe, then*, she thought. *I bet it's the blood-red rider*. Taking a chance, she said, 'So, what was this master of yours doing hanging around outside my house all night?'

Hob shrugged cheerfully. 'Don't miss much, do you? He was staking his claim.'

Bansi felt her stomach clench and knot fearfully. Echoes of her battle with the Dark Lord jostled her memory. 'Staking his claim? This is my home! He's got no right to claim anything here!'

The look of amused condescension on Hob's face now was infuriating. 'When a lord is as mighty as mine,' he said nonchalantly, sitting down again and reaching for his tea, 'who will deny him whatever pretty trinket catches his eye? The Dread Cruach has made his claim, and it's not for the likes of you to dispute it.'

Bansi's immediate instinct was to dispute it very loudly.

'But that's stupid! I mean, for one thing, he can't come and bagsy something that belongs to somebody else just because he's taken a fancy to it! Anyway, if he's so great and mighty and powerful, what could he possibly find in our house that he hasn't already got?'

Hob shrugged once more, as if the answer was obvious. 'A mortal bride.'

Bansi's mouth fell open in surprise. She was on the point of saying, 'But I'm too young to get married!' when she realized Hob couldn't mean her – he didn't believe she *was* mortal. And then, with a shock, she understood.

'Well,' said Asha O'Hara, sitting down just a little too close to Hob Under-the-Hill and putting her hand on his shoulder, 'isn't this nice?'

Chapter Eight

'No!' Bansi yelled. She snatched the mug from Hob's hand and set it firmly down on the table, ignoring both the splash of hot tea that stung her wrist, and her mum's shocked protestations – which lasted only a moment before she sank back into her enchanted daydream. Angrily, Bansi gripped the vial tighter, thumb furiously pushing. 'Get out! You go back to your master and tell him to forget it! My mum is married already – *happily* married!'

Hob was genuinely puzzled. 'Why the fuss, changeling? I've told you – you can have anything you want in return for helping. Better still – whatever you want, in exchange simply for standing by and doing nothing. It's a good bargain. We'll even replace the woman with an enchanted carving so perfect her husband'll never know the difference. It'll still feed you and clothe you – you'll hardly notice any change yourself.'

'For the last time, I am *not* a changeling, and you are *not* taking my mother!' Bansi glared at him, fists clenched, her anger almost drowning her.

He gazed back, unconcerned and uncomprehending. 'The Dread Cruach has claimed her, girl. She's taken his fancy, and he's decided to have her. There's nothing you can do.'

For a moment, the world seemed to Bansi to be just the two of them, eyes locked, with her mother somewhere in the background, as shadowy as her own enchanted daydream. Then Hob picked up the mug again, raised it ironically as if proposing a toast, and took another appreciative gulp.

Bansi flexed her fists again, filled with the primal urge to lash out and hurt him. Hob, smiling with calm uncaring confidence, set the mug down and reached for another biscuit. She heard her own breathing, loud and angry; felt her fingers wrapped tight around the glass, her thumb pressing hard against the rubber.

The stopper shot from the mouth of the vial and bounced on the floor behind Hob, hitting the skirting board with a loud *pock*.

Hob turned sharply, as if ready for danger; Asha O'Hara looked round dreamily; and without thinking Bansi upended the vial, tipping half its contents into Hob's mug. Her thumb stoppered the end as she closed it once more in her fist.

Hob, seeing nothing, shrugged once more and

turned back to her. He took a bite of his biscuit and spread out his hands as though appealing to reason. 'I don't get it, changeling child,' he said. 'You might as well take all the rewards the Dread Cruach has to offer. There's no point trying to oppose him; you can't win.'

'That's what the Lord of the Dark Sidhe said,' Bansi snapped. 'He was wrong, too.'

Hob's eyes widened. 'The Lord of the Dark— Wait a minute! Ah, hang on there – you're not . . . Oh, now it makes sense! Now it *all* makes sense!' He leaped to his feet excitedly. 'You're the child of the Blood of the Morning Stars! Which means that this lovely lady is of a royal line! Not only a beautiful mortal, but a direct descendant of one of the greatest faery kings who ever lived! What a prize! Just wait till I tell the Dread Cruach! He won't change his mind now, even if he'd ever have done before.' He grinned at Bansi again. 'And I know of one or two faery folk who'd be delighted to know where you live, young one, so you'd better not stand in my way, I can tell you.'

He laughed and, sitting down, picked up his tea once more; but Bansi snatched it away and set it down defiantly.

'Get out,' she said coldly. 'Get out of my house; keep away from my mum. She's not yours, or your master's either.'

Hob reached deliberately across for the drink, still smiling. 'Get out, is it?' he asked cockily. 'Or you'll do what?' Settling arrogantly back into the chair, he drained the mug.

The effect, as the hot liquid hit the back of his mouth, was both immediate and alarming. He gasped; turned purple; rose to his feet, stumbling and choking, clutching at his throat. His appearance changed, flickering wildly between his casual disguise and the elegant, top-hatted appearance of the night before, with strange traces of other shapes and forms dancing and storming around him.

'What . . . how . . . what did . . . ?' he gagged, almost doubling up on the kitchen chair.

Bansi held up the vial. She felt surprisingly calm and controlled. 'Iron filings,' she said. 'I don't want to hurt you; but I'm not going to let you take my mum. So you can tell your boss to find some nice single girl in his own kingdom, if he wants to get married – and to make sure he asks her properly, instead of just enchanting her and planning a kidnapping.'

Hob snarled and spluttered angrily, his composure gone. Spitting and retching, he tried desperately and ineffectually to dislodge the iron filings from the back of his throat. 'I'll kill you for this, child!' he gasped. With a sudden effort he launched himself from his seat, arms reaching to strangle her. Bansi reacted instinctively; her arm lashed out, flinging the rest of the iron filings straight into his face.

There was a scream; a sulphurous smell of burning; and then Hob was gone, only a wisp of smoke betraying the fact that he had ever been there.

Bansi's legs felt unexpectedly weak. She sank into the nearest chair, head in her hands, and waited for the sudden feeling of nausea to go. She breathed deeply, just once, in and out again, and felt better.

But only until she looked up. Her mother was standing over her, arms folded, wearing a face of fury.

'If you have any kind of explanation for that behaviour, young lady,' Asha O'Hara said firmly, 'I would just *love* to hear it!'

Chapter Nine

'Can you see them back there, Eileen?' Nora Mullarkey asked, peering through the crazed windscreen as the dark green Morris Minor Traveller roared along the narrow country road to Ballyfey.

Granny turned and looked behind them. The rear windows were almost as badly cracked by this time, and it was hard to tell; taking a risk, she wound down her own window and leaned out.

'No sign of them, Nora,' she yelled against the wind. 'No, wait – is that them?' The road wound and curved, but just for a second she thought she'd caught a glimpse of white, then a flash of red, far behind. It came again; and then the road straightened for a length, and just before they reached the next curve Granny had a clear view: all three riders in red were galloping fiercely, their untiring horses maintaining the distance between them. 'Aye, there they are.' She drew her head back in and wound the window up. It had been much the same all the way back, with the riders on their tail, dropping back but making ground where they could cut across country. 'Best head for mine then, Nora – no sense in letting them know where you live, too. Good job you didn't have to stop for petrol on the way back, that's all I can say.'

'Aye, well, there's a thing,' Mrs Mullarkey answered distractedly. 'Ever since our wee trip to the Other Realm, I've hardly had to fill up with petrol at all.'

'Really?' Granny said, casting another look backwards to check on their pursuers. 'That's awfully clever, now, isn't it? Those brownies ought to set up in business.' She half smiled in spite of their situation as she recalled how an entire tribe of the little people had not only thoroughly valeted the car but had apparently serviced the engine; there wasn't a faster car now in the whole county. She'd often had cause to regret that, but not today; any slower and the riders behind them would have caught them by now.

'*After four kilometres, turn left*,' the sat-nav said as they screeched round a blind bend on the wrong side of the road. '*Then you have reached your destination*.'

'I'm not sure if it's just down to the brownies,' Mrs Mullarkey said thoughtfully. 'There was an awful lot of magical power floating about all over the place, if you remember. I'm wondering if it might have been something to do with that. But whatever the cause, it's been a big saving for me.'

'It might well have just saved the both of us,' said Granny.

'Aye, well, perhaps. But don't count your chickens, Eileen. We're not home yet.'

'Maybe not, Nora; but we're just five minutes away. And then I'm going to call my wee Bansi and make sure she's OK.'

'Ach, don't fret, Eileen. I'm sure she's absolutely fine.'

Bansi was not absolutely fine. She was having the worst argument of her entire life. Faeries, she thought unhappily, could make grown-ups so unreasonable.

It was bad enough that, as far as her mum was concerned, Hob was the innocent victim of Bansi's bad temper. Worse still was the fact that she didn't seem able to properly hear what Bansi was saying; the enchantment clearly still held, and ran deep. So deep that it was futile to argue, but Bansi couldn't help herself.

'Mum, he's been in my room! He's taken my key ring, and my notice board, and—'

'Don't be so ridiculous, Bansi! As if any grown-up would want those silly things! Anyway, that wasn't Bob; it was me. I decided it was time for a clear-out.'

'*What?* You just took my things without asking? Where are they?'

Bansi's mum dismissed her anger with a wave of the hand. 'I gave them to the rag-and-bone man. They were in such a state, Bansi; I couldn't bear to touch them. I had to wear three pairs of gloves. You should be glad I got rid of them . . .'

'*Glad?* Mum, I needed those things – I *really* needed them. And don't you see – you wouldn't normally do something like that! *He's* making you behave this way!'

'Oh, now I'm getting *really* angry, Bansi! Bob Underhill is a nice man, and you're acting as if he's some kind of—'

'He is not a nice man! Didn't you see how he just *vanished*?'

'Can you blame him? I wouldn't stick around if someone else's child behaved like that to me! That was so *rude*, Bansi!'

'No, Mum, I mean *really* vanished!'

'Yes, and *I'd* really vanish, too! Anyone with any self-respect would! I'd be out that door like a shot, and I wouldn't come back! And if Bob doesn't come back, I'll never forgive you!'

'You don't under*stand* . . .'

'I understand perfectly! For some reason my own daughter is jealous of my having a little happiness for once!'

The words hit Bansi like a slap in the face. 'Mum!

What do you mean? You're one of the happiest people I know!'

Her mother laughed a joylessly ironic little laugh. 'It may look like that to you, Bansi; but I haven't been happy for years. Not really. Your dad's a sweet man, but . . .' She left the sentence hanging.

'Mum, you're under an enchantment! Hob Under-the-Hill is making you think things you don't really think!'

Her mum looked at her with one of those slightly sad faces grown-ups sometimes make when they think you're being silly and they know best. 'When you're older, Bansi, you'll understand. Bob Underhill is a wonderful man.'

'Mum, he's a *faery*!'

Later, Bansi couldn't tell what had made her forget the prohibition on speaking directly of the people of Tir na n'Óg. Perhaps it was the dreamy look on her mother's face when she spoke about Hob; perhaps it was the unconscious thought that if the Dread Cruach already knew where she lived there was nothing worse that could come of saying the word. Or perhaps it was just desperation to make her point, to try to get across the nature of the threat her mother faced. Whichever it was, it had the wrong effect. Asha O'Hara's expression grew grim and set and furious.

'Bansi O'Hara!' she snapped. 'I did *not* raise you

to be a bigot! Just because Bob may seem a little . . . *different* to you, just because he's lively and funny and wears colourful shirts, that is no reason to call him names! You go to your room right now, young lady, and do not come down until I tell you!'

'But, Mum—'

'No buts, Bansi, just go!'

'Mum!'

'You're not too big to be dragged upstairs,' Bansi's mother told her firmly and coldly, 'and I'll do it if I have to.'

'We'll just make it!' Mrs Mullarkey declared. 'Those wee hoodlums on horseback won't catch us before we reach your front door now!'

'You have reached your destination,' the sat-nav put in.

'Aye,' Granny said grimly as the car swung onto the gravel drive of her home, 'but somebody else got here first.'

Sure enough, the first little man in scarlet was there already, poised in front of the house. His expression was triumphant; his posture confident and sure. In his hand whirled a viciously loaded sling. He stood on the doorstep, blocking the doorway, cutting off their only route to safety.

And behind them, the horsemen were coming.

Chapter Ten

The little man raised the sling higher, as if ready to fire. The expression on his face made it clear that he thought he had won.

Mrs Mullarkey soon put him right about that. Gunning the engine, she accelerated straight towards the front door.

The little man's smile dropped. With a shout, and just in time, he leaped high in the air, somersaulting over the roof of the car and – though the occupants couldn't tell – vanishing in mid-twist.

The car slammed into the door, popping it open with a dreadful splintering of wood. Quick as blinking, Mrs Mullarkey ground into reverse and flicked the steering wheel. The car slid round, its flank parallel with the wall, and skidded right up against the house. There were sparks and the grinding, tearing sound of steel on stone; the car jerked to a halt and – just as the three horsemen galloped up, hooves spraying gravel – Mrs Mullarkey opened the driver's door right into Granny's hallway.

'Quick!' Out she scrambled, into the safety of the house.

'Well, now, Nora Mullarkey,' Granny complained, clambering after her, 'just look what you've done to my front door!'

'Hmmmph,' Mrs Mullarkey grunted. 'I suppose you'd have preferred me to just say "excuse me" nicely and hope that wee horror got out of the way?'

'I'd have *preferred—*' Granny began; but exactly what she would have preferred remained unsaid. They were interrupted by the *whhhttt* of several sharp projectiles embedding themselves in the wall.

'What the—' Granny began. 'Now they're tearing great holes in my wallpaper!'

'That's nothing,' Mrs Mullarkey retorted, 'compared to what they've done to my car!'

'Which is nothing compared to what your car's done to my house!'

'Which is nothing compared to what they'd have done to the both of us if they'd caught us, Eileen O'Hara, and don't you forget it!'

Behind them, another volley of elf-shot skittered off the roof of the car and onto the tiled hall floor. The two old women edged back towards the kitchen.

'This is ridiculous,' Granny said. 'Under siege in my own home! Well, I'm not standing for it. Come on, Nora, time to fight back.'

Mrs Mullarkey looked sceptical. 'And how do you propose to do that?'

Granny was already mounting the stairs. 'Come on and I'll show you,' she said.

'Right,' Mrs Mullarkey said as they entered Granny's bedroom. 'So you have a plan, do you, Eileen?'

'I do,' Granny said. 'Just open up my wardrobe and get out what you'll find in the bottom of it, will you?'

The bottom of the wardrobe turned out to contain a large stack of shoe boxes. Mrs Mullarkey lifted a couple out; they were surprisingly heavy, and rattled. Setting them on the bed, she removed the first lid. The box was full of little shiny spheres.

'Steel ball bearings! Very crafty, Eileen. They won't be so full of themselves after we fling a few handfuls of these out the window on top of them.'

Granny grinned. 'Better than that, Nora! Do you remember the time we were wee girls and got ourselves in big trouble for scaring old Mr Magill's cat and breaking his front window?' She held up two clearly home-made, but equally clearly well-made, catapults.

Now it was Mrs Mullarkey's turn to grin. 'Ah, now you're talking, Eileen,' she said, taking the proffered weapon. 'Although, to be fair, it was *you* whose shot went wide and broke old man Magill's window. Even in those days, I was too handy with one of these things to ever do something so silly.'

'What! The nerve of you, Nora Mullarkey! I was always the better shot! You were the one who couldn't have hit a barn door if you were inside the barn!'

'Is that right?' Mrs Mullarkey said, grabbing a shoe box and setting herself up in position. 'Twenty euros says I can knock one of those wee blighters off his horse before you can!'

Granny grinned and armed her own catapult. 'That'll be twenty euros you'll owe me, then, Nora.' She opened the window, took aim, and fired. Moments later, there came a surprised yelp from outside.

'Ha!' Mrs Mullarkey said. 'That was a lucky shot if ever I saw one. Anyhow, it doesn't count unless he falls right off.' She took aim herself. 'Take this, you wee hallion!' she yelled, and let fly. 'And stay away from my car if you know what's good for you!'

Bansi stamped up the stairs to her bedroom. She'd prolonged the argument as long as she'd dared, but somehow, even though – or perhaps because – her mother was under an enchantment, she hadn't been able to bring herself to the point of outright and open defiance. Besides, the angrier she'd become, the more her mother had talked down to her, treating her as if her point of view was of no consequence – just because she was young. And even though she knew it wasn't really her mother's fault, it hurt.

Furious and frustrated, she slammed her open hand against the closed bedroom door. It stung her palm; she didn't care. Grabbing the handle, she twisted and pushed much harder than was necessary.

Then she stopped, sudden bewilderment dissolving into bright hope. For the bedroom, which she had left in such a mess, was now completely, wonderfully tidy. And only one explanation made any sense.

'Pogo?' she said, hardly daring to believe it. 'Pogo!'

There was a pause. It felt as if the whole world was silent and waiting.

'Come on, Pogo,' she said. 'I know you're here!'

There was another pause, during which nothing seemed to move.

Bansi folded her arms determinedly. 'Oh, come on, Pogo,' she said, with just a hint of impatience. 'Don't play hide-and-seek with me!'

Something shifted on the lowest shelf of the book-case. A large and mostly unread reference book slid outwards and toppled onto the carpet; and there, framed in the gap between an encyclopaedia and a copy of *Myths and Legends of Ireland*, stood a figure that Bansi had been aching to see: a little brown man, dressed in a loincloth, with wild shaggy hair and a grumpy expression.

'Ah, how did you know it was me?' he grumbled.

Bansi ran to him and knelt down; she wanted to pick him up and hug him, but she felt he would never submit to such indignity; so she settled for bending forward and planting a kiss on the top of his head.

'Careful, now, you'll mess up my hair.' Pogo scowled, pushing the reference book carefully and neatly back into place; and despite her misery Bansi smiled.

'I'm so glad you're here,' she said.

'Aye, well,' the little brownie said, stepping down from the bookcase and hopping up onto her bed to perch on her pillow, 'before you start on all that – have you no sense? Do you not remember the dangers to mortals of using the word "faery"? You'll have drawn the attention of every faery being for miles around!'

'I know,' Bansi said, standing. 'But I don't see how it could make things any worse.'

'Well,' Pogo admitted grudgingly, 'to be fair, it might have made things better. I don't know if I'd have found you myself so quickly otherwise. But what's the matter?'

Bansi sighed, unsure of where to begin. She flopped down onto the bed herself, and turned to face him. 'My mum's been enchanted because some creepy Dark Lord type wants to marry her. He was outside our house all night. And his servant's been in our kitchen all afternoon.'

Pogo's eyes widened. 'That's bad, right enough. What does this Lord call himself?'

'The Dread Cruach. Lord of the Nightlands, or something . . . Oh, and ruler of the . . . Red Court, I think. But what's going on, Pogo? How come there are any Good People here at all? I thought there was no way to our world from Tir na n'Óg except at Midsummer or Midwinter; and I thought the only gateway was in Ballyfey!'

'Aye. Well.' Pogo seemed somehow awkward, ill at ease. 'The thing is, you remember what the prophecy said?'

Bansi nodded impatiently. 'Something like . . . *When the Blood of the Morning Stars is returned to the sacred earth of Tir na n'Óg, the land will wake up and the one who returns the blood will get the inheritance of Derga.*'

'That's most of it, more or less,' Pogo agreed gruffly, 'though it's not the land, but the power of the land. And you forgot the second bit. The whole prophecy goes: *When the Blood of the Morning Stars, joined and flowing together at last, is returned to the sacred earth as the light dies, then shall the power of Tir na n'Óg awaken. Then shall the ways between the worlds reopen. And the one who returns the blood to the land shall come into the inheritance of Derga.*'

Bansi's heart sank. 'Pogo, you're not going to tell me that this is all to do with the prophecy, are you? I thought that was over and done.'

'Nothing's ever over and done,' Pogo retorted. 'Everything we do makes a new future.'

'Yes, but—'

'I know, I know. You thought it was over for you. And I have to say, I'd hoped it was, too. You're a brave girl, Bansi O'Hara, and you faced danger well. But now you may have to face it again. And it may not be the last time.'

Bansi closed her eyes for a moment, as if to hold something inside. Then she breathed out, slowly. 'All right, Pogo,' she said quietly. 'Tell me what I need to know.'

Chapter Eleven

'The first thing we need to look at,' Pogo began, 'is the second part of the prophecy: *When the Blood of the Morning Stars is returned to the sacred earth, then shall the ways between the worlds reopen*. That's what's happening. The ways between the worlds are reopening.'

Bansi shivered. 'Pogo – are you trying to tell me that because of me, my world's going to be plagued with Good People now? No offence,' she added, realizing that perhaps she'd been rude; 'if you ask me, every house should have a brownie. But some of these others – the Dark Sidhe, or the Dread Cruach . . . Are they going to be popping up everywhere all the time now?'

Pogo shook his head. 'Not the whole time,' he said. 'And not everywhere. Remember what I said before – about why Midsummer and Midwinter were the times the gateway opened?'

Bansi thought hard. 'It was something to do with them being . . . border times, wasn't it? The end of one thing, and the beginning of another?'

Pogo nodded. 'It was. Magically, those are the strongest times, when light gives way to darkness or darkness to light. But there are other border times – many others. And now that the power of Tir na n'Óg is awakening . . .'

'The gateway will open at those times, too,' Bansi finished for him. 'Or – gateways? You told me before that there used to be *lots* of gateways, didn't you? Is that part of what the prophecy means – that all of the ancient gateways will reopen, too? How many are there?'

Pogo shrugged. 'No one knows. But the one that's open here, now – the one that brought me here; up through an underground station, it goes – it's not one of the ancient gateways, as far as I can make out. It doesn't seem to me that there's ever been one here before, and why a new one should suddenly open instead of any of the ancient ones I just can't work out. Unless . . .' He paused, as if the thought that had just occurred to him was not one he enjoyed. 'Unless . . . I hate to say this, girl; but I think it might be down to you.'

'Me? Pogo, how could I possibly have opened up a gateway to the Other Realm?'

'No, I don't mean that. I mean . . . the inheritance of Derga is yours, right? You have the power of your ancestor now, as promised by the ancient prophecy.'

Bansi shook her head. 'I don't think so – not really. Or, at least . . . if I *did* inherit the magic of Derga, I think I must have used it all up against the Dark Lord.'

Pogo tutted. 'Nonsense, girl. You mean to tell me you've felt no spark of the ancient power since Midsummer?'

'No. None at all.'

'Nothing? You've not found yourself influencing others more easily? You've had no foretellings of the future? No glimpses of something others couldn't see?'

Bansi thought. 'I suppose there was something, last night . . .' she said slowly. 'The first time I saw Hob Under-the-Hill – the Dread Cruach's servant – it seemed as if Mum couldn't see him.' She paused, remembering. 'In fact – it kind of looked as if no one else on the whole street could.'

'But you did,' Pogo said.

Bansi nodded again. 'And then, when he came to the house this morning, he seemed surprised that I recognized him from the night before. Is that the sort of thing you mean?'

'That's it exactly. Being able to see through a faery glamour is powerful magic, though it may seem nothing to you when it happens. Anything else?'

'Um . . . just before I saw him yesterday, I got this creepy feeling.' She closed her eyes, trying to catch her thoughts. 'And last night – I think I had some weird dreams.'

Pogo seemed unsurprised. 'Aye. Knowledge beyond mortal abilities. Being able to see things as they really are. All signs of faery power of some kind. Like I said – you're the child of the Blood of the Morning Stars, the heir of Derga.'

'But then why haven't I felt anything since Midsummer? How come this is the first time these . . . these powers have done anything?'

'Well, this is what I'm thinking. See, I've always thought of the prophecy as containing three separate promises: when the prophecy is fulfilled, the power of the land will awaken, the ways between the worlds will reopen, and the one who fulfils it gets the inheritance of Derga. But what if they're linked?' He looked at her meaningfully. 'What if, for instance, the inheritance of Derga *flows* from the power of the land? And what if it flows through the reopened ways?'

Again Bansi shook her head. 'I don't get what you mean.'

'I mean: what if the power you've inherited from your ancestor comes to you *through* the land of Tir na n'Óg itself, now its own power has awakened?

And what if, in order to grant you that power, the land of Tir na n'Óg has opened up a new gateway, right near where you are, now that another border time is at hand?'

'You mean – you mean a gateway's opened up near here . . . because of *me*? Because Tir na n'Óg is trying to give me . . .'

'Your inheritance. Aye, it could well be.'

Bansi's stomach lurched, as if the floor had given way under her. 'And now my mum's in danger . . . and even if we manage to keep her safe, there's a gateway from the Other Realm in our local tube station! What's to stop . . . *Good People* just pouring through it any time they like? And, Pogo!' she exclaimed as a new and horrific thought gripped her. 'Does that mean anyone who goes into the tube station at sunrise or sunset will be transported to Tir na n'Óg?'

'No, no,' Pogo hastened to reassure her. 'It's not like the gateway in the stone circle. It's more . . . *wild* than that. More like the old days, the old magic of Tir na n'Óg. You've been reading the ancient tales, have you?' he added, nodding at the bookshelf and, in particular, the copy of *Myths and Legends of Ireland*.

'Some of them. They don't all make sense, though.'

'Aye, well, that's how faery magic is to mortals. It

doesn't all make sense; but there's a sense to it all the same. So you've read of how mortals would find themselves in the Other Realm, but not every mortal who used a particular road would find it led them there. So it is now, with this new gateway. Most people will be safe using the station, and not even know there's anything magical . . . but there may be some who find themselves taken to Tir na n'Óg through it. Only while the way is open, mind; and once it closes it may open again and it may not.'

Bansi felt a sudden rush of relief. 'Of course,' she said. 'The gateway near Granny's house only opened for two days in the summer – on Midsummer's Eve and on Midsummer's Day. So this one won't open for any longer than that, will it? And I first saw Hob yesterday, so today's the last day, isn't it? In a couple of hours it'll close and . . .'

Her voice tailed off as Pogo fixed her with a stare.

'There's the thing,' he said. 'This is what happens when you mortals mess around with the natural order. You see, there's a border time that marks the midpoint of the land's descent into darkness. It comes halfway between the autumn equinox – when day and night are the same length, and darkness and light are in perfect balance – and Midwinter's Day, the shortest day of the year: the moment of darkness's greatest power. But there's more to it than that. In ancient times, it was when folk had to decide which of their livestock would be slaughtered to help them live through the long winter ahead, and so it became a border between life and death; between survival and destruction. Do you see?' He leaned in fiercely. '*Humans* made this border time; they created it out of their fear and need, out of blood and death and meat and . . . well, you can imagine what kind of faery would be drawn to that. So they created festivals around it, to control it and tie it down and make sure that the two worlds were brought close only for as short a time as possible. There've been many names for these festivals, this season; but here and now, Bansi, you know it as Hallowe'en.'

'But Hallowe'en's weeks away!' Bansi protested; and then she stopped, the conversation with her mother the previous evening nudging at her mind.

'Aye,' Pogo nodded. 'But now – and for no other reason but money, mind – mortals have stretched out the season: filling your shops with it, decorating with it, buying and selling it, making mischief, playing tricks and begging for treats in its name, first for days and then for weeks beforehand, until the edges of Hallowe'en extend way out beyond where their borders once stood. And now that the prophecy is fulfilled and the land of Tir na n'Óg has the power once more to touch the mortal world, the two will bleed together until the festival is over and the sun sets on All Saints' Day.'

'Pogo, what are we going to do? In that time, there could be an invasion! A whole army from the Other Realm could cross over.'

'It's not likely,' Pogo assured her. 'The tribes and kingdoms that are set on conquest – well, most of them are at war with one another, or maintaining an uneasy peace with their neighbours. They wouldn't spread themselves so thin as to make war on the mortal world as well. No, most of the faery beings that cross over during the next few weeks – and they will, make no mistake about that – will only want to make mischief and to make merry. There'll be a few like your Dread Cruach, who'll take it into their heads to steal away a mortal wife or a mortal husband for no other reason than that they can, and who'll enjoy the sport of the stealing as much as the marriage that comes after. There'll be others who steal babies or children and exchange them for changelings, I dare say, but there's maybe little we can do about that . . .'

'But we're going to try, aren't we, Pogo?'

Pogo looked at her. Bansi's face was set and determined.

He sighed. 'Aye. We'll do our best, little though that may be. Now, child: tell me everything you know and have heard and have seen about this Dread Cruach, and his servant Hob; and then we'll make a start.'

Chapter Twelve

'That was mine!' Granny yelled. 'Got him! That's twenty euros if you please, Nora!'

'What?' Mrs Mullarkey blustered, letting fly with another steel ball bearing. 'That was mine, Eileen O'Hara! It's *you* owe *me* twenty euros!'

Granny glared sideways at her old friend, and armed her catapult again. 'Nora Maura Margaret Thingummy Mullarkey,' she said, firing. 'I declare, you always were a sore loser!'

'Sore loser nothing! It's just that *my* eyesight's good enough to see when *I* knock one of those wee rapscallions off his horse!'

'There's nothing wrong with my eyesight, Nora Mullarkey; nor with my aim, either. It's me who knocked that wee fellow off his horse, and you know it! And it would've been sooner, too, if they didn't keep disappearing round the corner! What do they think they're doing, riding round and round the house like that?'

Mrs Mullarkey sighed dramatically and released

another missile. 'All right, Eileen, tell you what: forget that one, and forty – no, *fifty* euros on the next one. Which'll be mine. Fair enough?'

Granny raised her eyebrows scornfully and shot. 'As long as you don't try to wriggle out of it again, Nora; though knowing you . . .' She took aim once more. 'Is it just me, or is it getting foggy out there?'

'That'll be your eyesight, Eileen,' her friend said dryly. She drew back, ready to take aim, and stopped. 'Here! Where've those wee devils got to?'

'Can you not see them?' Granny asked innocently. 'Maybe it's your own eyesight that's the problem?'

'Nonsense! It's all that fog that's suddenly appeared! It'll be some kind of magical trickery, no doubt!'

And indeed, the house was quickly and efficiently being surrounded by fog – thin, misty and insubstantial, yet still enough to hide the horsemen as they galloped round and round like figures from some nightmare carousel.

'I don't like this, Eileen,' Mrs Mullarkey growled. 'They're up to something. I reckon they've conjured this fog so they can sneak something nasty up on us.'

Granny rubbed her chin thoughtfully. 'Well,' she said, 'maybe we can unconjure it before they can do whatever it is they're planning.'

'How on earth do you propose to do that?' her

friend snapped, peering vainly through the gathering haze. 'You're not going to pretend wee Bansi's been giving you lessons, are you?'

Granny sighed. 'Nora, it's a magic fog. You know as well as I do how to beat the Good People's magic.'

'For goodness's sake, it's *fog*! It's not like you can make it go away by hitting it with a horseshoe! See?' Mrs Mullarkey fired a steel ball bearing into the approaching thickness. It traced a path through the cloudy white, and disappeared.

'That's as may be, Nora,' Granny said, 'but I was thinking of using something a little larger. It occurs to me that if these wee men have made a fog by *riding* round and round the house . . .'

A light came on in Mrs Mullarkey's eyes. 'Maybe we can *un*make it by *driving* round and round the house! Eileen, sometimes – just *sometimes* – you're not as daft as you look! Come on!'

'Hang on a second, Nora!' Granny opened the wardrobe and started piling the boxes of ball bearings onto the bed. 'There's a wee wheelie suitcase in the back bedroom, if you wouldn't mind fetching it. I just want to try calling Bansi once more.'

'Och, Eileen!' Mrs Mullarkey muttered. 'You've tried half a dozen times already and haven't got through! I reckon those wee horrors have done some kind of magic on the phone lines.'

'I know, Nora,' Granny said, pulling the handset from her cardigan pocket once more, 'but you never know, do you. It might be different this time.' She set the phone on speaker mode, pressed the redial button, and fetched another shoe box. Mrs Mullarkey rolled her eyes and headed off on her errand.

As before, there was no answer, and no ringing tone – just a pause and then an artificial voice, reciting as before: *'The number you have dialled is temporarily unavailable. Please try again later. The number you have dialled is temporarily unavailable. Please try again later.'*

Granny's heart sank. She placed the box on the bed and reached for the off-button; but before she got to it, the message changed.

'The number you have dialled is not available from this location. We know where your granddaughter is. If she has the cloak of Conn, we will make her return it to its owner. If not, you will be persuaded to do so when you see her in our hands. You cannot warn her. The number you have dialled is not available from this location. Do not try again later. You will not be successful.'

The line went dead.

'Nora!' Granny yelled.

'Keep your hair on; I'm coming!' Mrs Mullarkey grumbled, dragging the suitcase into the room. Then she saw Granny's expression. 'Eileen, what's wrong?'

'Get this case loaded up with ammo, and let's get it in the car!' Granny ordered. 'We're going to find a working telephone. Bansi's in danger!'

The next couple of minutes were a frenzy of activity. Every shoe box was emptied out into Granny's little suitcase, until it was full to the brim. They zipped it up; bundled it down the stairs; wrestled it somehow through the driver's door and into the back of the car, knocking their walking sticks onto the floor to make way for it.

'I don't like it,' muttered Mrs Mullarkey as she took her seat. 'It's too quiet. Where are they? Why aren't they firing at us?'

'I told you, they're not firing at us because they've gone off to get Bansi. Now, come on!' Granny said, winding the window down and priming her catapult just in case.

The door slammed; the engine roared into life. 'Are we still going to drive round and round to try and clear this fog away?' Mrs Mullarkey asked.

'Forget that now,' Granny said. 'We'll do it on the way back. First, we're going to find a telephone!'

'All right, then. Once more unto the breach, old friend.'

With a painful grinding of steel against stone, the car lurched unusually slowly from the door. The barrier of mist parted in front of it, revealing . . . more mist.

'Careful now, Nora; mind you don't drive all over my plants!' Granny cautioned.

'Any plants you have left'll be all covered in hoof prints, Eileen.'

'You know as well as I do that *their* horses don't leave hoof prints! And mind the wall, too – we should be nearly at the gate by now.'

Mrs Mullarkey eased back still further on the accelerator, and the car crawled forward. Glancing back, Granny could see that they had cut a tunnel in the fog, through which the house was still visible.

A minute or so passed.

'Surely we should have reached the gate by now?' Granny said.

'You'd think so, wouldn't you?' Mrs Mullarkey said. 'There's something strange about this, and no mistake.'

On they crawled.

'You don't think those wee upstarts have knocked down my garden wall, do you!' Granny suddenly exclaimed.

'If that was it, we'd surely have hit the main road by now,' Mrs Mullarkey pointed out. 'Maybe even the hedge on the other side of it.'

And then the last layer of fog peeled back in front

of them, and they were through the barrier of cloud. The car jerked to a halt. Both of them stared at the scene in front of them. Granny cast a look back; the house was no longer visible through the tunnel they had made. She looked through the cracked windscreen again.

'Nora,' she said quietly, 'where in the world are we?'

They both looked down into a wild green valley resplendent with flowers brighter than any they had ever seen before. The setting sun shone a rich, dazzling gold, which cast an extraordinarily vivid light over the landscape. It was at once like a dream, and the most real thing either of them had ever seen.

The sat-nav gave a sad little beep. The words CANNOT LOCATE SATELLITES appeared at the top of its screen; below them the little blue car icon sat alone, cast adrift on a white and roadless background. Granny cast one more look back behind them. The fog was melting away, and through it an unfamiliar landscape was coming into view. Of her house, there was no sign.

'Technically, Eileen,' Mrs Mullarkey said, 'I don't think we're anywhere in the world at all.'

It had begun to grow dark without Bansi quite noticing it. She had filled Pogo in on everything that had happened since she and her mother had left the tube the previous evening, and he in turn had told her why he thought the underground station might be the focus of the new gateway.

'It's another border thing,' he said. 'The border between what's *on* the earth, and what's *in* it. Between the world where you live and breathe, and the earth where the dead lie buried. In ancient times, mortals used to think the faery folk lived inside the hollow hills – that's the meaning of "sidhe". They didn't know those hollow hills were ancient burial places, the graves of a people who had gone before.'

He was interrupted by a noise from outside – a growing hubbub, as if some kind of party was going on in the street.

'What on earth—' Bansi began. She went cautiously to the window and looked down. Gathered on the pavement below, and spilling out into the road, was a great crowd of people – but the strangest-looking people, dressed in the strangest clothing. Some of them carried flaming torches, which lit their faces eerily in the gathering dusk. Their faces were merry, like revellers out to celebrate; but it was a cruel merriment, like that of playground bullies. As Bansi looked, two of them produced instruments and struck up a wild music, and several of the crowd cheered and broke into a ragged dance that was, even so, oddly graceful.

'Um, Pogo,' Bansi said, 'either someone's trying to break the world record for Most People Trick-or-Treating the Same House at the Same Time, or we're surrounded by Good People.'

Pogo's face creased into a frown.

'We need to get Mum,' Bansi said. 'Just in case of trouble.' Her face paled. 'Pogo, do you think they've come to get her?'

Pogo shook his head. 'Likely as not, it's just faery folk making merry,' he said sourly. 'They've found the gateway, and they want to come and play.'

'A crowd that size? You think they've just turned up outside our house by coincidence?'

'Well, you did use a word you shouldn't have, not so long ago.'

Bansi went to the door and opened it. 'I'm going to get Mum. Do you think we're safest here?'

'Safer than downstairs, anyway,' Pogo said. He moved to the window. 'I'll wait here, and keep an eye out – I'll come and get you if there's any trouble. Yell if you need me.'

Bansi stepped out of her bedroom, turned on the landing light . . . and stopped. Something was wrong. It was so obvious, and yet so impossible, that for a moment she froze, trapped between two conflicting messages – one from her eyes, one from her memory. It made no sense. She moved cautiously along the landing and reached out, confirming by touch what her sight was telling her.

The stairs were in the wrong place.

She rubbed her eyes; shook her head again. It made no difference. The stairs had somehow moved. Confused, she turned, thinking she should fetch Pogo and ask his advice – and again she froze, horror sinking like cold stone through her stomach.

Her bedroom door was no longer there. In its place stood nothing but solid wall.

Chapter Thirteen

'Pogo?' Bansi called. There was no answer. She tried again: 'Pogo!'

Still no response.

'Mum!' she shouted, and listened. This time, after a moment, she thought she heard something. 'Mum!' she called again. Once more, a faint sound which might have been a reply came from downstairs. Cautiously she followed it.

At the foot of the staircase, she found herself in a hallway she did not recognize. She stood on the bottom step and gazed along a narrow, gas-lit, wood-panelled passageway which led only to what was obviously a front door. It would probably, she decided, take her either out to her own street and into the crowd of faeries, or to somewhere completely different from where she might not be able to return. Neither seemed like a good idea.

She turned to climb back upstairs, and stopped for a third time. Above her, the stairs now ended in a blank wall, as if the people who had built the house had simply forgotten to include the next floor. She felt the tug of despair, but pushed it away and, face set and determined, climbed back up.

The wall showed no sign of having been newly built; it was of a piece with the wall that ran up alongside the staircase. She pushed against it; knocked with her fist. It was completely solid. She called out once more: 'Mum!' There was no reply. 'Pogo!' she yelled. Again, nothing. She turned, looked back down the stairs – and recognized the beige carpeting of her own home on the floor below.

Relieved, she hastened downstairs and found herself in her own hallway – facing the kitchen when the front door should have been ahead of her; but still, it was an improvement. 'Mum!' she called again; and this time there was a definite reply – faint and faraway, but clearly a voice calling back in answer to her. It seemed to come from the kitchen, so she moved forward to open the door.

At the last moment, she paused. What if this wasn't the kitchen? What if, by some magic, it was the front door, transformed? What if it led to the street? The thought of the faery host streaming from the street into her house filled her imagination.

But they can't come in, she reminded herself. *They can't enter a human home unless they're invited.*

Taking a deep breath, she opened the door.

It led onto the landing. There, ahead of her, was the door to her own bedroom.

Almost trembling with relief, she ran to it and seized the handle. Only then did it occur to her that if the kitchen door had led back here, there was no reason to assume this one would lead where it should.

She paused, handle in hand. But what was the alternative? Taking a deep breath, she turned the knob and pushed.

What she saw made her stare in horrified fascination. In front of her was the landing she had just crossed. And through her bedroom door, she could see – her bedroom door. Framed in it was what could only be her own back view.

She turned. At the other end of the landing, the same thing – her own back view, framed in the doorway. She moved to one side, and so did the other Bansi – except somehow, it wasn't another Bansi. It was her. And beyond her was the same scene, repeated and repeated and repeated like the tunnel in a hall of mirrors, Bansi after Bansi after Bansi standing in the same doorway.

Summoning all her courage, she stepped forward; and all her echoes did the same. But as she crossed the landing, the door began to swing shut. She ran to grab it, but too late; the clunk of its closing came from before and behind her. Now panicking, she seized the door, pulled it open, ran through – and found herself alone in the darkened kitchen. The door swung shut behind her. She turned and opened it again; the guest bedroom lay there. Another turn brought her back to the landing, but a landing transformed again, with no stairs and too many doors. Not thinking, desperate to keep moving, she reached out for the nearest one . . .

. . . and something told her to stop. It was the same uneasy alertness that she'd felt just before seeing Hob for the first time. She paused, one hand outstretched towards the handle. Slowly she withdrew her hand, and the feeling diminished; she reached out again, and it returned in full.

What was it Pogo had said? *Knowledge beyond mortal abilities. Being able to see things as they really are.* And with that came another thought: all those hints of knowledge had come when there were faery people nearby – or perhaps it was faery magic that was the trigger, but in either case, her home was both under an enchantment and besieged by a crowd of Good People. Perhaps he was right; perhaps that knowledge was there now for her to use. It had warned her about Hob; it had warned her about the Dread Cruach; it would be foolish to ignore its warning now.

She reached out for another door, and felt nothing

– not a hint of unease. She almost pulled that one open there and then, but something told her to keep going, to test them all if need be. The next one and the one after that produced a shudder of foreboding; quickly she snatched her hand away. The next one along after those made her feel slightly uneasy; three more produced no reaction; and another made her skin crawl; so did the one after that.

She put her hand on the next door handle; and it was as if her entire body breathed out, letting go of some terrible tension she hadn't known she'd been carrying. It was like waking from a bad dream into warm, comforting sunshine. She shuddered again; but it was a *good* shudder, as if she was shaking off something that had been holding her down. Almost unaware, following her instincts, she turned the handle and pushed; and – as if a radio somewhere had just been switched on – the sounds of merriment and music from the street outside suddenly filled her ears. She stepped forward, and was in her own bedroom once more.

Pogo glared. In the dusk, the only light in the room shone in from the street outside – from the moon, the street lamps, and the flickering torches. 'Where've you been?' he said, his harsh tone betraying his anxiety. 'I was just coming to look for you!'

Bansi felt her knees buckle beneath her as she collapsed into a sitting position on the bed. 'The house is wrong,' she said. 'I mean,' she added, seeing Pogo's frown give way to a look of concern, 'it's been enchanted.' She took a deep breath and tried to compose herself. 'None of the doors lead where they should; the stairs keep moving around; when you go through a door and then back again you don't end up where you started.' Tears of relief and frustration prickled her eyes. 'I thought I was never going to get back here – and I couldn't find Mum.'

Pogo shook his head gravely. 'Ach, this is serious. That sort of magic hasn't been seen in the mortal world for centuries. The power is returning to Tir na n'Óg, all right – and it's not all for the good.'

'So . . . are we trapped here?'

Pogo nodded. 'Until morning, at least.'

'And what about Mum? How do we get to her?'

'We can't,' Pogo said bluntly. 'It's a miracle you found your way back here as it is. The Dread Cruach'll be behind this – it'll be a magic prepared when his servant was here earlier, probably to keep you or anyone else away from your mother. At least there's no question of anybody sacrificing anyone this time, that's a mercy – but I don't know any way this magic can be broken. And I dare say they've planned some way of having her out of here by dawn.'

'Pogo, we can't just sit around and let them kidnap my mum!'

'If you know of any way of stopping them, be sure and let me know!' He stared at her for a moment, and then his look softened. 'Don't give up hope, girl; but for now, with the enchantment that's been placed on this house, we've no way of doing anything. And since there's a crowd of faery folk making merry in the street outside, climbing out of the window and standing guard at the door is out of the question, too.'

'Yes, and what do *they* want? I don't believe it's just coincidence, them turning up and surrounding the house.'

As if in answer, a shout came from the street outside: 'Bansi O'Hara!'

Bansi looked at Pogo. 'Did one of them just call my name?'

'Sounded like it,' the brownie agreed, his face creasing into a still deeper frown.

'Bansi O'Hara!' the voice came again. It was a high, light, almost musical voice, but there was something cold and unpleasant about it. 'Bansi O'Hara! We wish to trade! You have something that belongs to a friend of mine – and we have something we know you value highly.'

Bansi's heart chilled. Glancing at Pogo, she rose and moved towards the window, positioning herself where she could just look down on the crowd below. The darkness in the room and the light shining up from the street gave her the advantage of seeing without, she hoped, being seen.

The caller was a little man, all dressed – as far as she could tell by the light of the flaming torches – in clothes of red. On his apple-cheeked face was an almost pleasant, but somehow not quite real, smile. Beside him two more little men, similarly attired and with the same coldly cheerful expressions, stared up at the window.

Held tight between them, struggling vainly and clearly in pain, stood Bansi O'Hara's granny.

Chapter Fourteen

'That's all we need,' muttered Pogo, appearing beside her. 'I wonder how they managed to capture the daft old biddy.'

'I know you can hear me,' the little man called. The celebratory mood of the crowd seemed to have heightened; dancers whirled past him as he spoke, laughing and chattering, and at the edges of the crowd a few of the creatures broke into raucous singing. Yet the little man's voice carried clearly to her as he continued, 'And I know you care for your grandmother. You won't want to see her hurt. Give us what we want, and you can have her back unharmed.'

'Do you know what it is they're after?' Pogo asked, quietly urgent. 'Is it something you can afford to give them?'

For a moment, Bansi's mind whirled. Pogo's questions, the sight of her grandmother – and how had they brought her here? – and the little man in red, standing triumphantly outside her house, all pressed in and filled her thoughts. But something was nagging at the back of her mind; something was trying to push into her awareness. She closed her eyes; focused; tried to block out all distraction.

'That's not my granny,' she said; and only when she had said the words did she realize they were true. 'It *looks* like Granny, but it isn't her.'

Pogo stared at her. 'What? How would you know that?' Then he scowled. 'And that'll be the daftest question I've asked all day,' he said. 'You're Derga's heir. Of course you know. Knowledge beyond mortal abilities.'

Bansi stared down at the figure, still struggling between her two apparent captors. It looked like Granny; it moved like her. But something about it *felt* wrong. She concentrated; it almost felt like – if she only knew how – she would be able to see the real form of whatever it was that was impersonating her grandmother. It was the same feeling as having a word stuck in your head, knowing you know it but not being able to remember it. 'It's not her,' she repeated.

Pogo stared down at the scene outside, concentration etched on his wrinkled face. 'You're right,' he said after a moment. 'It's not her. It's not mortal at all. That's a mercy. But what do we do now, I wonder? I don't like the idea of being trapped in here till dawn – and maybe longer. It's my guess the magic will fade then, but there's no guarantee; and nor can we be certain these ones in the street below will all leave with the sunrise.'

The little scarlet-clad man called again, 'I know you can hear me, Bansi O'Hara. Do you want your grandmother here to think you don't care about her?'

From where she stood, Bansi could see the fake-Granny look up with a face of despair, looking so much like her real granny that her heart was wrenched. Fury at the trickery welled up inside her. 'That's *not* my grandmother!' she yelled out.

The little man's face hardened. He waved his hand impatiently; one of his fellows twisted the fake-Granny's arm behind her back while the other produced a wickedly curved blade and held it to her throat. Bansi gasped involuntarily; a maggot of doubt squirmed at the back of her mind. Could she have made a mistake? She looked again at the captive, saw her granny's eyes widen with apparent terror, and for a moment came close to calling out again.

But the feeling of wrongness persisted. There was an odd flickering around the figure, one which – she realized – had nothing to do with the light of the flaming torches. She stared, not quite sensing something happen inside her. It was like the moment of getting lost in a game or a task – the point where instincts and mind and body fall in line, all working together with none dominating the others. The fake-Granny began to blur at the edges, her appearance unravelling. Bansi looked down at the street, seeing with a second sight that overlapped the first and allowed her, over what was visible to the human eye, to see the shape of things as they really were. She became half aware that other figures in the crowd were shifting at the edges of her vision, so that what seemed to be strange humans in fancy dress were revealed to be something far stranger: short, squat goblins dressed in rags; bizarre tree-like people – or people-like trees – with serious faces; half-human creatures with faces of green or blue or violet. But strangest of all was the shape that appeared to be her granny and yet was really, she could now clearly see, nothing more than a roughly carved, lifeless hunk of wood.

The image of her granny that overlaid the log flickered. For just a moment it vanished from sight, leaving the deception clear for all to see.

'Did you do that?' Pogo said, startled; and Bansi, distracted, felt something slip. Next moment, the second sight was gone, and the scene was as it had been; but the scarlet-clad faeries angrily cast the fake-Granny aside, and it lay, still and wooden on the street, looking less like a real person every moment.

A few of the crowd laughed, obviously seeing this as a game to be played out for their entertainment, and the musicians struck up a new tune.

The first little man looked up at the window, his smile fixed but his eyes unblinking. 'You'll wish you'd taken that trade, false though it may have been,' he called. 'We will have what we seek, and we'll take it by force if we must!'

He stepped back, his eyes scouring the darkness behind the glass until – it seemed – he saw Bansi standing in the shadows, and locked her gaze with his.

'You have no iron in the house to defend yourself with,' he said, his voice high and loud and clear and full of mockery.

Bansi stepped forward and pushed the window up. 'That's what Hob Under-the-Hill thought,' she said defiantly. 'He was wrong, too. There's more where that came from.'

A few of the faery beings clearly understood her; perhaps they had heard what she had done to Hob. The music stopped, suddenly and discordantly; the celebratory mood faded; there was a sudden uneasy shuffling. A disturbed muttering ran through the crowd, and the little man's smile grew colder as the murmurs reached him.

'Well, now,' he said, 'are you bluffing, or speaking

true? That's a question, isn't it? And here's another: when your mother invited a faery gentleman into your home today, how was that invitation framed? Is it only the one charming hobgoblin who may set foot within – or are there others who may enter besides?' He stepped forward, his expression confident and challenging. 'Is there, perhaps, another who has *already* entered – and what sort of creature might it be?'

The mood of the crowd shifted again; now Bansi sensed a sort of anticipatory hunger as they drew closer together and stared up at her.

And then she became aware of a new sound in the sudden silence: an animal sound, a predatory snuffling, as if some great beast was scenting out its prey. It was coming from the landing outside her room.

'This is your last chance, mortal child!' the little man called out. 'Invite me in, give me what I seek, and you will be safe. Otherwise . . .'

He left the sentence hanging. But next second, something threw itself against the outside of her bedroom door so viciously that it shook in its frame.

Chapter Fifteen

Bansi felt her heart leap in fright. The door quivered dangerously under the force of a second blow.

'What is it?' she asked Pogo anxiously.

The brownie's eyes were wide. 'There's dozens of things it could be,' he said. 'If we're lucky, it could be an illusion.'

'It might not be real?' Bansi said as the door shook fiercely once more. 'Is there any way of telling?'

'If it can't rip our throats out and tear us limb from limb, it'll be an illusion.'

'That's not terribly helpful,' Bansi said, moving hurriedly to the corner of the room to pull up a fold of carpet, and under that, a loose floorboard. 'I'd like to find out before it gets to that point.'

A third blow came. There was an ominous wooden cracking, and a sound as of some powerful creature grunting.

'Whatever this thing is they're after,' said Pogo, 'it looks as if they want it badly. Do you know what it is?'

Bansi was sure she did. She reached into the hiding place under the floor; her hands touched coarse fur. Quickly she drew it out and unfolded it – the cloak, made of a single untrimmed grey pelt, which the Dark Lord's malevolent servant Conn had used to transform himself into a savage wolf.

'That thing!' Pogo exclaimed. 'Aye, now – that'd be worth someone going to this trouble for! An object of power like that.'

Bansi looked at him. 'An object of power . . .' she said, struck by a sudden thought.

'Aye,' Pogo said. His brows knitted angrily. 'Or, at least, a channel. I don't like the idea of just handing it over.' He flinched and looked round as another huge blow shook the door. 'But I'd say we have no choice.'

Bansi didn't answer. The thought that had just occurred to her seemed ridiculous, but the more she played with it the more plausible it seemed. She laid one hand flat on the grey fur and stroked it; it felt subtly different from the other times she'd touched it, as if it were . . . not quite alive, but almost *waiting* to live.

'Maybe we do,' she murmured.

The door shuddered again, cracking visibly; now a fracture ran down the centre for half its length.

'I hate to say it,' Pogo said, 'but I think it might be time to surrender.' He turned, and his jaw dropped.

Bansi was draping the wolf-skin cloak over her own shoulders. 'What do you think you're doing, girl?'

'Getting us out of here. I hope.'

Pogo's face stiffened. 'Are you mad? Putting on that thing?'

'Have you got a better idea? And before you say "give up", are you sure they'll call this whatever-it-is off if I *do* give them the cloak?'

The whatever-it-was slammed against the door again. This time they both saw the door buckle down the length of the crack.

'But what about your mother?' Pogo asked.

Bansi bit her lip. 'Even if that thing wasn't outside the door, we can't find her,' she said. 'Not with the house enchanted like it is. Anyway,' she added, hoping she was right and not daring to think about the alternative, 'they'll be too afraid of the Dread Cruach to harm her. And she'll be safer inside the house if we draw them away.'

'But this cloak—'

'Pogo!' Bansi snapped. 'They lied about having my granny; they're probably lying about calling this creature off! If it's real, it'll tear us apart whether we surrender or not! We've got to get out of here!'

As she spoke, the door shook again. Wood cracked. The split in the door lengthened.

'There's no time,' Bansi said. 'I've got to try this.'

She drew the collar of the cloak around her neck; it joined seamlessly, sending a pulse of enchantment through her fingers.

'I don't like it,' Pogo grumbled. 'Messing with dark magic . . .'

Ignoring him, Bansi pulled the grisly hood of the cloak over her head. She felt her skin crawl and her hair bristle angrily as the inside of the wolf's scalp settled onto it. And then she felt something more: a tingle of enchantment; the pulsing of power flowing through her and into the cloak. Without thinking, guided by that magical instinct she was beginning to recognize, she drew the cloak around her; it clung greasily, wrapping its limbs round hers. She shuddered; but even as she did so, the cloak was starting to feel like a part of her. Her vision dimmed – no, shifted somehow; the leaping hues of torchlight outside the window had faded, but the faint light and dark shadows of night had intensified, making familiar shapes stand out strangely in the gloom around her.

A threatening smell assaulted her nostrils: a scent that spoke of danger and blood. She growled, her hackles raised, all her instincts preparing her for conflict. This was *her* territory, *her* hunting ground, and no other beast, however fearsome, was going to drive her from it.

A challenge came from behind her; a loud bang, a cracking of wood. Fury and blood-lust in her heart, she wheeled. Something landed on her back – nothing large, but still something that had no place there. She twisted her head, teeth bared, to snatch and devour it. It was making a sound; and deep within the recesses of her mind the sound had a meaning.

'Bansi!' it was saying. 'Bansi! Bansi!'

She snapped and snarled, unable to reach it. Still the sound persisted: 'Bansi! Bansi!' Slowly its meaning forced its way past the animal savagery of her instinctual mind, until it broke through some mental barrier and she realized what it meant.

It was her name.

And she remembered. She was not a wolf. She was a girl in a wolf's shape, with a wolf's instincts and senses, but she was not a wolf. The thing on her back was her friend Pogo. This was her bedroom. And she had to leave, now, before the bedroom door gave way completely and some creature from the realm of Faery broke through.

Whirling, she aimed herself at the lower right-hand pane of her bedroom window, and leaped.

Chapter Sixteen

The window burst around her; glass shattered and showered, wheeling in fragmented plates towards the street below. Her animal mind was aware of shouting; of a smell of panic; of the heat and light of flames; of the grip of small fingers on her fur and a weight on her back. Guided by instinct, her body twisted in the air; she landed, colliding with a soft body that collapsed under her. Rolling, she sprang to her feet, but from all around arms reached out; bodies blocked her path; hands grabbed at her. A snarling, snapping wildness of teeth and claws and fury, she forced her way to the edge of the crowd; but her enemies were many, too many, and they were dragging her to the ground, bringing her down. She felt her passenger torn from her back. Enraged, she howled, thrashing vainly against her captors.

There was an explosion of blackness, a confusion of wild whirring wings. The air around her was filled with furious beating; startled, she reacted, twisting her head to snap savagely at this new threat.

'Not me, you daft twit!' a voice cawed from above her. 'Run!'

Suddenly she was able to struggle free. A clamour of dark birds was bearing down on the mob, engulfing them, the scene now a hurricane of black feathers and flailing limbs; protecting themselves, her enemies had no time for her. She wriggled through the crush of bodies, found herself released, and sprang away.

At the end of the street she hesitated, the wrongness of her passenger's absence tearing at her like the loss of a cub.

'We've got him! Keep going!' the raven shouted. A moment later something landed on her back with a soft thump; she felt familiar fingers grip her fur. Instantly she was off again, leaving the street behind.

The first little scarlet-clad man saw her go. Fighting his way through the black whirlwind of birds, he set up a wild halloo that echoed through the streets ahead of them.

From somewhere else, and somewhere else again, it was answered.

Hearing it, she ran. Animal cunning and the instinct of the hunted drove her on, the raven flying low and close to her, the brownie clinging to her back. She kept to the shadows and dark verges, cutting through unlit gardens and deserted yards, following the trails of the sly city foxes to keep herself safe. But the strong urban smells confused her senses and misled her; and the continuing echoes of the hunting cry pursued her, harried her at every turn and drove her relentlessly towards the lights of the main street.

'Bansi! Bansi! Stop!' hissed the little man on her back, tugging urgently at her; and she remembered that 'Bansi' meant her and forced herself to understand. In an unlit alley close to the brightness and busyness of the main thoroughfare she halted, panting, and tried to think how to become herself again. Vaguely she remembered how she had once seen Conn shrug the skin off; and she pushed towards that memory; and as she did so, it was as if she pushed her wolfness away, reaching out towards the Bansi who held the memory in her mind. She pushed and wriggled towards her own self, and all unknowing her wolfish body pushed and wriggled away from its wolfish nature, until the skin fell away and she was Bansi O'Hara once more, standing in the unfamiliar darkness of a familiar place and feeling very afraid.

'Are you all right?' Pogo asked worriedly.

Bansi, staring down at him through human eyes, nodded. 'That was weird. It was like . . . like I was only half me.'

Pogo seemed unsurprised. 'There's more animal to you mortals than you know. Bring it to the surface with magic – especially dark magic like that – and it's no wonder if it tries to run away with you.' He hugged himself as if for warmth. 'We should keep moving.'

Bansi scooped the cloak up and fastened it round her throat. 'Where to? We can't go back to the house yet.'

She flinched suddenly as her hair was beaten by a flapping of dark wings. The raven alighted on her shoulder.

'Too right,' it said. 'I just took a look – the streets back there are full of them, and they're coming this way.'

In that case, there was only one route to take, and Bansi took it. Slipping from the alleyway, she moved towards the main road.

'I don't like this,' Pogo muttered from beside her. 'You're not exactly inconspicuous, you know – a wee girl wearing a wolf-skin cloak and carrying a raven on your shoulder.'

But as they stepped out of the side street, Bansi saw that Pogo was entirely wrong. The High Street seemed to have taken on some kind of carnival atmosphere; it thronged with what looked like people in Hallowe'en fancy dress. They had colonized it from pavement to pavement and made it their own, mixing merrily with the early partygoers, the late-home commuters, and the just-off-to-the-pubbers. A line of revellers was dancing down the centre of the road, unheeding of the angry hooting of buses and cars and taxis; Bansi saw a tall, striking woman with a vampire-pale face, all in crimson and black, pause to kiss a passing mortal and leave him staring after her, clearly enchanted in more ways than one. The artificial lights had all been somehow dimmed, leaving the scene lit by fire and moonlight. It was a festival of Tir na n'Óg, transplanted to her own neighbourhood and dressed in Hallowe'en colours. There were skeletons and banshees, spectres and ghouls; and Bansi could tell that many of these otherworldly costumes hid creatures no less strange and unearthly. In the midst of all this wildness and colour and revelry, one girl in a wolf-skin cloak with a raven on her shoulder looked perfectly in keeping, if not a little mundane.

'Are they *all* from Tir na n'Óg?' she whispered.

'Aye,' came a voice from under her cloak, and she realized that Pogo had found a hiding place. 'But I wouldn't worry. They're here to make merry as much as to make mischief, I reckon. Not everyone in the Other Realm is after you, remember.'

'I think there's enough of them after her to be

getting on with,' the raven muttered. 'Let's keep moving.'

Moments later, at the head of a wild mob, the little man in scarlet burst onto the main street; but Bansi had already disappeared into the bustling crowds.

Chapter Seventeen

It felt to Granny O'Hara as if they had been driving for hours, yet the sun had still not entirely set. Everything seemed strange: the landscape; the flora; even the colours of dusk were somehow brighter and more intense than seemed right. Thankfully there was one thing that remained constant; one comforting thing that was the same as ever. She and Mrs Mullarkey were arguing.

'Of course we're in Tir na n'Óg, you daft old trout,' Mrs Mullarkey was saying. 'In the name of goodness, where else could we possibly be?'

'Well, I don't know, do I?' Granny retorted. 'We could be in the Land of the Bumbly-Boo for all I can tell!'

Mrs Mullarkey heaved a dramatic sigh. 'Eileen, you know as well as I do there's no such place as the Land of the Bumbly-Boo.'

'Six months ago, Nora, I'd have said there was no such place as the land of Tir na n'Óg; but now I've been there! And it looked very different from this place.'

'Well, maybe we're in a different *part* of Tir na n'Óg.'

'Maybe we are,' Granny snapped, 'and maybe we're in a different place altogether, and how are we going to get home? And how, come to that, am I going to warn my wee Bansi that those hallions in red are coming to get her?'

Mrs Mullarkey cast an automatic glance at the sat-nav. The message on its screen now read: UNABLE TO CALCULATE ROUTE.

'Bansi'll be fine,' Mrs Mullarkey assured her, but with something less than her usual unassailable confidence. 'What with that magic she got from fulfilling the prophecy and being the heir to what's-his-face, she'll have no problems dealing with them – if she has to at all, of course.'

'She's only ever had that magic happen the once, Nora,' Granny pointed out.

'Aye, well, it probably only pops up when it's needed. You mark my words, any of them wee red fellows turn up on her doorstep with their threats and their elf-shot and she'll likely set their rear ends on fire . . . Here!' she added, bringing the car to a sudden halt. 'What's that?'

Granny peered into the gathering twilight. The car's headlights lit only a small path in front of them; but beyond that, something was twinkling. 'Some kind of light,' she said.

'Well, I can see that, you silly old biddy. The question is, what kind of light? And more to the point, who's making it?'

'It could be someone we can ask directions from,' Granny suggested hopefully.

'Directions? To where? What are we going to say? "Excuse me, but can you tell me the way back to the mortal world, please?" I don't think so.'

'Well, why not?'

Mrs Mullarkey sighed. 'For one thing, Eileen, because even if they knew they'd not tell us. You know as well as I do that the Good People are full of wickedness.'

'Not the brownies,' Granny pointed out.

'It's not going to be a brownie waving a light about like that and drawing attention to himself, is it?'

'But it could be some other kind of wee helpful person . . .'

Mrs Mullarkey snorted contemptuously. 'Rubbish. Brownies aside, there's not a one of . . . of *them* as would want to help a mortal human.'

'You don't *know* that, Nora. Anyhow, it can do no harm to go and find out where that light's coming from.'

'*You* don't know *that*, Eileen.'

Granny sniffed. 'Well, if you're too scared.'

Mrs Mullarkey bristled. Without saying a word, she ground the car into first gear and eased it forward.

Yet although they moved towards the distant light, they seemed to get no closer. Mrs Mullarkey shifted up through the gears; the car accelerated over the bumpy ground; but the light stayed ahead of them.

'Maybe it's some kind of illusion,' Granny offered.

'Aye, no doubt,' her friend agreed grimly. 'But whether it's Good People trickery or just some trick of the dusk remains to be seen.'

On they drove, bumping and rocking on the uneven ground; and now they were clearly gaining on the light.

'It's some kind of lantern, would you say?' Granny asked.

'I would,' Mrs Mullarkey answered her uneasily. 'Now what does that make me think of?'

'Well, how would I know, Nora? I'm no mind-reader. But look! It's moving off to the left! Don't lose it, now!'

And then, oddly, just for a second the lantern moving ahead of them seemed to blink off and on again.

'That's weird,' Granny said. 'Did it jump just a

wee bit further away there? Hang on, though – it's stopped! Quick, Nora, and we'll catch it!'

Nora Mullarkey pressed down on the accelerator, but only for a moment. Suddenly she lifted her foot and stamped hard on the brake. The car slewed round, rocking and bumping and jarring, the small patch of ground in the headlights whirling madly in front of them, and skidded to an abrupt stop at a right-angle to its direction of travel.

'Nora!' Granny scolded. 'What on earth do you think you're doing?'

Mrs Mullarkey was uncharacteristically silent for a moment. Then, in a small, measured tone that was quite unfamiliar to Granny, she said quietly and without moving, 'Just roll down your window and look out, will you, Eileen?'

Granny, puzzled, did as she was asked. And then she gasped.

The ground was, quite simply, not there. The moon was rising high above them; its ghostly light shone against the door of the car and, below that, against the side of a sharp rocky cliff that dropped away for what seemed like miles. Far, far below, the water of a rushing river reflected silvery-white. They had missed falling to their deaths by seconds.

Across the chasm, the light that had led them on swayed for a moment and then extinguished itself.

Granny turned to her friend, who sat stone-still and facing forward. 'What—' she began.

'A will-o'-the-wisp, Eileen,' Nora Mullarkey said in a shaken voice. 'I should have guessed sooner. I should have remembered. They carry a lantern; they use it to lure lost travellers to their doom. And this one was nearly the end of us.'

If anything, Granny found her friend's unsettled mood more disturbing than their near-death experience. 'Aye, well,' she said. 'Better late than never, I suppose.' Then, when there was no response, she added, 'Still and all, Nora, it *was* very careless of you. Mind you, I suppose it's only to be expected at your age that your memory might start to go—'

Mrs Mullarkey's head snapped round. 'At *my* age?' she said. 'At *my* age? I may be a few months older than you, Eileen O'Hara, but there's nothing wrong with my memory that wasn't wrong with yours when you were twenty!'

Granny allowed herself a secret smile, and went straight on the attack. 'Is that so? I'd have thought that if *I* was setting myself up as some kind of expert on the Good People, and if *I* knew there was one of them that lured people to their doom by waving a lantern about, then it might not be the sort of thing to slip my mind if I was in Tir na n'Óg and someone started waving a lantern around the place right in front of me!'

'So we're in Tir na n'Óg now, are we? I thought we were in the Land of the Bumbly-Boo, according to you!'

'Oh, now, I never said that, Nora.'

'Well, you said something of the sort, Eileen.'

As the familiar rhythm of their bickering continued, Granny could see the fire returning to her friend's spirit. The engine started; slowly and cautiously the Morris Minor Traveller turned away from the cliff edge and onto safer ground.

A little later, the argument having run its natural course and with both of them still – though neither of them would admit it – shaken after their narrow escape, they found a lonely spot in the shelter of a grove of trees in which to rest until dawn. The engine was stilled; the headlights extinguished. The only light came from the screen of the sat-nav, still displaying its white featureless map and its hopeless message: UNABLE TO CALCULATE ROUTE.

'Can you not turn that thing off, Nora?' Granny asked.

Mrs Mullarkey shook her head. 'I don't know what's wrong with the silly thing, Eileen. I've pressed the button, I've unplugged it, but it won't switch off whatever I do. I dare say it'll run out of battery soon enough.'

Granny nodded and settled back in her seat. 'I hope my wee Bansi's all right,' she said as she closed her eyes.

'I'm sure your wee Bansi's fine,' Mrs Mullarkey said. 'She'll be fast asleep in her bed right now, and dreaming sweetly.'

Chapter Eighteen

Bansi was far from being fast asleep, although she could easily have believed she was dreaming. The street was growing more alien and unreal by the moment: many of the faery folk – including some of the strangest – were making no attempt to disguise themselves now. Even Pogo had emerged from his hiding place and was riding on Bansi's free shoulder. No one gave him a second glance.

As she pushed through the crowds Bansi saw tall, elegant tree-women laughing together under a street lamp; small grey goblins dancing merrily to a piper's tune; handsome, delicate, ethereal human-shaped beings with faces of blue, or lilac, or pale green; creatures she might have called dwarves and elves and pixies for want of better names, and others for which she could think of no name at all. She saw a woman who looked old and bent and almost crippled, but who was skipping through the crowds more nimbly than a six-year-old. In the window display of the off-licence a red-faced cluricaun lolled, happily nursing a bottle of whiskey that was bigger than he was. A little way along the road an impossibly handsome man in velvet and lace, who – Bansi was sure – must have been one of the sidhe, leaped high into the air, turning somersaults above the heads of the onlookers, each leap surpassing the last and earning him a greater cheer than the one before.

'Best keep moving,' Pogo muttered, anxiously scanning the crowd.

'Too right,' muttered the raven. It flapped its wings nervously, filling the corner of Bansi's vision with black feathers.

They pushed along the thronged street, squeezing their way through the crush of revellers, twisting and turning and doubling back and back again, both to keep moving and in the hope of shaking off any pursuit. On every side faeries and half-enchanted mortals danced and caroused; competing snatches of songs, raucous and yet unutterably tuneful, burst around them like exchanges of fire in some merry battle of sound. The bright lights of locked shops flickered and dimmed; street lamps began to haze and melt and re-form into tall flaming beacons as the scene continued its slow transformation from ordinary London street into otherworldly festival of Tir na n'Óg. On they pushed, as all around the celebration grew wilder.

'Pogo,' Bansi said after a while, 'will you do something for me?'

She didn't turn her head, but she could feel Pogo's gaze burning into her. 'You don't need to ask,' he said. 'I said before I'd give my life to protect you, and I will.'

'Then,' Bansi said hesitantly, 'will you go back to the house – see if you can find out if Mum's OK?'

Pogo drew in a sharp breath. 'And leave you here?' he said. 'Alone?'

'Hang on a second!' said the raven indignantly. 'What do you mean, *alone*? I'm here, ain't I?'

'Oh, aye,' Pogo muttered, 'and a fine lot of help you'd be!'

The raven fluffed up its feathers resentfully. 'I like that! Who was it came to the rescue when you needed it, eh? Who organized a whole army of rooks to help you get away? Who grabbed you right out of the hands of one of those little red blokes and plonked you back on Bansi's back? Who—'

'All right, all right,' Pogo growled. 'You've made your point. But I still don't trust you to look after her if I'm not here.'

The bird bristled. 'Oh, don't you! Let me tell you, sunshine: when it comes to trouble, a sharp beak and a good set of claws are more use than a talent for housework!'

'Maybe,' Pogo retorted, 'but if you haven't got the—'

'Pogo,' Bansi interrupted. Hearing the urgency in her voice, the little brownie stopped in mid-flow and turned his face to her again. 'Please,' she went on. 'I'm really worried. Just check she's there and she's OK. We'll be here on the High Street.'

Pogo heaved a sigh. 'I should be here,' he said. 'Looking after you.'

'If you're looking after Mum,' Bansi said, 'you *are* looking after me. If I have to go back to Tir na n'Óg to rescue her, I'll be in a lot more danger than I am now.'

Pogo sighed again. 'All right,' he said. 'I don't like it, but I suppose you're right. I'll be back in about ten minutes. Just stay on the High Street and I'll find you. Only . . .' He reached round behind Bansi's head and gently but firmly took the raven by the throat. 'If you leave her,' he said softly; 'if she comes to any harm while she's in your care, but especially if you abandon her: I know this really good recipe for sage and onion stuffing. And I'm not afraid to use it.'

Slipping down from Bansi's shoulder, he turned to nod at her, and then the crowd surged and eddied and she felt herself swept away from him on its tide.

The raven said nothing for a minute or two, but made a great show of being on guard as the whirl of the crowd carried them along. It felt as if the street was continuing to fill; as if more and more revellers were joining the throng. Bansi found herself pressed in, her view of the scene cut almost to nothing as taller figures jostled around her, pushing merrily this way and that.

'Mebbe I should go for an aerial view?' the raven suggested presently. 'Just to check none of those little red fellas is around.'

'They might see you, though,' Bansi pointed out, 'and then they'd find us.'

'Hadn't thought of that,' the raven admitted. 'Suppose they might be on the lookout for big black birds, mightn't they?'

Bansi nodded. 'That was amazing, by the way. Where did you get all those other birds from? Are they . . . you know, under an enchantment, like you?'

The raven shook its head. 'Naw,' it said. 'Whoa!' it added, flapping its wings anxiously as the swirling of the crowd almost swept Bansi off-balance. 'Mind yourself! No, they're just ordinary rooks. I met them after I left your house this morning – I stopped off for a quick bite of roadkill up near the common, and suddenly I'm surrounded by all these birds wanting to know what's going on. Which is weird. Took me by surprise, I can tell you. 'Cos ordinary birds can't normally say much beyond "Clear off, this is my patch" or "Look out, there's a scary thing" – and that's not really proper talking, just body language, warning calls, that sort of thing.

'But then I thought: in the old tales, animals are always talking to people, aren't they? All the magic that's going on here ain't anywhere near as strong as it was back then – but I guess it don't take half so much magic to get real birds talking to enchanted birds, does it? Anyhow, they were all unsettled. So we talk a bit, and then I think: well, I can go back to my tree and wait another five hundred years, or I can hang around here with my new pals and maybe give you a hand if you need it. After all,' it continued hopefully, 'you might get the hang of your magic one of these days and turn me back into . . . well, me. Seems a safe bet: a couple of extra days if you can't, against the best part of five hundred years if you can. So we've been keeping an eye on your house all day. Saw that bloke with the top hat going in this afternoon. Saw that mob gathering outside. Oh, and saw you through the window putting on the cloak and changing into a wolf, in case you're wondering how we knew it was you. That was a trick and a half, that was. Oi, watch out!' it added, flapping its wings furiously as a sudden surge from behind pushed Bansi dangerously off-balance.

Bansi stumbled and righted herself, but the crowd surged again. Suddenly everyone around her was moving in the same direction, and although she fought against the flow, seconds later she found herself at the edge of a circular opening in the heaving mass. She dug her heels in and pushed backwards, but those behind her were packed too tightly and she was held there. Quickly she scanned the perimeter for signs of danger, looking at all the faces. None of them looked back; all eyes were on the performance they had pressed forward to see.

In the middle of the circle was, of all things, a dog. And not just any dog; Bansi recognized it as a Rottweiler that lived on her own street, a horribly aggressive brute that would hurl itself at the windows, barking furiously, every time anyone passed by.

It wasn't barking now. On the contrary, it looked terrified; for on its back, riding it as if it were a horse and forcing it to perform tricks for the cheering spectators, was a little laughing cluricaun. He wore a green jacket and a red cap, his nose and cheeks were flushed bright red, and in one hand – the hand that wasn't tightly holding the dog's studded collar – he held a little brown bottle. And Bansi recognized him.

'Blimey!' the raven croaked. 'It's Flooter!'

Bansi stared, half delighted to see another friend in this crowd of strangers, but half uneasy; for like all his kind, Flooter lived in a state of perpetual drunkenness, and this made him less than the wisest of allies. He had, in the end, been a huge help during her Midsummer troubles, but how much of this had been intended and how much entirely accidental she could not be sure. She tried to ease back into the crowd, painfully aware of how exposed she was, but the onlookers were pressed tightly together and there was no room for her to move.

Flooter was now riding the dog madly round the ring. As he rode there came a burst of laughter from a knot of spectators not far from where Bansi stood, and something began to blossom in the centre of the circle – a hoop made entirely of flame, standing upright a few inches off the ground and blazing hotly, its flickering light reflecting orange against the surface of the road and the faces of the watchers.

The galloping cluricaun saw the hoop, and his face took on a crafty grin. 'Through the ring of fire, ish it?' he yelled. 'Ish that what you want, eh? An' what'll you give me if I do?'

'Whiskey!' roared the crowd.

'Whishkey?' Flooter cried delightedly. 'Wey-hey! Come on, Fido!'

He wheeled the frightened dog round and aimed it squarely at the centre of the hoop. The Rottweiler's eyes bulged fearfully, but it seemed to have no choice. Through the flames it leaped, and a great cheer went up all around. Flooter, buoyed up by the crowd, waved the hand that held the bottle and swept round for another go, the next leap being longer and more daring. Again he circled, acknowledging the cheering of his audience, and made a third leap that was more spectacular still. The roar of approval was deafening.

'Here!' he shouted as he circled for the fourth jump. 'Youse'll like thish! Look – no handsh!'

He let go of the dog's collar as he leaped, and waved both hands in the air as he passed through the blazing hoop. The resulting cheer was the loudest yet.

'Look!' he shouted again as he came round once more. 'No feet!'

This time, he lifted both hands and feet clear of the dog as it jumped. Bansi, knowing how poor the cluricaun's sense of balance could be, wondered how he managed to stay on; but stay on he did, to another great and appreciative roar.

'Here!' he yelled triumphantly, sweeping round for the next pass. 'Look – no bottom!'

The dog leaped.

'Whoopsh!' Flooter tumbled from the Rottweiler's back and went rolling dizzily across the circle to an undignified stop right at Bansi's feet.

This time the roar that went up was one of

laughter. It was still hanging in the air as the circle broke up and the onlookers melted back into the rest of the crowd. But Flooter hardly noticed, for he was staring up, delightedly bewildered, into Bansi's face.

Bansi pressed one finger to her lips, eyes widening in a plea for silence; but Flooter was not one to take hints easily.

'Banshi!' he burbled happily, completely failing to take in her frantic gestures. 'Banshi O'Hanshi! . . . No, no, I mean, Banshi O'Hara! That'sh grand, sho it is!' And then, wobbling to his feet, he raised his voice and, to Bansi's horror, yelled out, 'Hey! Hey, everybody! D'you know who thish is?'

Bansi crouched down, frantically whispering, 'Flooter, please! Be quiet!'

The raven joined in: 'Shut it, you daft twit!'

But Flooter's mouth was running away with itself. 'It'sh Banshi O'Hara! Would you b'lieve it! The child of the Blood of the Morning Shtarsh! The girl who beat the Lord of the Dark Sidhe! My ol' pal Banshi, who— Here! What'sh the matter?' he went on; for Bansi, unable to get him to stop, had risen to flee.

But too late; for there – right in front of her – stood three little men dressed all in scarlet. Their eyes were wide with triumph; their arms reached out eagerly to seize her.

Chapter Nineteen

Bansi reacted instinctively. She threw herself backwards as the little men, greedy-eyed, reached out to grab her; and she twisted, pushing through the crowd, somehow anticipating the shifting steps of the dancers and merrymakers. Behind her she heard the wild halloo being raised, and her blood chilled as answering cries came from all too near and all around her.

Then she was fleeing almost blindly, a sudden panic seizing her. Through resisting knots of people she forced her way, not knowing if she was running into the arms of her enemies; on her shoulder the raven flapped its terrified wings. Hands reached out from nowhere to grab at her. The crowd suddenly seemed to be one single formless adversary, barring her way, herding her towards her pursuers; yet it was her friend, too, pushing them away at the last moment. She turned, turned again, her path frantically confused, not knowing which way she was facing, but entirely focused on escape.

Then the crowd once more parted in front of her, a narrow avenue opening up, and she ran, desperate for the advantage of even a few metres.

It was as she reached the pavement that she realized where she was being herded. She looked round, almost turned, but the little men in scarlet were on her heels and their allies were closing in from both sides. There was no choice. On she ran, into the mouth of the tube station.

The barriers lay open in front of her, their custodians caught up in the great wave of revelry. On she ran. Racing for the steps, she saw a surge of bodies rushing up them towards her: a new wave of ghostly partygoers freshly arrived from Tir na n'Óg. She swerved, leaped for the down escalator an instant before the newcomers emerged from the stairwell to flood in front of her. The escalator was empty; down she ran. Above, her pursuers fought their way vainly through the new arrivals. She did not look back. The escalator carried her downwards. On she ran.

Only as she hit the next level down, only as her feet struck the hard surface of the underground corridors, did she remember that there was no other exit. The corridors led only to the platforms; the platforms only to the trains. She could but hope the trains were still running on this strangest of nights.

Whether they were or not, the platform was crowded with figures: figures strangely still and quiet, after all the hurly-burly up above, as if lost in some kind of dream. With a great effort, Bansi pushed her way through them and made herself as small as she could.

'I don't like this,' muttered the raven.

'No,' Bansi agreed quietly, 'but if the next train comes soon . . .'

As she spoke, a rattling sound on the tracks heralded its approach. All eyes on the platform turned to the tunnel, where a light now blazed in the darkness. Like a great dragon, the tube train burst from the tunnel's mouth and slowed to a standstill.

There was something odd about this train, Bansi observed as the doors slid open. It had an old-fashioned, wooden look, as if someone had resurrected the original carriages from Victorian days and added an engine to match.

'I don't like this, either,' the raven said. 'I'm going to *kill* that Flooter. If he hadn't started yelling your name like that . . .' Its voice tailed off, leaving no sound on the platform but the eerie thrum of the engine.

Bansi stepped forward, and then hesitated. The strangeness of the train was so much at one with the strangeness of the night that she didn't know what to think about it; but before she had the chance, a shout came from behind her.

She turned. The first little man in red was there; he had seen her and was trying to force his way through the unyielding crowd towards her, calling out to his companions to show them where she was.

Once again she had no choice. Just as the train doors began to close, she slipped on board. The doors slid shut behind her.

Pogo was worried. As a brownie, well used to remaining hidden, it had not been so difficult for him to slip through the crowds unnoticed, but the back streets still held dangers for him. He could not know whether all their enemies were now hunting for Bansi among the crowds, or whether some, in groups or alone, were patrolling the area between the High Street and Bansi's house.

He had been forced, therefore, to move cautiously. More than once he had been startled by a cat or an urban fox – creatures which had more to fear from him than he from them – and once by a faery man trying to woo a mortal woman, just like the old days. It had taken him longer than expected to return to Bansi's home.

Once there, his job had not been easy. The street was deserted now, but he had forgotten about the magic that had so confused and frightened Bansi: the enchantment that made doors and stairs and corridors lead anywhere but where they were supposed to. By its very nature this magic had for some time confounded his instincts, making it at first impossible for him to locate Bansi's mother inside the house. And when at last, with a tremendous effort of will and concentration, he had unravelled the mystery of the enchantment enough to apply his brownie instinct with any degree of certainty, he had felt his heart sink.

The house was unoccupied.

There was no doubt about it: Bansi's mother was not there. Where she might be, he could not tell; nor whether she had left recently or long before. He might just have missed crossing paths with her; she might have been taken by the Dread Cruach shortly after he and Bansi had made their escape; she might even have slipped from the house while Bansi was lost inside it or while they were distracted by the scarlet-clad man and his demands, and gone to join the revelry. But however and whenever it had happened, one thing was certain: she was gone, and in a city of over ten million people, he had little hope of finding her.

Chapter Twenty

Almost all the seats in the carriage were occupied and, looking around, Bansi could see that none of the occupants appeared to be faeries. They were mortal, each one appearing every bit as preoccupied and closed-in-on-themselves as any Londoner on the tube. None of them showed any sign of awareness that this train was unlike any other they had ever taken; but to Bansi, the differences were clear.

For one thing, the bench seats on which they sat were upholstered in leather: a worn, antique leather that spoke of history and ancient things. For another, the windows seemed to have a tint to them that darkened the blackness of the tunnel outside in an extraordinary way, and all were hung with stiff green curtains. The floor was made of a grooved and polished board; no straps hung from the ceiling; the walls appeared to be panelled in dark, glossy oak. Perhaps most unusual of all was that the carriage interior was lit by gas: gently flickering lamps lined the walls at intervals, filling the compartment with an unfamiliar – although not unpleasant – smell, and a pale and misty yellow light.

'This is a bit creepy, don't you think?' the raven muttered, and Bansi realized that something else was odd: not one of the passengers had reacted to the appearance on their train, late in the evening, of a girl in a cloak made from a wolf's skin and with a raven perched on her shoulder.

The train rocked on through the darkness. The traveller in the seat opposite – a pinkly clean and chubby young man, dressed as for a day at the office – glanced up briefly, then returned to his newspaper. Further up the carriage, a couple of women murmured absently to one another. There was a faint, rhythmic *tsss-tsss-tsss* from somebody's head-phones. Otherwise all was still, all was quiet, except for the clacking of the wheels against the tracks. On the train ran, on and on, and soon it occurred to Bansi that they should already have reached the next station. Yet still the train travelled onwards, and no one seemed to notice how long their journey was taking.

The gas lamps began to sputter, growing gently dimmer one by one. The light in the carriage grew faint, taking on tones of moonlight and sepia and lending to the already dreamlike scene a deeper sense of unreality. On Bansi's shoulder, the raven shivered and drew in closer; across from her the chubby young man folded his newspaper and closed his eyes. The tinny hiss of the headphones fell silent. The light continued to fail until it was no more than a feeble orange-brown glow that scarcely illuminated them at all; and still it faded and fell away.

As the light from the gas lamps weakened almost to nothing, the door at the rear of the carriage opened and a tall gentleman entered. He was pale of face and dressed in a black tail-coat and well-pressed trousers, with a white high-collared shirt and a plain cravat. His thin black hair was slicked back to reveal a high forehead, his face was aged and kindly, and he wore a peaceful smile. In one hand he carried a candle, whose delicate flame illuminated his head and shoulders in an ethereal halo. Behind him came a woman, round and apple-cheeked, all in burgundy velvet and carrying before her a candle of her own. Behind her came another woman dressed straight out of history, and behind her, another man, and another, and so the strange procession moved gracefully through the carriage. Each figure carried a candle; each wore the same peaceful expression. Some were clothed like living exhibits from a museum; others wore modern dress, or dress that had been modern not so long ago. On they came, on and on, like contented sleepwalkers, until the line stretched beyond the doors of the carriage in both directions, the ghostly light of their candles bathing the scene in a dreamlike glow as they processed through.

Suddenly Bansi's heart lurched; her mouth fell open in surprise and shock. Coming towards her, walking gracefully between an old woman in black evening dress and a young man in a scarlet soldier's uniform, smiling serenely and bearing a candle of her own, was her mother.

Bansi tried to speak, to call out, but some enchantment had fallen on her and taken her voice. She tried to stand, to reach out and touch her, but her body refused to obey. It was as if she was truly dreaming, and the rules of the dream had changed. Powerlessly she watched the procession as it passed, her eyes fixed on her mum, willing her to turn and look at her; but Asha O'Hara seemed lost in a dream of her own, and looked only straight ahead, that calm smile never leaving her face. The procession moved onwards, and Bansi could only watch as her mother continued down the aisle and passed on through the door and into the next carriage.

After an achingly long time, the last of the walkers appeared: a tall, elegant, glamorous woman dressed all in satin of emerald green. As she stepped through the door she began to sing: a soft and gentle song in a strange and beautiful language, with a melody that made Bansi think of blue skies and green trees and yellow sun, of warm air and cool streams. And then the walkers in front of her took up the song, joining in with sweet summer-filled harmonies that spread like ripples down the line until their voices seemed to echo through the whole train.

The singers moved on, stepping gracefully along the carriage and through the door, until at last the woman in green satin passed over the threshold.

Immediately the gas lamps spluttered into life again, and Bansi found herself able to move. Without hesitation she sprang to her feet.

'Here – you're not going after that lot, are you?' the raven asked nervously.

'They've got my mum,' Bansi said, moving up the carriage. Ahead of them, the song echoed back through the open door.

'But . . . but . . . Oh, bloomin' 'eck!' the bird muttered. 'Do you think it's safe?'

'You don't have to come with me if you don't want to.'

The raven ruffled its feathers and flapped its wings once in agitation. 'Easy for you to say. I've *got* to come. I think the brownie was serious about that sage and onion stuffing.'

As they hurried up the carriage, the passengers around them seemed to be awakening from a trance.

A young man stretched his legs across the aisle and then tutted with irritation as Bansi leaped over them. She heard a woman complaining to her friend about the state of the underground. 'And what was all that business with the lights flickering just now?' the friend added in agreement, and then Bansi passed through the door into the next carriage and left them behind.

The next carriage was completely packed with commuters and evening travellers. Bansi pushed her way through it, aware that the sound of the singing from up ahead was growing fainter and further away.

The carriage after that was only half full, and not all the travellers in it were ordinary Londoners. Whether they were faery, mortal or ghost Bansi couldn't be sure, but a number of them were in historical dress, just as many of the walkers had been, and she heard a woman complain loudly about rationing and the blackouts. On she ran, following the sound of the singing.

The next carriage was empty except for a handful of wounded soldiers, dressed from all ages of history, who stared at her with glassy, shell-shocked eyes.

The carriage after that was entirely empty – of seats as well as passengers. It felt now as if she was running downhill – as if the train was plunging down into some subterranean darkness. Through the open door ahead of her, candlelight glimmered.

The carriage after that scarcely looked like a carriage at all. It had the windows of an underground train, and the floor was the same grooved board as in the others, and the same gas lamps hung on the walls; but the walls themselves looked almost as if they were carved out of rock. Ahead, the singing grew louder for an instant and then faded. On she ran.

And then, although she had passed through no more doors, she found that she was no longer in a carriage at all. The grooved board beneath her feet had turned to soft earth; the gas lamps that lit her way had become flickering torches of fire. The windows had vanished. Glancing behind, she saw that she was in a long tunnel that stretched back further than she expected; of the door through which she had come, there was no sign. But ahead of her, the faint sound of singing drew her on.

Then she was emerging from the mouth of the tunnel into the fresh night air. From high above, the moon shone down, brighter and larger than normal, lighting up the landscape before them. Below them a hillside fell away into a wide valley; in the moonlight the waving grass looked like the waters of the sea. Across the valley the landscape rose into the darkness of a forest.

'Bloomin' 'eck,' muttered the raven. 'This is bad.

This is really bad. We're in Tir na n'Óg again. And we're lost.'

Bansi stared all around, eyes and ears alert. But of the walkers from the train, there was no sign. Of their song, there was no sound.

Her mother was gone.

Chapter Twenty-One

As Pogo made his cautious way back to the High Street, all his thoughts were focused on Bansi. Despite the enormous number of people in the city, despite the noise of the festivities, he knew he could find her – firstly because he was sure she wouldn't have gone far but also, more importantly, because by now he knew her so well. His brownie instinct, his sense for mortals, was attuned to her as it had never been attuned to any other human.

So it was not only surprising but worrying when, reaching the area in which he had left her, he could not sense her anywhere.

The street was still a torchlit carnival, a festival of mayhem and mischief, a wild waking fantasy under the moon. The hubbub of talk and laughter made it difficult to concentrate; the roaring of groups within the crowd and the delirious bursts of music and singing cried out for his attention. Pogo ignored them. He had made a promise months before to watch over Bansi, to protect her with his life if necessary, and he intended to keep that promise. Denying all distraction, he closed his eyes and searched for her.

And then his eyes snapped open again, for what he was feeling made no sense. It was as if Bansi was near – and yet she was not on the street. She was . . .

She was *underneath* it.

It took him only a moment to realize what that might mean. Then, all caution forgotten, not caring who might see him, he was running, pushing his determined way through a forest of legs towards the tube station, utterly heedless of the revellers who towered above him.

As he neared the underground he could sense her more strongly, almost directly beneath his feet and far down under the road – but then, suddenly and swiftly, she was moving away from him. A train, he realized: she must be on a train. He stopped, focused and concentrating, knowing that however far she moved he could maintain his awareness of her as long as he didn't allow himself to become distracted. It was as if he was locked onto a signal; and the signal, he knew, could not be broken.

He moved more slowly now towards the opening to the station, keeping his awareness of Bansi at the front of his mind. He knew where she was, he knew in which direction she was travelling, and he would know where and when she left the train she was on. He could make his way there easily; he would be able to find her. There was no need to worry.

Except that suddenly, completely unexpectedly, the signal blinked out. He simply lost awareness of her. He had no idea where she was.

Pogo halted, aghast. There were only two possible explanations, and neither appealed to him. Either Bansi had been killed, or she was no longer in the mortal realm. So shocked was he by this new development that for a moment he failed to realize something else was tugging at his senses – his instincts, warning him of danger. Glancing up the street, he became aware that a wave of foreboding was sweeping through the crowd. All around, the festivities were grinding to an abrupt halt, the merrymakers seeking shelter at one side of the street or the other, creating a clear path up its centre.

Shaking himself, Pogo turned and leaped out of the way, just as a dreadful figure on horseback galloped from the station's mouth. In the torchlight his clothes, the colour of rich, deep rubies, shone darkly. The hood of his robe of midnight blue shadowed his face so that it could not be seen, but still, there was no mistaking the air of menace he carried. His immense steed gleamed as white as freshly picked bones; something about it made it difficult to look at. Out of the station he galloped, tall and arrogant in the saddle. This was the Dread Cruach, come to claim his bride.

Pogo watched him go, trembling in the shadows as the great horse thundered through the swiftly parting crowds.

It was of small comfort to Pogo that the Dread Cruach would find the O'Hara house empty and his intended bride gone – though at least, he reflected wryly, this almost certainly meant that Bansi's mother was not already in their enemy's hands. But it left the problem of what to do now. If Bansi lived – and he refused to believe otherwise – then she could only be in Tir na n'Óg. Asha O'Hara, on the other hand, could be anywhere. If she was nearby, chances were that her unwelcome suitor would find her and take her – but what could he, Pogo, do to stop such a terrible and mighty faery lord?

There was no ideal solution. If Bansi was in Tir na n'Óg, he had a good chance of finding her – he knew her better now, was more attuned to her than when he had last hunted for her there. More than that, the land itself had changed since the prophecy was fulfilled: the magic of Tir na n'Óg was returning, and with it the magic of all its peoples – even the smallest magic of the smallest people.

And it was, after all, Bansi he was sworn to protect.

Besides which, it was possible Asha O'Hara was already in the Other Realm. If she was not, but the Dread Cruach found her, she would be taken there soon enough.

His mind made up, Pogo crossed over to the underground station and slipped inside.

Chapter Twenty-Two

'OK,' said the raven. 'Hang on. Let me think. It might not be that bad. We could ask someone for directions.'

Since the raven was sitting on her shoulder and huddling into her for comfort, it wasn't easy for Bansi to stare disbelievingly at it, but she did her best.

'Sorry?' she asked incredulously. 'Ask someone for directions? I mean, aside from the fact that it doesn't look like there's anyone for miles around, most of the people I met here last time wanted either to kill me or eat me.'

'Well,' the raven said, 'strictly speaking, the ones who wanted to eat you wanted to kill you as well. It's not really an either/or thing, is it? Mind you, there's a lot of faery folk can't be doing with all that killing and eating mortals business. In fact, it's pretty rare, really. As long as we're careful, we should be all right. Anyway, have you got a better idea?'

And that was where Bansi was at a loss. They'd already searched back down the tunnel, which now led to a great hall inside the hill, but the hall was deserted and there was no sign that anyone had lived there for a long time. Neither was there any sign of an underground railway system or, for that matter, of the city of London – both of which had been at the other end of the tunnel when Bansi had come down it. They were clearly stuck there.

'No,' Bansi grudgingly admitted. 'But there doesn't seem to be anyone around here to ask, does there?'

'Hmmm,' the raven said. 'No, you're right. It's funny; I'd have expected to see a fire or something burning somewhere – I reckon you can probably see for miles from here in the daytime, and you'd think there must be someone living somewhere nearby. Doesn't look like it, though. Tell you what – let's get moving, shall we? Better to go in the wrong direction and then find someone who can help us than just stay here for ever, eh?'

Reluctantly Bansi had to agree. With the raven still perched on her shoulder, she set off down the hill. The going was easy – surprisingly easy, in fact, so that before long she felt herself breaking into a run.

'Here, steady on!' the raven croaked. 'We might have a long walk ahead of us here! Shouldn't you save your strength?'

But Bansi didn't want to save her strength. She felt herself not bursting with energy exactly, not even overflowing with it, but just . . . flowing with it, as if it was running through her on its way somewhere else. Down the hill she bounded, her body exuberant despite the turmoil of her emotions. Reaching the bottom of the valley, she turned, keeping the dark forest on her left, and fell into a steady run, the wolf-skin cloak streaming out behind her. But then the sight of something glimmering through the trees made her stop.

'What's the matter?' the raven asked.

Bansi peered into the dark shadows of the forest. 'I thought I saw something.'

The raven looked, too. 'Can't see a thing,' it said after a moment. And then: 'No, wait, hang on – what's that?'

The light was visible again, though it was difficult to tell what its source was, or from how far away it shone. It flickered gently, in a way that suggested a small fire, or perhaps a burning torch.

'What do you think?' Bansi asked cautiously.

'Why don't we get a bit closer and see?' the raven suggested. 'If there's any danger, you can always turn into a wolf.'

Bansi had almost forgotten about the cloak, but she felt no easier thinking about using it again. The idea of returning to that savage animal way of being made her shudder.

'I know,' she said. 'You could fly on ahead and have a look.'

'Uh-uh,' the raven said firmly. 'No way. I'm not leaving you for a minute. We might get separated, and then what? I'm allergic to sage, you know. And onion makes my eyes water.'

'I don't think he was thinking of putting it in your eyes,' Bansi said dryly, turning uphill towards the dark shadows of the looming trees.

Her legs felt spring-driven; there was no sense of tiredness in her as she raced up the slope, keeping her eyes fixed ahead. The light, flickering between the trees as she approached, almost seemed to be calling her on – although now it seemed to be moving as well, drawing slowly away from them.

'You know what?' muttered the raven nervously. 'Maybe this isn't such a good idea, after all.'

Bansi ignored it and plunged into the woods.

The moonlight that fell amongst the trees was just enough to illuminate the forest floor – and to create eerie night shadows that wavered at the edges of her vision. Bansi ran, her feet finding a narrow foot-trodden path that pointed her towards the glimmer in the distance. Skirting twisted roots, leaping loose stones, avoiding unexpected dips and hidden animal holes, she found herself dashing like a deer along the track, her breath clear and easy in her lungs, her shoes surprisingly quiet against the dry earth. She felt as if she could run for ever.

Yet the light in the distance seemed to get no closer.

'This is a bit odd, isn't it?' the raven ventured after a while. 'We should have caught up by now.'

'You'd think so, wouldn't you?' Bansi said. 'It doesn't look like it's moving that quickly.'

'It's definitely moving, is it? I've been trying to work that out. Not easy to tell with your eyes stuck either side of your head. No depth perception, see. It's not a campfire, then, anyway.'

'I think it's probably a lantern,' Bansi said. 'Someone lighting their way home, maybe.'

'A lantern?' the raven said uneasily. 'Hang on – that rings a bell . . . What does it make me think of?'

At that moment, the light ahead of them moved suddenly to the right, as if turning a sharp corner. Bansi saw her chance – by cutting the corner she could gain on the lantern-bearer, perhaps even catch up.

The raven saw a moment too late what she meant to do. 'No!' it squawked. 'Don't leave the path!'

But Bansi was already charging headlong into the deeper darkness where the trees were thicker.

'Hang on!' the raven insisted. 'Stop! It ain't safe!'

Bansi slowed. 'You said it yourself – we're lost. We need someone who can tell us where we are.'

'Yeah, but— Look, just stop, will you? I've got a really bad feeling about this all of a sudden.'

Reluctantly Bansi stopped. 'We're going to lose any chance of catching up.'

The raven shook its head. 'Naw,' it said. 'I bet you anything it's waiting for us.'

Bansi looked. The light had indeed halted. It was gently swaying from side to side as if waiting for her, as if beckoning her on, but it was no longer moving away.

'Don't reckon you'll ever catch up with it,' the bird advised her gloomily. 'It's a trick, see. I've heard about these things – not for centuries, mind, and never seen one till now. Will-o'-the-wisp, it's called. Carries a lantern; leads lost mortals astray – and into danger, if it can. We'd be best turning round and going back the way we came, before we end up in bigger trouble than we're in already.'

Bansi needed no further convincing. She turned – and was startled to see her path blocked by an enormous tree, its mossy trunk silver-green in the moonlight. All around it other trees stood, densely packed and unyielding. Thick brambles grew between them, making her route impassable.

And yet Bansi knew she had just come this way.

On her shoulder, the raven groaned softly. 'Too late,' it said.

Bansi looked round. Though there had been no sound, though she had detected no movement, the trees of the forest seemed to have crowded in on them from all sides. Only one way remained open for them – the way the far-off lantern had been leading them all along. She turned again, looking for an alternative, but – although she could detect no movement from them – the trees seemed to be crowding ever closer; it was as if they were herding her somewhere. Their very nearness was somehow menacing. She was left with no choice.

Reluctantly she moved deeper into the forest, eyes searching for a path that would lead back the way she had come. There was none.

In the distance the lantern-light swayed, swung, and blinked out. A thin, high cackle of impish laughter drifted through the forest.

Chapter Twenty-Three

A very long way away, Granny O'Hara – despite her best efforts to rest – was still wide awake. She felt no sense of exhaustion, and try as she might she couldn't keep her thoughts from turning to her granddaughter.

Eventually, unable to remain still and quiet any longer but not wishing to disturb her friend, she sat up and, as quietly as she could, reached for the car door handle.

Mrs Mullarkey didn't stir as Granny softly opened the door. Her eyes remained shut tight; her head, resting against the seat-back, didn't so much as twitch; her hands stayed folded in her lap.

Only her mouth moved. 'Now I hope you're not thinking of doing anything so foolish as going outside, Eileen,' she said.

Granny jumped. 'Goodness, Nora! I had no idea you were awake!'

'Aye, well. I just don't seem sleepy, Eileen, and that's the truth of it.' Mrs Mullarkey opened her eyes and fixed Granny with an unblinking stare. 'Odd, but there you are.'

Granny closed the door again and looked at her friend, illuminated in the glow from the sat-nav's screen. 'It's maybe not that odd, Nora. We're trapped in the land of the You-Know-What, completely lost, with no way of getting home, and we've been inches from death once already. I dare say anyone would lose sleep, given all that.'

Nora Mullarkey straightened herself up, as if to iron out a crick in her back. 'That's as may be,' she said, 'but the thing is, Eileen, I don't feel one bit tired. Not one bit. And you'd think I might do, after the day we've had. Anyhow,' she went on, 'if we're not going to get any sleep here, we might as well do something.'

'And what might that be?' Granny asked.

'To be honest,' Mrs Mullarkey said, turning the ignition key, 'I have no idea. But that's no reason we shouldn't get moving.'

The sat-nav beeped mournfully as the engine fired and the headlights blazed into the darkness. Its display still read, UNABLE TO CALCULATE ROUTE; its on-screen map was still blank and featureless apart from the lonely little blue car.

'Well, you were wrong about this thing running out of batteries,' said Granny. 'Looks like it's just going to keep reminding us how lost we are.'

'Aye,' Mrs Mullarkey agreed, shifting into reverse. As she swung round to pull out of their parking spot, the headlights lit up a tree right in front of them, and Granny started in surprise.

'Nora!' she said. 'Doesn't the windscreen look a bit . . . well, *better*, don't you think?'

Mrs Mullarkey, craning backwards as she reversed, tutted in exasperation. 'What on earth do you mean, *better*?' she asked.

'Not as broken. As if some of the cracks have just . . . I don't know, healed themselves or something.'

Nora Mullarkey shook her head and swung the car round. 'What a thing to say, Eileen. How on earth could a window get better?'

'Well, that's how it looks to me, Nora,' Granny huffed.

'It'll be your old eyes playing tricks on you, no doubt.'

'If your own eyes weren't so old and doddery you'd see I'm right, so you would!'

The Morris Minor Traveller roared off into the darkness of the Tir na n'Óg night.

A long way away, Asha O'Hara awoke to find herself lying on soft grass by a tree on the shores of a wide lake. The enormous yellow moon reflected brightly from the water; the air was warm against her skin but fresh as cool water in her throat; the stars twinkled dreamily in the velvety sky above her. She did not know where she was, but she was not afraid.

There was a rustle in the branches of the tree; she raised her head to see a pair of round eyes looking down at her, silver moonlight glittering palely within them. In the darkness, and against the silhouettes of the gently waving leaves, she could not make out the shape of their owner; but this did not seem odd. Nor did it seem strange when the creature spoke to her.

'Oho!' it said, in a voice like a rusty gate. 'And what might you be, then?'

She smiled but said nothing, unsure how to respond.

The thing shuffled a little, and stepped down onto the next branch. 'A pretty mortal woman, I'll be bound,' it said. 'And what brings you to Tir na n'Óg? Lost, are you? All alone?' There was something hungry about the way it said this, and for a moment something like claws or teeth flashed in the darkness.

Asha O'Hara's smile slipped. She tried to speak, but could think of nothing to say.

The indistinct shadow of the creature moved down towards her through the dark branches. The huge round eyes gleamed coldly. 'No one to take care of you?' it said. 'No one to miss you? No one to know when you have gone?'

Its gaze pinned her to the spot. She felt unable to move; it was like the moment when dream turns to nightmare. And yet, she felt hazily, there was someone who could take care of her, who could protect her, if she could only remember.

The widening eyes came closer. The harsh voice spoke again, its hunger growing clearer by the moment. 'Come, then, my pretty,' it said. 'Come with me.' Its eyes shone now with what seemed like more than just reflected moonlight, as if they were casting some kind of spell upon her. And then the name she had been searching for emerged through the haze of her thoughts and she clutched at it desperately.

Bob Underhill, she meant to say. *I'm here to find Bob Underhill*. But just like in a dream, the words when she spoke them took on a life of their own, and she heard herself say, 'I seek the protection of Hob Under-the-Hill, Chatelain of the Red Court.'

The shadow stopped on the branch it had reached. It shuffled restlessly from side to side, its great eyes narrowing suspiciously. 'What want you with Hob of the Nightlands?' it asked.

She wasn't sure, to be honest, but her mouth spoke for her in a voice that was strangely certain: 'I am to be wed to his master, the Dread Cruach.'

And when she had said it she felt it to be true, although somewhere in her mind there was a shade of doubt and the memory of a tall Irishman with twinkling eyes and curling hair.

'Ah,' the creature said, and its still-gleaming eyes grew small. 'Ah. Wed, you say. To the Dread Cruach. Who would undoubtedly be displeased should his bride disappear, no? Who would be greatly angered if her bones, picked clean and dry, were discovered beneath my tree. Whose vengeance would surely be terrible if he so much as suspected her remains were hidden in the lake and the cold dead finger of blame pointed this way, hmmm? And is one meal, however sweet and tender, worth risking such retribution? Perhaps, perhaps.' It paused, as if considering. 'And yet, and yet. Might it not be better to earn his favour, to turn his temper aside, by telling him where his bride might be? Yes, yes. And perchance to earn more besides. Perhaps one day when he tires of the pretty mortal, perhaps one day when his eyes light on another to take her place, perhaps one day when he has no further use for her – perhaps then he will be glad to remember me, no? And in Tir na n'Óg, no flesh loses its sweetness . . .' The eyes widened again, full of bright malice. 'Wait here, pretty one. Wait here, and your prince will come.'

There was a great *whoomph*, as if an enormous pair

of wings had suddenly unfolded to beat the air just once. The blackness of shadow filled her vision for an instant and was gone. She looked up, trembling, to see a distant winged figure silhouetted against the moon and moving swiftly away from her into the night. It turned, banking sharply, and vanished against the dark sky, only the occasional blinking of stars betraying its path.

Still lost in the dreamlike fog of enchantment, and not truly knowing if she was awake or dreaming, Asha O'Hara fled into the darkness.

Chapter Twenty-Four

'So are we just going to keep driving around for ever?'

Mrs Mullarkey glanced sharply at her friend and then peered into the darkness at the small patch of landscape caught in the beam of her headlights. 'Have you got a better idea, Eileen? You're not going to suggest we stop and ask for directions again, are you?'

Granny shrugged. 'Oh, I don't know. But we might well be going around in circles for all we know – or getting further away from where we need to be.' She pointed off ahead of them and slightly to the right. 'Is that another of them Wispy Willy things?'

'Don't make yourself out to be dafter than you already are,' Mrs Mullarkey tutted, casting a glance in the direction indicated. 'You know fine rightly it's "will-o'-the-wisp", even if you know precious little else about it. And, aye, it looks like it might be. I tell you, if I ever catch one of those wee rascals, I'll wring its neck.'

On they drove, studiously ignoring the distant, flickering light. And yet, curiously, they appeared to be drawing closer to it, and it did not seem to move away.

'You know,' said Granny after a while, 'I don't think it's that Wispy Willy fellow at all. Maybe we should head over to it and have a look. I think it's maybe a campfire or something.'

'That's just what he wants you to think,' Mrs Mullarkey said. 'He'll wait till we start chasing him, and then he'll move away. Or maybe he's already sitting on the edge of a cliff or some such, just waiting for us to come and fall over it. I've half a mind to turn the car round and go a different way.'

'Ach, don't talk nonsense,' Granny retorted. 'Sure, you can tell it's not a lantern.'

'Hmmph,' her friend snorted. 'You think that if you want, Eileen; but I'm glad it's not you driving, that's all I can say. You'd have us off after that wee hallion and over the edge of another cliff in no time, the way you're talking. It's a will-o'-the-wisp, I'm telling you.'

But as the flickering light grew into an orange glow, it gradually became clear that this was indeed a campfire. Soon they could just make out a dimly lit figure sitting at it, tending to something in a small pot slung from a tripod over the flames. Nearby stood a lone tree; the flames of the fire cast dancing islands of glimmer and shadow over its trunk and lower branches, turning it into something mysteriously alive.

'Shall we get closer just for the fun of seeing him trying to pick up that fire and run off with it, then?' Granny asked innocently.

'Very funny, Eileen,' Mrs Mullarkey snapped.

'So are we going to stop, then?'

Mrs Mullarkey tutted and stood on the brakes. The car skidded to a halt, wearing two long grooves in the earth behind them. They sat with the engine running, looking out at the campfire and the man – they could now see it was a man – tending to his supper and taking no notice of them at all.

'I don't see any point in going over there, Eileen,' said Mrs Mullarkey at last. 'Whoever it is, it'll be . . . one of *them*, won't it? And you can't trust a thing they say.'

'Maybe, Nora – but I'm sure I remember in the back of my head some old stories about Good People helping lost travellers. Do you remember the tales old Miss Maguire used to tell us in school when we were wee girls? Heavens, I haven't thought of those in years.'

'Aye, but in most of those stories,' Mrs Mullarkey pointed out, 'it'll have been wee girls the Good

People helped who've been driven out by wicked stepmothers. Or young men who've been set an impossible task by a cruel master. I don't remember any stories about the Good People ever helping two old ladies in a Morris Minor. Anyhow, I don't believe any of that being-helpful business ever happens in any of the tales of old Ireland.'

'And is it only the Irish who ever had dealings with the Good People, do you think?' Granny said.

Mrs Mullarkey looked thoughtful. 'You may have a point, Eileen,' she said, 'which makes twice since we were wee girls. All right, let's see what he has to say. But let's go armed.'

She slipped her catapult into one cardigan pocket, and Granny did the same.

'Right,' Mrs Mullarkey said, scooping up a handful of steel ball bearings, 'let's see what this fellow has to say for himself. But any funny business and he'll get one of these right up his nose.' She slipped the little silver spheres into her other pocket and patted it reassuringly.

'Now, Nora,' Granny admonished, 'remember what Miss Maguire used to say about the moral of those tales? The sister who was polite, whatever the provocation, was always the one who got the help. And the one who was rude always came to a sticky end.'

'Aye, well, she would have said that, wouldn't she?' Mrs Mullarkey retorted. 'She was the teacher who used to skelp you on the backside with a hair-brush if she thought you were even thinking about being cheeky.'

'Used to skelp *you* on the backside, you mean. Some of us were always polite in school.'

'Some of us were always the wee sneaky teacher's pet when it suited them, you mean, Eileen O'Hara.'

'And some of us couldn't be polite if we tried, Nora. So maybe you ought to stay in the car and wait for me to come back, and I'll go and see if I can get any help.'

'What, and have you turned into a toad or something because you're too daft to recognize Good People trickery? Not that a toad wouldn't be an improvement in some ways, of course; but if you were a toad with wee webbed feet instead of hands, I'd always end up being the one who had to put on the kettle and make the tea. In fact, maybe *you* ought to stay here while *I* go and ask for directions.'

'Not a chance!' Granny exclaimed. 'I'm not having us both ending up going to sleep for a hundred years just because you can't remember your pleases and thank yous!'

'My manners are better than yours any day of the week, you stupid old haddock!'

'They are not, Nora! You've no more manners than a jar of pickles!'

Mrs Mullarkey looked outraged. 'A jar of pickles, indeed! Come on, Eileen, I'll show you manners and no mistake!'

She reached for her walking stick, heaved herself out of the car and slammed her door behind her. Granny sighed and followed.

The man sitting by the fire was still stirring the pot that hung over the flames. He was dressed in clothes so ragged you might have thought he lived outdoors, and the dancing firelight flickered over his weather-beaten face so that it was impossible to tell whether he was old or young. He looked up and nodded in greeting as they approached. Mrs Mullarkey nodded in return, but said nothing.

'Good evening,' said Granny, using her politest voice – the one she usually reserved for priests and police officers. Mrs Mullarkey cast a ferocious glare at her.

A smile broke over the man's face, giving him suddenly a wise and kindly look. 'And a good evening to you, ladies from the mortal realm,' he said. 'Will you sit down and share the warmth of the fire?' He indicated two rocks, large enough to serve as seats, that stood close by the tree on the opposite side of the flames.

'Why, thank you, kind gentleman,' Mrs Mullarkey replied in an unrecognizably courteous tone. Granny, who had been just about to say that the rocks didn't look very comfy and perhaps they'd stand after all, cast a glare of equal ferocity back at her.

'You'll sup with me, now won't you?' the man said, picking up a bowl and ladling into it from the pot a most delicious-looking stew. A gloriously tantalizing aroma drifted from it, mingling wonderfully with the smell of woodsmoke. Granny's mouth began to water; but she remembered Mrs Mullarkey's warning and it occurred to her that the food might be enchanted or poisoned.

Mrs Mullarkey had clearly had a similar thought. 'What?' she said scornfully, with a dry, barking laugh. 'And let ourselves both be— I mean,' she amended hastily, her tone changing as she caught Granny's eye, 'my thanks, good sir, but I'm afraid the good food of Tir na n'Óg is too rich for fragile old ladies such as ourselves.'

The man threw back his head and laughed, a deep and hearty laugh of genuine merriment. 'A good answer, madam, and one mannerly enough for all the courts of Tir na n'Óg! But I cannot eat while my guests remain hungry. Surely an apple from this tree could do you no harm?'

Granny looked up and saw that the tree was

indeed laden with large apples, their smooth skins shining in the firelight. They looked utterly delicious, and again she felt her mouth watering. Thinking that the man must be right – fruit growing on a tree was obviously quite a different prospect from food cooked in a pot by hand – she began, 'Well, perhaps—'

Nora Mullarkey cut in before she could accept. 'Thank you, good sir, but no. The pleasure of your company will be food enough for us. But please don't let us stop you eating.'

The man grinned broadly. 'Another wise answer,' he said, dipping a spoon into the bowl, 'and one with which I can find no quarrel. So then: what brings you here, Nora Mullarkey and Eileen O'Hara?'

Granny stared. 'How do you know our names?'

Mrs Mullarkey tutted. 'Really, Eileen. Have you no manners?' She turned back to their host. 'You must forgive my friend, good sir, for being so rude as to answer a question with a question.'

This was greeted with another good-humoured smile. 'No offence is taken, Nora Mullarkey; and you, Eileen O'Hara, shall have your answer in due course.'

He paused. It was Granny who first realized what he was waiting for.

'Ah,' she said. 'Well – as to what brings us here:

we were hoping for some directions. We want to get home.'

'Do you now?' the man asked teasingly, between mouthfuls. 'I'm not so sure about that. Not yet, at least; for I believe you may have a quest to accomplish first.'

Mrs Mullarkey pursed her lips impatiently. 'And what kind of quest might that be?'

Closing his eyes, the man tilted his head back as if thinking.

'Two captives must you free,' he said at last.
'One race must you win.
And the first step is to find
that which you knew not you had lost.'

The two women leaned forward expectantly and waited. After some moments, however, it became clear that the man had said all he was going to say.

'I don't suppose you'd care to expand on that?' said Mrs Mullarkey.

'Ah now, Nora Mullarkey,' the man said teasingly, opening his eyes and winking at her, 'have you no respect for tradition? And surely you know the old stories? Besides,' he added more seriously, 'if I speak to you too plainly, there may be a price to pay. Few things are given for free. As to your question, Eileen

O'Hara – how is it indeed that I know your names?' He paused, appearing to consider his words carefully. 'There are three answers I could give you. The first is that the old ways are returning, and with them the old magic. The second is that I know some of the secrets of those who have trapped you here, and they are no friends of mine.

'But the third is that, for good or ill, you have a reputation in this land. Many have heard of the part you played in the defeat of the Lord of the Dark Sidhe; and many of us are grateful. So, this much it is fair to tell you as payment for the service you have done:

'Blood of your blood, Eileen O'Hara,
and bone of her bone:
these you must find,
'ere you go home.'

Instantly Granny was on her feet. 'Blood of my blood? You mean my wee Bansi, don't you? Where is she? What's happened to her? *How* do I find her?'

The man held up his hands. 'I can say no more, Eileen O'Hara. But all you need to help you on your quest is there.'

He pointed; and Granny and Mrs Mullarkey turned to see what he meant. There was nothing there, however, except for the old and battered Morris Minor Traveller.

'What do you mean, all we need—' Granny began, turning back to him.

But the man had vanished.

Chapter Twenty-Five

Bansi walked on into the ghostly forest, dry dead leaves crunching beneath her feet in a monotonous rhythm that seemed to have been going on for hours. The trees, their bone-fingered branches reaching towards the pale moonlight, surrounded her menacingly and, though they seemed utterly still, pressed in eerily on all sides. However she tried to escape them, only one way was ever left for her to go.

'This is creepy,' muttered the raven for the fourteenth time.

Bansi nodded. Neither she nor the bird had seen any of the trees move, but there was no doubt that somehow they were herding her. She tried not to think about where or why.

Through the forest she caught sight of a flicker of firelight in the distance. *Another will-o'-the-wisp*, she thought at first; but after some time it became clear that the light was not moving, and that she seemed to be drawing nearer to it. Before long she realized that she was seeing not one flame but more – perhaps many more – burning close together. The way before her began to straighten as she walked, and soon she found herself looking down a sort of long avenue walled with trees. At the end of it, she could just make out a tall and roughly stained wooden gate. On top of each gatepost stood what looked like a large smooth white stone, which somehow cast a light away from her – or perhaps two lights; for now she could see that there was a ring of little flames facing inwards in flickering pairs, curving round from the gate itself.

As if it had seen her, the gate creaked open.

Bansi stopped. In the silence, her heart seemed to pound like a hammer. The back of her neck prickled fearfully; a shudder seized her and wrung her out.

'Yeah, gives me the willies and all,' the raven said, flapping fretfully on her shoulder. 'What're we gonna do?'

The question hung in the air; Bansi groped for an answer but could think of nothing. And then it came to her: why *shouldn't* she do nothing?

'We're going to stay here,' she said, quietly but determinedly. 'We can't go back, but we don't have to go forward.'

She folded her arms and, staring at the gate ahead, stood firm.

The raven bobbed nervously on her shoulder, its

eyes darting about. 'How long do you reckon we're gonna stand here, then?'

Bansi shrugged.

'Careful!' the raven complained, wings fluttering agitatedly as Bansi's shoulder moved beneath its feet. ''Ere,' it added in sudden alarm, 'what's that noise?'

The sound above them had begun quietly, but even as the raven spoke it grew louder, escalating rapidly from a gentle creak into a terrible cracking. Bansi looked up in sudden alarm to see an enormous bough, its branches like skeletal arms against the night sky, bending and snapping under its own weight. It blotted out the moon above as it came away from the gigantic trunk and swung towards her like an executioner's axe.

'Look out!' screeched the raven, flapping from her shoulder in panic; but Bansi had already turned to run. Air rushed past as the great limb fell at her. Its branches raked her back, tore at her shoulders, and brought her crashing to the hard earth. She felt her knees graze against a rough root.

'Blimey!' croaked the raven. 'Are you OK?'

Bansi pulled herself out from under the branches that held her, freeing herself from the tangled grasp of gnarled, finger-like twigs. 'Um . . . yeah, I think so,' she said, brushing herself down. 'Just a bit scratched, that's all.'

'Thank goodness for that,' the raven said, settling back onto her shoulder. 'Just for a second there, I could actually *smell* sage and onion.'

Bansi managed a tiny smile, and turned to look at the huge bough that now lay across the path behind them; and that was when she began to tremble. It was huge, and heavy, and would certainly have crushed her if its bulk had landed on her. She had, quite literally, been inches from death.

'That was too close,' she said shakily. 'Do you think it was trying to kill us?' She looked up at the enormous tree. A great gash showed pale in the moonlight against the dark and mottled trunk where the bough had torn off. 'Or just scare us?'

'If it was trying to scare us, it did a bloomin' good job,' the bird said. 'Still,' it went on in what was clearly meant to be a defiantly cheery tone, 'it didn't move us much further along, did it? They'll have to do better than that if they're trying to get us through that gate.'

As if in answer, another cracking sound came from above them. Bansi leaped aside as another thick branch crashed to the ground. There was another creaking noise, and another, and another. Her heart pounded in sudden alarm. An unseen creature screeched terrifyingly in the trees behind her; a furious howling answered it from the other side of the path. Another branch fell, catching her shoulder a glancing but painful blow. With an ear-splitting shriek something darted across her path, scraping her face with a leathery wing. The creaking above her became the harsh cracking of wood, echoing from tree to tree. Something clawed at her hair from behind. The raven cawed in terror. Another branch fell, dangerously close.

The forest was chasing her.

Bansi ran. Branches dropped like bombs all around her, scraping her, bumping her, thudding and thumping heavily on the ground, chasing her onwards. Brambles fell at her, lashed and scratched her face, her arms, her back. She dashed in desperate headlong flight, hardly seeing where her frightened steps were leading until it was too late.

The gate slammed shut behind her.

'Oh, bloomin' 'eck,' the raven said, flapping in agitation. Its voice seemed loud against the sudden silence. 'I *really* don't like the look of this.'

They were in an enclosed clearing – or rather, garden; for it had clearly been cultivated. Around it ran a high circular fence over which wild brambles and creepers climbed.

The fence was made of bones.

On top of each grisly white picket sat a human skull in whose sightless eyes a bright flame burned.

These were the lights that she had seen from the other side of the gate; it was two of these skulls that she had mistaken for smooth white stones. She shuddered again – there was something almost alive about the way the fires flickered in the horribly dead sockets – and looked away, towards the strange centrepiece of the garden.

It was a hut, a sort of log cabin; but one like no other building Bansi had ever seen, for it stood on legs carved and painted to look like the long, bony legs of an enormous bird. The effect would have been unnerving even without the ordeal in the forest and the fence of bones. By the eerie light of moon and skull it was horrifying. The skill with which the legs had been crafted only added to the horror, for they looked almost real, and as the firelight flickered on their surface Bansi found herself almost believing she had seen them move just a little.

That was when she became aware of a new noise in the silence of the night. It was a soft, scratching sound, *skritch-skritch-skritch,* as if someone was gently tearing up the coarse grass underfoot.

Bansi stifled a scream of terror as she suddenly saw that the legs were neither carved nor painted. They were real. They were alive. The sound she had heard was the sound of one foot, one monstrous chicken-claw, scratching at the earth.

The hut turned as if looking for something, its movements jerky and birdlike. The light from the ghastly skulls threw dancing shadows onto its wooden surface as it brought its door round to face Bansi and the raven, and then squatted down in front of them.

Like the eye of some bizarre Cyclops, the door of the hut swung open and a pale yellow light spilled out.

'A visitor!' rasped a voice. It was not a pleasant voice. 'Come in, my dear.' Then, when Bansi did not move, it snapped, 'Enter! There is nowhere else to go! Or would you insult me by refusing my hospitality?'

Bansi looked around. There was only one gate; it was shut tight, and – even if she could get through it – behind it lay the unfriendly forest. The idea of staying in the sinister garden, under the fiery stare of those macabre skulls, did not appeal. And she could remember stories, too, in which insulting a faery proved to be most unwise. Hesitantly she moved towards the doorway.

'Out of the frying pan,' the raven croaked softly, 'and into the fire.' It paused, and then whimpered, 'I wish I hadn't mentioned frying pans . . .'

Chapter Twenty-Six

Bansi could feel her skin crawling as she entered the hut, as if every little hair on her body was trying to stand on end. She stood as tall as she could, trying to appear unafraid – which was not easy, with the raven trembling on her shoulder like a cornered mouse. Still, she was glad of its company.

As she stepped over the threshold, the door clicked shut behind them.

The hut was lit by scattered candles – tall, fat blocks of wax giving off an uneasy yellow glow which left pools of shadow at the edges. In their pale light, Bansi could see all manner of unpleasantly strange things dotted around the room: a jar which appeared to contain some kind of preserved creature, hard to identify without its skin; a kitchen knife, whose handle of horn was inlaid with an eye that blinked at her as she looked at it; a shelf of books that seemed to shuffle nervously at the edge of her vision but stopped dead if she looked straight at them; a glass globe like a paperweight, with a dead toad frozen in its centre like a fly in amber. The room itself was horrendously untidy and badly kept; cobwebs hung from the ceiling corners and dust lay on every surface. Of the person who had called her in, there was no sign.

Her eye was drawn again to the glass globe with the toad in it. There was something unusual about the glass, a pale, almost invisible mauve tint that seemed to sparkle somehow. Almost without thinking she moved to pick it up; and then withdrew her hand, aware of the need for caution and wary of offending her unseen host.

'Pick it up, child!' the voice rasped suddenly, making her jump. She cast her eyes around to see where it had come from. There was a shadow in the corner that she had taken for an empty chair, but as she peered at it, it moved, and there came a loud thump like someone banging a heavy stick on bare floorboards. 'Pick it up, I say!'

Heart pounding, and making sure not to turn her back on the unseen speaker, Bansi reached out her hand again. Tentatively she lifted the globe, ready to drop it at the first sign of danger. There was certainly something magical about it; as she raised it, the mauve colour deepened and the sparkles became more defined, until there appeared above the toad a rich violet sky spattered with stars, while beneath its feet she could now see a rich green grass that looked fresh and real.

'Well, Paddock,' the voice grated, 'what say you? Who is this come to visit: a pair of hands to serve me, or a tasty morsel for the pot?'

The toad's eyes snapped open.

Bansi felt herself tremble. She held the toad's gaze, keeping herself aware of the shadow in the corner, and resolved to use the wolf-skin cloak if necessary.

The toad held her gaze without blinking. Then it spoke, slowly and ponderously, in a deep and croaking voice that carried clearly through the glass globe and made it vibrate softly in Bansi's hand:

'If you put the child into the pot to sate your appetite,
Then your belly will be hungry once again tomorrow night.
If you let her live, a servant-girl to sweep and keep your home,
You'll have use of her much longer than a single day alone.'

It gazed at her for a moment longer, as if reflecting, and then slowly closed its eyes again.

'Hmmmph,' the voice grunted. 'Aye. You speak

wisely, Paddock, though my belly aches with hunger.' She stood suddenly and stepped out of the shadows, revealing herself to be a hideous old woman with an extraordinarily long and hooked nose and chin, like a very real and very terrifying picture-book witch. Bansi suppressed a shudder of horror as the hag – for that was certainly what she was – shuffled across the room towards her, beady eyes fixed hungrily on Bansi's face. Halfway towards her she paused for a second, and then, with a speed so swift and unexpected it was frightening, closed the distance between them and seized Bansi roughly by the upper arm. 'You would make a tender meal, girl,' she croaked, licking her wrinkled lips with a blood-red tongue, 'and if you prove a poor worker then you still may. But at least I need not go entirely hungry this night.'

And with the suddenness of a snake, she snatched the raven from Bansi's shoulder and held it tight in one bony hand. The raven cawed in alarm and struggled against her grip, but to no avail.

The hag leered wickedly at Bansi. 'Pluck it and prepare it,' she said, 'and then light the fire and boil it.' Releasing Bansi, she reached for the kitchen knife.

'No!' Bansi cried, and her hand went to the hood of the wolf-skin cloak. She tugged it over her head, automatically slipping the heavy glass globe into her pocket to free her other hand, and drew the cloak around her. Instantly she felt the magic begin to work: the cloak clung, becoming part of her; her vision shifted as before, simultaneously dimming and sharpening. She could see the hag's eyes widen in surprise and shock before her; she felt her anger turn to hunger and a desire for the taste of blood. As she dropped on all fours, a savage growl escaped her, and she crouched, ready to spring.

The figure before her took a step back, and she growled again, anticipating the joy of the chase. Instead the creature flung out one hand and said:

'Cast aside this dark disguise.
Let truest nature to my eyes
By no enchantment be concealed
Nor hid by any magic shield.'

The wolf stopped, confused; for suddenly she didn't feel like a wolf at all. She felt like a girl in a wolf's body. She remembered that she wasn't really a wolf, and that her name was Bansi, and she felt the pelt she wore begin to loosen.

And she remembered that this creature in front of her was a hag who wanted to enslave her and eat her friend the raven. Anger flowed through her, and she felt the wolf-skin tighten around her again, and she forgot everything except the anger and the hunger and the thirst for blood. She growled again and stalked forward, her mind purely and fiercely animal. The warm scent of fear filled her nostrils, and she snarled and sprang. Something black fluttered into the air as her prey tumbled to the ground beneath her, but she ignored it and bared her teeth, ready for the kill.

Her prey was strong, but she was stronger; it tried to force her head away, but she pushed back, bringing her snapping jaws nearer and nearer to its throat. But once more it spoke, harshly intoning the same rhyme as before:

'Cast aside this dark disguise.
Let truest nature to my eyes
By no enchantment be concealed
Nor hid by any magic shield.'

Once more she felt her skin loosen as power flowed from her enemy's hands, and the fierce animal nature slipped away. Suddenly she was Bansi O'Hara, fighting a hag who was much, much stronger than she was, who threw her off and leaped on top of her, bony fingers clasped around her throat.

'For that, child, you will surely die!' the hag hissed venomously.

Her gnarled hand reached for the knife with the eye in its handle.

Chapter Twenty-Seven

Bansi fought frantically, but the hag was much more powerful than she was. The knife drew closer.

The hag leered hideously, showing sharp black teeth. 'You will be my sweetest meal for many a long night!' she cackled. 'What say you, Paddock?'

Bansi shuddered, and waited for the death-blow, but it did not come. She felt a stirring in her pocket, as if the toad were shifting within its glass ball, and hope glimmered within her as she realized that the hag was waiting for the creature's advice. Then the toad spoke, its voice carrying clearly through the fabric of her fleece:

'Though mortal, she bears magic that is of the realm
of Faery,
And whilst she may not wield it well,
'tis wisest to be wary,
For greater power she may hold, and magical
defences

Too strong for you to overcome, yet hidden from
your senses.
If so, to pierce her with a knife
Could be enough to end your life.'

The hag squatted heavily on top of Bansi and glared down at her. 'Hah!' she muttered. 'Perchance too dangerous to kill, eh?' She paused, chewing her wrinkled lip and mumbling to herself distractedly. 'Well. We shall see,' she said at last. 'Your life is spared, girl. For now. My house needs cleaning; my fire needs tending.' Warily, knife still poised, she rose and hauled Bansi roughly to her feet. 'Do your work well,' she said with a glance at the raven, which fluttered fearfully against the wall atop the highest bookshelf, 'and obey me in all, and your pet shall live. Otherwise, it dies, and you shall serve it to me for supper. And you shall not use *this* against me again,' she added, tugging the wolf-skin cloak painfully off over Bansi's head. Tossing it carelessly into a corner, she snapped her fingers and held out her claw-like hand, adding, 'And now, what's mine.'

It took a moment for Bansi to understand. Then she reached into her pocket and pulled out the little glass ball. Inside, the toad sat motionless, eyes closed. It did not move as she returned it to the hag.

The crone closed her hands around the ball for a

moment and then set it down. She reached out and seized Bansi's upper arm in a painfully strong grip. 'Time to work, girl. Now that you belong to Grandmother Bone, it will always be time to work.'

Far away, Granny and Mrs Mullarkey stood by the open back doors of the car in the warm flickering glow of the campfire and gazed in at the objects strewn on the floor of the rear compartment.

'I told you, Eileen,' Mrs Mullarkey said. 'There's not a thing there that's of any use to us.'

'There must be, Nora,' Granny said firmly, leaning in and beginning to sort through the objects for the fifteenth time. 'He said that everything we needed to find Bansi was over here, and there's nothing here but the car and all this stuff you keep in it.'

'Oh, aye, he *said* that,' Mrs Mullarkey agreed sceptically. 'And if he was some tourist information guide telling us how to get the best out of our holiday, I might be more inclined to believe him. But this is one of the Good People we're talking about, in case you've forgotten, and what have I always told you about them, Eileen? You can't trust them. Not a one. And I don't see why this fellow should be any different.'

'Well, maybe so, Nora,' Granny said impatiently, pulling out an old picnic blanket and shaking it. 'But

I don't see what else we can do except keep looking, do you? We have to rescue Bansi, after all.'

'Aye, well,' her friend said. 'We've only *his* word for it that she's in Tir na n'Óg at all. We haven't *even* his word for it, if you think about it; only some silly old riddle about blood and bone. She's probably safe at home and tucked up in bed.'

'That's easy for you to say,' Granny snapped, folding the blanket up again with more force than was strictly necessary before flinging it back inside the car.

'Well, we can go on looking through all of this stuff until the cows come home, but that won't get *us* home. I keep telling you, Eileen, there's nothing here that's of any use to us at all.' Miss Mullarky paused, and a thoughtful look came over her face. 'Unless . . .' She reached into her handbag. After a little rummaging, she withdrew a small and dented hip flask, and unscrewed the top.

'Nora!' Granny said, scandalized. 'Things may be bad, now, but that's no excuse to take to the bottle when we need all our wits about us!'

Mrs Mullarkey rolled her eyes scornfully. 'Eileen, I'm only humouring you, here; but even so, if you'll just shut up a minute you might wish you'd thought of this yourself.' She produced a battered little metal cup and, filling it from the flask, set it on the ground by the car. 'Some of us,' she went on, 'believe in being prepared for all eventualities. And it just occurs to me that *if* our mysterious friend was speaking the truth, then there *could* be someone we both know round here who might be prepared to help us for the sake of a drink or two.'

Now it was Granny's turn to roll her eyes. 'Well, Nora, if that isn't wishful thinking then I don't know what is. What are the chances that, of all the places in Tir na n'Óg he could be, Flooter'll be around here somewhere?'

'How should I know?' Mrs Mullarkey said. 'Better than none, that's for sure.'

'It's not sure at all, Nora! It'll be *precisely* no chance, or as near as makes no difference!'

'Will it, indeed? I suppose you're going to tell me now that *you* know how the cluricaun travel, even if they don't know it themselves?'

'All I'm going to tell you, Nora, is that you're wasting our time and your whiskey!'

'Well, now, Eileen, if you have a better idea—'

A flash of movement caught their eyes, and together they looked down. The little metal cup was lying on its side, empty.

'Ach, you've knocked it over, Nora,' Granny said.

Mrs Mullarkey raised her finger to her lips, and shook her head. She righted the cup and refilled it, setting it down a little further from the car.

'Now, Eileen, what were you saying?' Mrs Mullarkey asked innocently.

Granny folded her arms contemptuously. 'You're soft in the head, Nora,' she said, 'if you think it was Flooter or anything else other than your own clumsiness that knocked that drink over.'

'Maybe, Eileen,' Mrs Mullarkey retorted, pointing at the cup with her walking stick, 'but if you look for a minute, you might well learn something.'

Granny shook her head, and turned to look. 'If that's Flooter, I'll eat my—'

There was a flash of movement. A small figure darted from the darkness beneath the car, downed the contents of the cup, and hurtled back into the shadows.

'Now, then, Eileen,' Mrs Mullarkey said triumphantly, 'what was it you were going to eat?'

'Well!' Granny exclaimed, not a little put out. 'Why would he be doing that? It's not as if we don't already know what he looks like!'

'Aye, but in the old stories the wee folk like to keep out of sight, don't they? Still, be that as it may . . .' She filled the cup once more and carried it towards the fire, setting it down near to the two rocks and the apple tree. Then squatting creakily down next to it, she peered back towards the car and the shadowed darkness beneath it. Granny joined her, eyes fixed on the cup. Watching, the two old women waited.

And waited.

After some minutes had passed, Mrs Mullarkey began to grow impatient. 'Come on now, Flooter,' she muttered. 'Stop your messing about.'

Nothing happened.

'For goodness' sake, Flooter,' Granny said. 'Come out, would you? We need your help. *Bansi* needs your help.' When there was still no response, she added, 'There might be a wee reward in it for you.'

Still nothing happened.

'Right,' Mrs Mullarkey said at last. 'Well, I'm getting fed up of this. If you don't want to help us this time, that's up to you, but you needn't think you're getting this!'

She went to pick up the drink as she stood; but in the firelit darkness she misjudged the distance. Her hand knocked against the rim of the cup and tipped it over; the liquid ran off into the earth.

'Ach, Nora, you *have* knocked it over this time—' Granny began; but before she could get any further there was an angry yell from beneath the car.

Granny and Mrs Mullarkey both turned, startled, as a small figure hurtled across the grass towards where they stood. It was a cluricaun, grey-faced and with a bulbous nose as red as his hat, waving his fists furiously and wearing an expression of pure incandescent rage.

It was not Flooter.

'Here!' the little man roared savagely as he careered unsteadily but speedily towards them. '*Here!!!* DID YOU SHPILL MY DRINK???'

Mrs Mullarkey drew herself upright and folded her arms. '*Your* drink? I like that! That was *my* whiskey, bought with *my* money, and— *Ow!*' she exclaimed as the little man reached her and, without stopping, drove one tiny fist into her shin.

'Shpill my drink, would ye?' he stormed. 'Put 'em up! Take that!' he went on, aiming a jab at Mrs Mullarkey's other leg. 'And that! And that! Heh! Weren't exshpecting that, were ye! And that, too! Hah!' He danced drunkenly around her, weaving between her legs and around her walking stick, not seeming to notice that few of his punches were connecting. 'That'll teach ye, sho it will! Take that! And that! And . . . whoopsh!' he added as he tripped over one of Mrs Mullarkey's feet and landed face down on the grass.

Next second, Granny had picked him up by the collar and was holding him at arm's length in front of her as he swung his little fists wildly and pointlessly.

'Here, now,' she said. 'Just stop that, you wee hooligan!'

The little man froze as if he had been slapped, and his eyes grew narrow and suspicious. 'How'd you know who I am?' he said. 'Who'sh been talking?'

Granny stared at him. 'What?' she said.

'Don't you try that "what" shtuff on me, missus!' the cluricaun fumed. 'How'd you know they call me Hooligan, eh? Shomeone'sh been shaying shtuff about me behind my back, haven't they? Who was it? I'll . . . I'll pulverize 'em! I'll pash 'em to a mulp! I'll . . . I'll—'

'Right, well, Mr Hooligan,' Mrs Mullarkey interrupted, 'how would you like some whiskey?'

Hooligan stopped in mid-flow and swung round, his eyes widening. 'Whishkey? Aye, that'd be grand. Thanksh very much. I had a whishkey, see, only shome old bat went an' shpilt it . . . Here!' He suddenly scowled darkly. 'Was that you? Did you shpill my drink? Ye did, didn't ye? Right, put 'em up! I'll mulverize ye, sho I will!'

Granny shook her head despairingly. 'I think we're wasting our time here, Nora,' she said.

Mrs Mullarkey shrugged. 'I dare say we are,' she admitted, 'but we may as well give it one more try. It's not as if we've anything to lose, now, is it?' She poured a little more whiskey into the cup; at the sound, the cluricaun became suddenly attentive. 'Right then, Mr Hooligan,' she said, speaking slowly and clearly. 'This is for you, if you'll help us. We're looking for a girl called Bansi. We think she's in Tir na n'Óg somewhere, and we need to find her. If you help us, you'll get this drink, and if you can help us all get home, there's a whole bottle of whiskey back at my house for you as well. Now – do you understand what I've just said?'

Hooligan, still dangling from Granny's hand, stared at the cup. 'Oh, aye,' he said, nodding so vigorously that he began to swing like a pendulum. 'You shaid the cup of whishkey's for me, and there'sh a bottle of whishkey for me as well.'

Mrs Mullarkey closed her eyes and pursed her lips in exasperation. She took a long, deep breath in. 'You're right, Eileen,' she said, pouring the drink carefully back into the flask. 'We're wasting our time. Come on.'

Granny nodded, and set Hooligan down, and the two women turned back to the car.

'Here!' Hooligan yelled furiously. 'Come back wi' my whishkey!'

'It's not your whiskey,' Granny said over her shoulder. 'Not unless you help us find Bansi.'

Hooligan stared at her, weaving slightly. 'Who'sh Banshi?'

'The girl who's lost,' said Granny.

'And what'sh that to do wi' me?' Hooligan asked petulantly. 'It'sh not my fault if people go round losing wee girlsh. Why should I help?'

'Because,' Granny said, opening the car door, 'if you do, you get a drink of whiskey now, and a bottle of whiskey later.'

Hooligan looked outraged. 'But it'sh *my* whishkey! That'sh what the other old bat said!'

'No,' Granny told him. 'It's only yours if you help us find Bansi.' She got in and closed the door as Mrs Mullarkey started the engine.

Hooligan stared at her. 'Who'sh Bansi?' he asked.

If Granny heard him through the door, and above the roar of the engine, she showed no sign. The dark green Morris Minor Traveller roared off into the night of Tir na n'Óg.

Hooligan stared after it for a moment.

'Hey!' he yelled. 'Come back wi' my whishkey!'

Pogo stood on a tall rock on a high mountain, and gazed out across a vast wide moonlit valley. He was beginning to feel completely hopeless about the prospect of ever finding Bansi. His brownie instincts would have told him if she was anywhere nearby, but he felt nothing – no awareness of her at all.

The whole vast land of Tir na n'Óg stretched out

before him, and he had no way of knowing where to start looking.

Asha O'Hara ran through a nightmare landscape, not knowing where she was or where she was going; no longer sure even of her own name. Sinister noises sounded all around her; hidden creatures cackled and bayed. The unnaturally bright moonlight cast terrible shadows at her feet and into her mind. Imagined terrors pressed in on every side.

Through the haze of her clouded, fear-filled thoughts, a face swam to the surface – the face of Hob Under-the-Hill. To Asha O'Hara, drugged by enchantment, it seemed like the face of salvation. Unthinking, unremembering, she plunged on into the night in search of him.

Chapter Twenty-Eight

'Right,' Pogo muttered to himself as he emerged back into the shadows of the empty platform. 'Let's start again.' He edged his way towards the escalator, keeping himself hidden from mortal view.

Not that there was any mortal eye there to see him; nor any faery either. The entire underground station seemed to be completely deserted. Few things are quieter than the footsteps of a brownie, yet the only sound Pogo could hear was his own footfall echoing down the tunnels.

Stranger and more worrying yet was the sight that met him as he reached the surface and hurried out of the station, for outside there was no one. Gone were the thronging crowds. The street was abandoned; no sign remained to show that this had so recently been the scene of wild and unearthly celebrations. Instead, the whole area had been transformed into some kind of ghost town. Nothing – not so much as a cat or a fox – disturbed the eerie stillness. Even the street lights seemed somehow dimmer, their light paler and more spectral, as if they were trying not to be noticed.

A movement from above caught his eye – a curtain twitching in the window of a flat above a shop. Just for a moment the face of a child appeared – a little boy, no older than three; and then the boy was snatched away, and the curtain was hastily replaced, and Pogo's sharp ears made out the sound of the boy's mother scolding him, her voice fading quickly as she hurried him away from the window and out of the room.

Silence returned.

Pogo looked up at the night sky and scowled darkly. Keeping to the shadows, he began to make his way carefully back to the spot where he had last seen Bansi.

He was hardly halfway there when a sudden noise from a side street made him jump – a clinking sound, like someone knocking over a bottle. It was not a sound that would have attracted his attention at any other time; but here and now, on a night when it seemed no other living creature dared to venture outdoors, it made him wary. Stealthily, eyes searching for anything he could use as a weapon, he moved towards the source of the sound.

It came again, brutally loud in the silence. He edged into the side street, making his careful way towards the low garden wall of the first house; and as he did so the glassy clink sounded a third time. It was coming from behind the wall. Cautiously he crept up to it and, ready for trouble, stood on tiptoe to peer over the top.

With heart-stopping suddenness he was eye-to-eye with a wild, hairy face which popped up from behind the wall and yelled, 'Wey-*hey*!' Alarmed, Pogo leaped backwards, slipped, and sat down hard and painfully on the solid pavement.

The face looked down at him and grinned. 'Pogo!' it said cheerily. 'How'sh about ye? Hope I didn't shtartle you. Here – what're you doing down there?' it added, its expression becoming more quizzical; and then it said, 'Whoopsh!' and disappeared behind the wall again with a noise like a dozen bottles being unexpectedly sat on.

With a despairing sigh, Pogo got to his feet. Behind the wall, Flooter was clearly having trouble with the bottles; the clinking noises were growing wilder and more furious. Then came a thump, a loud tinkling and a yelp, like the sound of a recycling box tipping over and spilling out a dozen bottles and a cluricaun, and moments later Flooter's face re-appeared at the top of the wall.

'Right, Pogo, sho . . . whoopsh!' he said, and disappeared again with another tinkling crash.

Pogo rolled his eyes and turned back towards the High Street.

'Here! Pogo!' Flooter's voice came from behind him. 'Hang on a— *Whoopsh!*' There was another rattle of bottles. Pogo did not look round.

He had almost reached the corner when it occurred to him that Flooter had not tidied up the bottles or righted the recycling box.

He tried to keep going; tried to ignore the little voice inside his head that whispered, *You can't leave it like that. It'll only take a minute to tidy it up*; but his brownie urge was too strong. Before he got to the High Street his feet were refusing to obey him. Another glassy crash sounded behind him, and this time it was like a voice that called, *Tidy me! Tidy me!*

'All *right*!' he muttered to himself as he turned. 'But just the bottles. There's no way I'm going inside the house!'

He hurried back to the wall and found the gate – just as Flooter came scooting out through it, colliding with him and sending him sprawling a second time.

'Whoopsh-a-daishy!' the cluricaun said brightly, landing flat on his back. 'Shorry, Pogo! Jusht thought I'd go round the long way!'

Pogo growled as he stood. He stalked past Flooter, through the gateway, and set the fallen box firmly on its base.

'Sho what're you doin' here, then?' Flooter asked, wobbling to his feet.

'I'm not rooting around in other people's rubbish, that's for certain!' Pogo snapped, starting to gather the scattered bottles.

Flooter grinned. 'There was a fine wee drop of whishkey left in that one,' he said, prodding a very empty bottle with one foot. 'Would've been a shame to throw it out. Not very enmironventally friendly.' He winked, and licked his hairy lips with satisfaction. 'Sho, anyway: what're you doin' here, Pogo?'

'If it's any of your business,' Pogo said impatiently, 'I'm trying to find Bansi.'

'Och, you won't find her round here,' said Flooter. 'She was here a couple of nightsh ago, mind.'

'Four nights ago, I'd say,' Pogo answered, glancing at the stars as he carefully began to replace bottle after bottle in the box. 'That's the thing about the mortal world; you can never tell how much time will have passed here while you're in Tir na— Hold on a second! How do you know she was here a few nights ago?'

Flooter shrugged. 'I seen her, sho I did. She had that raven with her. It'sh funny,' he added. 'It was all a great big party – everybody shingin' an' dancin' – and now it'sh all . . . quiet. Where'd you think everyone'sh gone?'

Pogo shook his head gravely. 'Just like the old days,' he said. 'They come into the mortal world singing and dancing and making merry, and the next thing you know the mortals are joining in, off their heads with enchantment – and drink, too, some of them,' he added, casting at Flooter a severe look which the cluricaun completely failed to notice. 'They don't remember a thing in the morning, but they wake with a feeling that something strange has happened – and with a sense of shame too, some of them, for they may have done things they'd never have dreamed of doing had they been in their right minds. And it may happen again the next night, and maybe the night after; but soon the feelings of strangeness and shame are so strong that they lock themselves in their homes as soon as night falls, and stay away from the windows for fear of it happening any more. In their heart of hearts they know what has happened – even the ones who would tell you they don't believe in such things – and it scares them. So they hide, and hope it'll go away. And it does; for then the faery folk move on, and find somewhere else to make merry.'

'Sho the party'sh shtill going on somewhere?' Flooter asked hopefully.

Pogo nodded. 'I dare say. It may come back here again,' he added, 'on the night the mortals call

Hallowe'en, when the veil between our two worlds is at its thinnest. By that time all the mortals round here will have convinced themselves it was just a foolish dream; and the magic of Tir na n'Óg will be at its strongest.' He put the last bottle back in the box and stood purposefully. 'Right,' he said. 'Can you show me where you saw Bansi? I mean, *exactly* where?'

Flooter tipped his head back and looked at Pogo quizzically. Then he tipped it back a little further, and overbalanced. 'Whoopsh!' he said. 'What d'you want to know that for, Pogo?' he went on, forgetting to get up.

Pogo glanced down at him, and then looked away towards the High Street. 'I know she's in Tir na n'Óg,' he said gruffly, 'but I've no idea where to start looking. So I thought maybe if I came back here, and started at the last place I know for certain she was, I could . . . follow her trail,' he tailed off weakly.

Flooter stared up at him. 'Can you do that?' he said.

Pogo sagged, as if all the hope had suddenly gone out of him. 'Probably not,' he admitted wearily. 'But I don't know what else to do.'

'Ah, cheer up there, Pogo,' Flooter said. 'Sure, you found her last time she was losht in Tir na n'Óg, now, didn't ye?'

'That was different,' Pogo told him tersely, folding

his arms tightly against his chest. 'Then, I had the whole of the fellowship of the Sacred Grove to help me look; and Tam, too.' He scowled, as if remembering something best forgotten. 'And it wasn't me who found her first, anyway. It was . . .' He paused, a sudden look of hope coming into his eyes as he straightened up and stared at Flooter. 'It was *you*!'

Flooter stared back in puzzlement. 'It was?' he asked. 'Oh, aye! Sho it was. Ah, well, there you go, Pogo; if a dough-head like me can find her, sure anyone can.'

'No, but don't you remember?' Pogo asked in excitement. 'You were just . . . *able* to find her somehow! Because you thought she had a wine cellar!'

'Ach, don't be daft, Pogo! Sure, what would a wee girl like that be doing with a wine— Ah, now, hold on a minute!' He raised one eyebrow knowingly and wagged a meaty finger at the brownie. 'You tricked me, didn't ye? You *told* me that she had—'

'Never mind that!' Pogo cut in. 'The point is, can you find her? And for goodness' sake, get up, would you?'

Flooter looked down at himself. 'Ish it me who'sh lying down, then? I thought it was yourshelf, sho I did.'

Momentarily speechless, Pogo raised hands and

eyes skywards. 'Look, just answer the question, would you? Can you find her?'

'How could I do that?' the cluricaun asked in bewilderment, hauling himself to his feet. 'It'sh not as if she has a wine cellar or anything, now, ish it?'

Pogo erupted in wide-eyed fury. 'Are you telling me you won't look for her because she doesn't have a wine cellar?' he exploded. 'Why, you . . . you . . .'

'Ah, don't be like that, Pogo,' Flooter said. ''Courshe I'll *look* for her. Nobody shaid anything about not *looking* for her. It'sh jusht . . . I prob'ly won't be able to *find* her. But I'll *look* for her, all right. Anything for me old friend Pogo.' He went to pat Pogo supportively on the shoulder, missed, and fell over. 'Whoopsh!' he said, an instant before landing face down on the pavement.

Pogo knelt urgently and rolled him over. 'So what you're saying is, you'll *look* for her, but you won't be able to *find* her unless there's alcohol involved.'

Flooter nodded blearily and rubbed his nose. 'That'sh about the shize of it,' he agreed. 'Nobody knowsh how the—'

'What about whiskey?' Pogo interrupted.

'Whishkey?' Flooter asked enthusiastically, sitting up. Then his eyes narrowed suspiciously. 'Ah, now, hold on a moment, Pogo. What would a wee girl like that be doing with whishkey, eh?'

Pogo shook his head. 'No, no, *she* doesn't have any; but help me to find her and *you* will. Remember that bottle of whiskey you got from her granny's friend?'

An ecstatically dreamy expression came over Flooter's face. 'Ah, now, Pogo, I do that,' he said. 'That was a fine wee drop of whishkey, that was. You don't tashte whishkey like that very often, I'm—'

'Right, well, find her again and you'll get another bottle. Only, Bansi's got to be home safe before you do.'

'Would it not do if I just found her—' Flooter began to ask.

'No,' Pogo said sternly; 'it wouldn't. Here's how it works, Flooter: once Bansi's safe I'll tell her you're owed a bottle of that whiskey; and she'll tell her granny; and her granny'll tell the other old trout; and then you'll get your whiskey – not before.'

Flooter screwed his face up in concentration. 'Sho . . . I need to find her . . . and then find you . . . and tell you where she ish . . . and then go back and keep her shafe . . . And then I get the whishkey!' he concluded, his expression clearing as he got to the easy bit.

Pogo nodded. 'That's it, Flooter. Do you think you can do it?'

Flooter rose unsteadily to his feet. 'I'm your man, Pogo,' he said. 'Leave it to me.'

'Aye, well,' Pogo said. 'I just hope you can do it. A lot rests on it.'

'I know,' Flooter said. 'A whole bottle of the besht whishkey.'

'I was thinking about Bansi's life,' Pogo growled.

'Oh, aye, that too,' Flooter agreed cheerily. 'Fear not, Pogo. I'll find her. After all,' he added, tapping his nose wisely, 'nobody knowsh how the cluricaun travel. Not even,' he went on, tapping more emphatically, 'the cluricaun.' The final tap was clearly a little too hard. 'Whoopsh!' he said as he fell over.

Pogo closed his eyes despairingly for a second. When he opened them again, there was no sign of Flooter.

'I hope you're right,' he muttered. 'I hope you can find her. Because if you can't – she may be lost for good.'

Chapter Twenty-Nine

'Lazy scullion!' screeched the hag. A sharp blow stung Bansi's ear; a strong, claw-like hand seized her shoulder painfully and pulled her roughly to her feet.

'What?' Bansi protested indignantly, trying to wriggle free. 'Ow! Let go! I've been scrubbing for hours! I've swept the floor! I've dusted the ceiling, and all those bookcases! I've—'

'You have let my fire go out!' the creature shrieked, twisting her round to face her. 'While I slept, you have let the fire die! Even now, the room grows cold!' She slapped Bansi hard, sending her tumbling to the floor. 'Light that fire, girl! Light it now, and light it well, or I'll make a good supper of your pet!' One gnarled finger shot out, pointing at the raven, which was still huddled fearfully atop the tallest bookcase. It shivered, and shrank backwards as best it could.

Bansi got to her feet, burning with anger inside, and went to the hearth. Her cheek throbbed from the slap, and her shoulder stung painfully where the hag's fingernails had bitten into it. Worse than either of those, though, was the feeling of rage and powerlessness.

The fire had completely burned down, leaving nothing but a few barely glowing embers; but despite Grandmother Bone's assertion, the room was still uncomfortably warm. With a resentful sigh, Bansi picked up some sticks and straw from a nearby basket and tried to remember what her dad had taught her about building a campfire.

'Ha!' the hag mocked, standing over Bansi as she hesitantly set the straw atop the embers and piled the sticks around it. 'Have you never laid a fire before?'

'I've never had to,' Bansi muttered to herself. 'We've got radiators.' Finishing her stacking, she stood and looked around the fireplace. 'Where are the—?'

She stopped, feeling slightly foolish as she realized that the faery folk were unlikely to use matches. But then, what did they use? Was she supposed to rub two sticks together?

The hag sneered at her confusion. 'What?' she taunted. 'Power enough to skin-change, and yet not the power to start a simple flame from the heat of the embers?'

Bansi stared at her in disbelief. 'You want me to light it by *magic*?' she asked.

Grandmother Bone grinned unpleasantly, the

black points of her teeth like sharp silhouettes behind her withered blood-red lips. 'Never has Paddock been wrong,' she said, 'though he may mislead the unwary. But I begin to wonder. Perhaps the power is all within your cloak of wolf-skin? Without it, then, you are powerless . . . In which case,' she went on, picking up the knife with the eye in its handle, 'you might after all make a better supper than a servant. Hmmm? What say you, Paddock?'

The toad, resting on a low shelf, stirred within its sphere, and its eyes flicked open. Then it spoke:

'Though magic lives inside the fur
That turns the girl to beast,
Without the stronger power in her
It could not be released.
And so, you take your life into your hands
If hers you end. My former warning stands.'

It regarded Grandmother Bone balefully for a moment, and closed its eyes once more.

The hag snarled wordlessly and glared at Bansi. 'Well, then,' she snapped after a moment. 'A tasty meal is better than a lazy servant; but a lazy servant is better than nothing. Something else shall I find for my supper, girl. When I return, make sure the fire blazes!' Throwing the knife down upon the table, she snatched up a cloak from the back of her chair and wrapped it round her skinny frame.

'But . . . that's not fair!' Bansi objected. 'You can't tell me to light a fire and not give me anything to light it with!'

Grandmother Bone glanced at the rough pile of sticks and straw that Bansi had made, and muttered:

'Heat that sleeps within the embers
Wakens now, and now remembers
What it is; and all its power
Blossoms, bursting into flower.
Light arises. Flame returns,
Glowing, dancing. Fire burns.'

Instantly there was a crackling sound from the fireplace, and Bansi saw a flame leap up into the straw. Within moments, a fire blazed there, wood snapping and popping in the roaring heat.

With a contemptuous nod, the hag glanced at Bansi and turned back to the fire.

'Burn,' she said, *'and blaze; destroy, consume.*
Your appetite becomes your doom.'

At these words, the fire blazed higher and hotter until Bansi recoiled for fear of being scorched. But within moments the fire died down again. All the straw and all the wood had been burned up, and there was nothing left.

'With all your hidden power, girl,' Grandmother Bone said scathingly, 'can you do that? We shall see. I go now to find a morsel for my supper – but if, on my return, I find you have not served me well, then our compact is broken and I shall see how tasty your pet may be.'

'That's not fair!' Bansi began, but the hag ignored her. Snatching up with frightening ease an object like a huge stone skittle with a rounded base, she strode to the door and flung it open. 'That's not *fair*!' Bansi repeated. 'I can't light a fire by magic!'

Grandmother Bone leered horribly, her hooked nose and chin almost touching. 'Then I shall light a fire on my return, and over it your bird shall be roasted.'

The door slammed shut behind her, with a click like a lock turning.

Almost immediately there was a flurry of wings above Bansi's head. She looked up to see the raven heading for the door. 'Come on!' it said in urgent panic. 'Let's get out of here!'

'But the door's locked!' Bansi said.

'I've got a beak, haven't I?' the raven insisted. 'Maybe I can pick the lock!'

It perched hurriedly on the door handle and leaned

forward to probe the lock with its beak. An instant later it was cawing in terror and flapping backwards into the air, a feathery bundle of noise and fear.

'It . . . it's got teeth!' it squawked, trembling. 'It's got *teeth*!'

Bansi looked. Around the inside of the lock a little circle of shiny brass teeth were snapping together – enraged, it seemed, at having just missed the tip of the raven's beak.

She tried the handle, but with no effect except to start the lock's little teeth gnashing more furiously. There would be no escape that way. Quickly she looked around the room, but this only confirmed what she was already sure of: there was no exit from the hut except the way they had just tried. The only other door led to Grandmother Bone's bedroom, a room just big enough to contain a small bed and a smaller chest of drawers. None of the windows opened, and in any case they were all too small for Bansi to squeeze through. They were trapped; or at least *she* was.

'Look, if I break a window then you can get out,' Bansi said.

The raven shook its head gloomily. 'Bet they're enchanted in some way, to stop you doing that. And even if they're not, you heard what the brownie said . . .'

'Oh, come on,' Bansi argued. 'Pogo wouldn't really hurt you.'

'If I saved my own skin but got you killed? I wouldn't like to risk it.'

'She's not going to kill me, though, is she? You heard what Paddock said. She thinks I've got some kind of power that might kill her if she—'

'If she loses her temper,' the raven said darkly, 'I wouldn't want to bet on what she'd do. And she would, if you broke her window and let me out. Anyway, all them skulls outside give me the willies, with their burning eyes and everything. I'm not facing them on my own. Nope,' it went on, 'I reckon my best bet all round is staying here with you, and you lighting that fire before she gets back.'

Bansi stared at the bird disbelievingly. 'But I can't *do* magic,' she protested.

The bird cocked its head to one side. 'Says you,' it said. 'Look, I was there when you beat the Dark Lord. I saw what you did. And like the toad said: if you wasn't magic, you wouldn't be able to turn into a wolf when you put that cloak on. So you *can* do magic, and Grandma Boney seems to think lighting a fire's a pretty easy trick. Come on,' it added, a pleading tone entering its voice; 'give it a go.'

Bansi sighed and started to lay the fire, setting out a large pile of straw and building a tent of sticks around it. 'I really don't think I can do this,' she said.

'Aw, come on,' the raven begged. 'Don't be like that! How's about a bit of positive thinking? Tell yourself you can, and maybe you will, eh?'

Bansi nodded uncertainly; and then the sense of the raven's argument sank in a little, and she said, 'OK. OK, I'll try. I'll really try.'

'Good girl!' the raven said enthusiastically. 'You can do it!' Then to itself it muttered tremulously, 'You'd better.'

Bansi clearly wasn't meant to overhear this last comment; but she did, and it made her realize how frightened the bird must be feeling. Her resolve strengthened, she knelt and stared into the fireplace.

'Go on, then!' the raven said nervously. 'What are you waiting for?'

'Shhh!' Bansi said. 'I'm trying to remember what she said. What was it? *Sleeping in the embers* . . . No . . . *The heat that sleeps inside the embers, wakes up and . . . and remembers . . . remembers* . . . Oh, it's no good!' she burst out in frustration. 'I *can't* remember! I don't know what the spell was!'

'Hang on!' the raven said, a note of surprise and awe creeping into its voice. 'Look at that! Something's happening!'

It was. Deep inside the pile of straw, a dim hint of red could just be seen.

'Is that . . .' said the raven; 'is that the fire starting?'

Bansi leaned in, to see if she could feel any warmth beginning. She could see more red now, as if the flame was spreading – and yet, it didn't quite look like a flame. It was the wrong sort of red, and although it was moving, the movement wasn't the flickering movement of fire. It moved again, and Bansi had only time for the absurd thought that it made her think for some reason of a nose . . .

. . . when the whole pile of sticks and straw exploded gently upwards, and there stood a little man-shaped figure.

'Wey-hey!' it said cheerfully.

'Blimey,' muttered the raven, 'that's all we need.'

'Found ye!' Flooter said happily. 'Right – what'sh next? Oh, aye – go tell Pogo where you are. Cheerio!'

And, just as Bansi was saying, 'Flooter! Wait!' the cluricaun wasn't there any more.

Moments later, his voice came from behind them. 'Hang on, though – where *are* you? I mean, where are *we*? Where'sh thish place?'

Bansi whirled. 'Flooter, before you go to get Pogo . . .'

'Oh, aye,' Flooter said. 'That'sh the nexsht thing, ishn't it – find Pogo!'

And again he was gone.

Moments later, he was back, standing on the table.

'Where *are* we, though?' he began.

'I'll tell you in a moment,' Bansi said, 'but first, I need you to listen to me, OK?'

'Righto,' Flooter agreed, swaying slightly.

'This is really important. Can you bring me a box of matches?'

''Courshe I can,' Flooter said proudly. 'What'sh a mox o' batches?'

Bansi sighed. 'A *box* of *matches*, Flooter. And maybe you should ask Pogo to bring them. Can you do that?'

'Oh, aye,' the cluricaun agreed. 'Get Mogo to bring a pox o' batches . . . No, get *Pogo* to bring a mox o' . . .'

'Matches,' Bansi said firmly. 'Tell him to bring matches.'

'Matches. Right. Bye,' Flooter said, and was gone.

Then he was back, this time on the narrow windowsill. 'But where *are* we?'

'We're in a forest,' Bansi told him, biting back a growing sense of panic as she wondered whether Flooter was up to the task, 'in a hut that stands on bird's legs . . .'

Flooter stared at her. 'Doeshn't that hurt them?'

'What?' Bansi asked, thrown.

'The wee birdiesh. Doeshn't it hurt them, a big

old hut coming along and shtanding on their legs?'

Bansi shook her head in despair. 'No, it's *got* bird's legs . . . the hut, I mean: it's got legs *like* a bird's, but they're the hut's legs, and it stands on them like . . . like you stand on your legs.'

'What, like thish?' Flooter asked, lifting up his legs, one at a time, to show her; and then lifting both at once for emphasis and falling off the windowsill. 'Whoopsh!' he added cheerfully as Bansi caught him and set him back on the sill, facing outwards.

'Look,' she said, pointing. 'Scary skulls with burning eyes, and beyond them, lots of trees. It's a forest. Tell Pogo: we're being held here by a hag. She lives in a hut that has bird's legs. And tell him to bring matches. And, Flooter,' she added, in a sudden burst of inspiration, 'if you can manage all that, you'll get a big bottle of whiskey.'

Flooter looked at her as if she were crazy. 'Sure I know *that*,' he said indignantly; and was gone.

'Great,' the raven said gloomily. 'My life's in the hands of a cluricaun who can't even remember which way's up, except when it comes to bottles. And,' it added with a shiver, 'Grandma Boney could be back any moment.'

Chapter Thirty

'Well, *that* was a waste of time,' Granny said tartly as the Morris Minor Traveller accelerated into the darkness. 'I told you we wouldn't find Flooter that way.'

'It *might* have worked,' Mrs Mullarkey retorted. 'We were just unlucky enough to get the wrong cluricaun, that's all.'

'The wrong cluricaun, indeed,' Granny tutted. 'And where might we be going now?'

'To be honest, Eileen, I have no more clue than you have. Where would you like us to be going?'

'I'd have thought that was obvious,' Granny said. 'I'd *like* us to be going to wherever Bansi is.'

The sat-nav beeped gently to itself.

'And *I'd* like that useless wee box there to switch itself off,' Mrs Mullarkey rejoined, 'but if wishes were road maps we'd none of us get lost, would we now?'

'Well, I'm only saying, Nora,' said Granny. 'And you did ask.'

'Perhaps I was hoping for something a wee bit more useful, then,' Mrs Mullarkey said, 'but if I was,

I'm after asking the wrong person, aren't I? I mean, I *know* that we need to find Bansi – assuming she's in Tir na n'Óg at all, that is, and that other fellow wasn't leading us up the garden path – but unless you can suggest something a bit more useful—'

'Make a U-turn when possible,' the sat-nav said, its perfectly measured voice somehow sounding even more like a newsreader than before. *'Then drive three point one kilometres, and turn left.'* It binged softly. The featureless map changed from white to green and a bent-back arrow appeared on the screen in front of the little blue car icon.

Mrs Mullarkey sighed. 'That's all we need. Eileen, could you try one more time to turn that thing off? It's bad enough having that screen on the whole time, not to mention all the beeps and bingy-bongies it keeps doing, but if it's going to start jabbering away at us it'll drive me mad.'

'Might it not be worth doing what it says?' Granny suggested.

Mrs Mullarkey heaved a weary sigh. 'Eileen, it works by listening to the wee satellites up in the sky. Only, there are no satellites in the sky above Tir na n'Óg, are there? So if it's giving us directions, it must be even more broken than it was before.'

'Make a U-turn when possible,' said the sat-nav.

'See?' Mrs Mullarkey said.

'Make a U-turn when possible,' the sat-nav repeated.

'Ah, shut up, you stupid thing,' Mrs Mullarkey growled, her foot pressing on the accelerator.

'Shut up yourself, you daft old trout,' the sat-nav said, its electronic voice as measured and polite as ever, *'and make a U-turn when possible.'*

The Morris Minor Traveller skidded to a startled halt, and the two old ladies inside it stared at each other.

'What did you just say?' Mrs Mullarkey asked.

'I said,' the sat-nav answered calmly, *'shut up yourself, you daft old trout, and make a U-turn when possible.'*

Mrs Mullarkey's mouth dropped open. 'Now just hold on a—'

'Make a U-turn when possible,' the sat-nav said again. *'Now would be nice.'*

'Oh, aye?' Mrs Mullarkey said suspiciously. 'And where will that take us if we do?'

'To a left turning three point one kilometres away,' the sat-nav answered.

'And what would we do there, might I ask?' Granny said.

'Turn left,' the sat-nav said, *'and drive eight point seven kilometres.'*

'Whatever for?' Mrs Mullarkey demanded indignantly.

'To turn right,' the sat-nav answered, still sounding

more like a computerized newsreader than anything else, *'and drive fifty-nine point six kilometres, and turn left, and drive thirty-three point one kilometres, and—'*

'Yes, but why?' Granny asked in exasperation. 'Where will this . . . this magical mystery tour take us?'

The sat-nav gave no hint of impatience, and yet something in its tone suggested to Granny that it felt it was talking to an idiot. *'To Bansi, of course,'* it said.

Time flows differently in the Other Realm, so it may have been just then, or earlier, or later, or all three at once, that Pogo, still searching the deserted High Street for any trace of a trail he could follow, looked up to see Flooter racing unsteadily towards him from the direction of the tube station.

'Did you find her?' he asked urgently as he met the cluricaun halfway.

'Find who?' Flooter asked. 'Oh – aye: Banshi. I did, Pogo, aye.'

'So where is she?'

Flooter screwed his face up in concentration. 'Let'sh see . . . she's in a foresht of birdsh' legs. No, that'sh not right . . . she'sh in a hut that'sh *got* bird's legsh, and all around that're lotsh o' shkullsh with burning eyesh, and all round that'sh a big dark foresht with lots of treesh. And that raven'sh with her, and they're being held prishoner by a hag. Here – what'sh the matter?'

For Pogo – as much as a brownie can – had gone pale, and sat down unsteadily on the road.

'Well,' he muttered, 'the good news is, I know where to find her. Every brownie knows exactly where those hags live.'

'Sho what'sh the bad newsh?' Flooter asked cheerily.

'Every brownie child,' Pogo began shakily; 'every brownie child is told of the terrible hags who live in the cottages that walk on chicken-legs. And each of us is told that if we are bad or lazy or disobedient, one of them'll catch us and she'll . . . she'll . . .'

'Ah, now, Pogo!' Flooter said in horrified sympathy. 'You don't mean to tell us that them hags eat brownies, do you?'

'It's worse than that, Flooter,' said Pogo weakly. 'If one of them catches us, she'll . . . she'll make us tidy her home!'

'I thought browniesh *liked* tidying houshesh,' Flooter said, giving Pogo a puzzled and wobbly look.

Pogo returned the look balefully. '*Human* houses, aye. That's what we live for. But those hags! Did you see how she keeps her home, Flooter? Never swept, never cleaned, full of grotesque . . . *things* that you have to touch when you're tidying them, and worst of all . . . you have to do her washing-up.'

'What'sh sho bad about that?'

'They eat humans,' Pogo said grimly. 'When you scrape out the pots and pans, you're scraping out bits of human flesh and bone. For a brownie, that's a terrible thing. And one of them has Bansi!' he exclaimed in horror. His fear for himself swept aside by his concern for Bansi, he rose to his feet, a determined expression on his face. 'Come on!'

'Sho don't I get that whishkey now, Pogo?'

Pogo glared at him. 'You do not. Not till Bansi's home and safe. Now go and look after her. I'll be there as soon as I can.'

'Right,' Flooter said. 'Go and look after her, get her shafely home, get the whishkey. Grand. Um . . . was there shomething elshe, Pogo?'

'The only shomething elshe'll be my toe on the seat of your trousers if you don't get a move on!' Pogo growled.

'Right. Fine. Go and look after Banshi, and Pogo'll be along with a mox o' batches. Got it.' And, again without Pogo seeing exactly how, he disappeared.

Pogo stared at the space where Flooter had been a moment before, a puzzled expression on his wrinkled face. 'Mox o' batches?' he said.

* * *

Bansi was staring at the restacked tinder and kindling, willing it to burst into flames, when there was a noise behind her. The raven exploded into flight, and she leaped up, her heart pounding with fear, half expecting to see Grandmother Bone bursting through the door.

Instead, she saw Flooter lying on his face under the table.

'Whoopsh!' he said cheerfully, picking himself up. 'I fell off,' he added by way of explanation.

Bansi felt a fearful lump grow in her throat. 'Flooter, please – try and remember this time,' she said. 'We're in a hut on bird's legs, in a forest, and we need matches.'

'I know that!' Flooter said. 'Sure, wasn't I here the firsht time you said it!'

'Yes, but we need you to tell Pogo!' Bansi said earnestly.

'What, again?' Flooter said. 'But I've only jusht told him! That brownie'sh memory ishn't what it used to be, I'm telling you . . .'

Bansi's mouth fell open. 'You haven't had time to tell him! You've only been gone a few seconds!'

'Ah,' said Flooter wisely. 'But time goesh differently in the mortal world, sho it doesh. It might have been jusht a few sheconds here, but it was . . . um . . . lots of sheconds there.'

Bansi's heart leaped. This seemed like the first piece of good news for a very long time. 'So Pogo knows we're here?' she said. 'And he knows about the matches?'

'Oh, aye,' Flooter said confidently.

Bansi felt just a little of the burden on her shoulders lift. 'Right,' she said to the raven, who was shivering once more on the high bookshelf, 'that improves our chances, doesn't it?'

The raven glared at Flooter. 'Yeah,' it said. 'As long as wobbly boy there doesn't keep scaring me like that, I might just survive till morning. But – don't stop trying with the magic, eh? Just in case Pogo doesn't get here in time.'

Bansi nodded and returned her attention to the fireplace.

'I still say we don't know if we can trust this thing,' Mrs Mullarkey muttered for at least the third time.

'And *I* still say, if you've got a better idea, Nora, let's hear it,' said Granny. 'And since you haven't come up with anything so far, then if the wee box thinks it knows where Bansi is, let's give it a go.'

'Turn right,' said the sat-nav.

'Bossy wee thingummy,' Mrs Mullarkey muttered, swinging the car onto a wide and bumpy forest track.

'Stubborn old cactus-face,' the sat-nav replied calmly. *'Now drive fifty-nine point six kilometres,'* it added. On its screen, the map was slowly becoming more detailed; it now showed the trees on either side of them in a darker shade of green, and a small crooked blue line a little way off to the left, which presumably indicated a river.

'My goodness, we reached that turning quickly, Nora,' Granny remarked.

'I suppose we did,' Mrs Mullarkey said, peering into the darkness ahead of them. 'The old car's going well today.'

'It'll be magic, I expect,' Granny said comfortably.

'Magic, indeed!' Mrs Mullarkey snorted. 'There's nothing magical about my car, Eileen O'Hara.'

'Apart from the fact that it got fixed by brownies, that is. And it hardly ever runs out of petrol. And,' Granny added, examining the windscreen again, 'it seems to be fixing all the cracks in the windows by itself. Oh, aye, and it's got a magic wee talky box. And it's going faster than it has a right to, as well. But apart from that, no, there's nothing magical about it at all.'

Mrs Mullarkey made no reply other than a gruff harrumphing sound.

'So how far to where Bansi is, do you think?' Granny asked.

The question was addressed to Mrs Mullarkey; but it was the sat-nav that answered. '*Five thousand, three hundred and forty-seven point six kilometres.*'

'*How* much?' Granny almost shrieked.

'*Five—*' the sat-nav began.

Mrs Mullarkey interrupted. 'Better get moving, then,' she announced, pressing the accelerator down by its final centimetre. 'We've a long drive ahead of us.'

The car roared like a beast of prey as it hurled itself furiously into the forest.

'Come *on*!' the raven croaked agitatedly.

Bansi bit back a sarcastic reply, remembering that the bird was in fear for its life. 'I'm trying,' she said, gazing at the tinder and kindling. 'But I just don't know how to do this.'

'Ah, sure, Pogo'll be here shoon,' Flooter remarked. 'He'll know what to do. Browniesh are alwaysh lighting firesh and tending them.'

Bansi nodded. 'And he'll have matches with him, too.'

'As long as he gets here in time,' the raven muttered. 'That's all.'

Bansi stared again into the heart of the cold fireplace and tried to imagine it bursting into flame.

Nothing happened.

'Come *on*!' the raven muttered again.

For what seemed like ages, nobody moved. Bansi tried to block out all thoughts of anything but fire; but the hearth remained as resolutely cold as ever.

'Burn,' she muttered. 'Burn.' She repeated it until it seemed to lose its meaning, and something in the back of her head began to wonder if it was really a word. Still nothing happened.

'Come *on*!' the raven hissed again, shifting from foot to clawed foot anxiously.

'Here!' Flooter said suddenly. He was staring out through the little window nearest to Bansi. 'Would you look at that? Sure, I've never sheen one of them before, and that'sh a fact!'

Bansi looked. Up in the sky, something like an enormous bowl was silhouetted against the huge round moon. Bansi strained to see. There was something or somebody in it, sitting upright and paddling away at the sky with a huge implement of some kind – paddling directly towards the hut, and, she suddenly realized with a sickening lurch of the stomach, moving incredibly swiftly. Already it was noticeably closer, and the silhouetted figure in the bowl had become horribly recognizable. There could be no doubt about it.

Grandmother Bone was coming home.

Chapter Thirty-One

'Right,' Bansi said urgently. 'There's nothing else for it. I'm going to have to break the window and let you out.'

'But . . . but . . . aw, heck, I suppose you're right,' the raven cawed. 'What about you, though?'

'She'sh coming in awful fasht, sho she ish,' Flooter said.

'OK,' said Bansi, picking up a heavy brass poker by the shaft. 'Keep low when you get out, and get in among the trees as quickly as you can. Here goes. Cover your eyes!' She swung the poker back, ready to bring its handle crashing into the window.

'Stop that!' cried an angry voice.

Bansi jumped, and almost dropped the poker with fright. She swung round, and a little gasp of hope and relief escaped her.

'What do you think you're doing?' Pogo snapped. 'You'll never get out through a window that size. How big do you think you are? You'll just make her angry, and then where will you be? Besides,' he added darkly, ignoring Bansi's attempts to interrupt, 'just think of the mess. Someone'll have to clear it up, you know. Not that there isn't enough mess in here already.' His eyes swept the room, taking in the full extent of the disorder and chaos in which Grandmother Bone lived. 'So the stories are true, then,' he muttered, his expression suddenly glazed and frantic. 'You might be here for ever, and still never get it tidy—'

'Pogo,' Bansi said urgently. 'Pogo!' But the little man seemed lost in some kind of horrified trance. 'Pogo!' she said again, kneeling and taking him by the shoulder. 'Did you bring the matches? *Pogo!*'

'What?' Pogo said, coming out of his daze. 'Eh? Oh – matches. I did, aye.' He shook himself as if to clear his head, and held up the little box in his hand, adding with a glare at Flooter, 'Once I finally worked out what that muttonhead there was blethering on about, that is. Mox o' batches indeed!'

'What about Mum?' Bansi asked. 'Have you any idea where she is?'

The brownie shook his head. 'She was gone when I got back to your house,' he said, kneeling to light the fire.

'I know,' Bansi began. 'I've seen her – here, in Tir na n'Óg; or, at least, somewhere between here and our world, I mean—'

'Never mind all that!' the raven suddenly

squawked in alarm. 'Grandma Boney's coming in to land! Oh, bloomin' 'eck, be *careful*!' Pogo, startled, had fumbled the box.

'What d'you expect, if you're going to go around shouting like that!' Pogo snapped, hurriedly scooping up spilled matches.

'Just get on with it!' urged the bird. 'Oh, thank goodness,' it added as the kindling took light beneath Pogo's skilled hands. 'Thought I was a goner then, I really did.' It fluttered shakily back up to the top of the bookcase and huddled there, small and shivering.

Bansi cast a glance through the window. 'She's here!' she hissed. 'Pogo! Flooter! Hide!'

'Eh? What'sh that?' Flooter said; and then, 'Whoopsh!' as Pogo bundled him inside an old and roughly hewn wooden trunk, whispering threats as to what he'd do to him if they were discovered.

The lid had barely closed when the door burst open and Grandmother Bone stamped in, shaking mud off her boots. In one hand she carried her huge and oddly shaped stone paddle, which she set down by the door; over the other shoulder she held a small sack.

'Ha!' she spat, an edge of surprise and disappointment in her voice. 'The fire burns. So the bird is safe – for now.' She stared chillingly for a moment at the raven. 'I am lucky, then, to have found some morsel to appease my hunger.' Reaching into her sack, she produced a loaf and a small hunk of yellow cheese which she set down on the table. 'Now, child,' she rasped, hobbling to her chair, where she sat down and clapped her gnarled hands together imperiously. 'Serve me my supper!' A crafty look came over her face as she added, 'But firelighting by magic is hungry work, is it not? Cut enough for both of us. Only a little for you, but you must eat something.'

Bansi looked at her mistrustfully, suspecting some trick – poison, perhaps. But if the hag was planning to eat from the same loaf—

'Go on, girl!' Grandmother Bone snapped.

Unwillingly Bansi picked up the knife with the eye in its handle – and stifled a shriek as she felt it blink, its eyelashes stroking the palm of her hand. The sense of shock and disgust was so great that she almost dropped it but, looking up, she saw her captor glaring ferociously at her. As quickly as she could, she began to cut.

'Not too much,' the hag cautioned. ''Tis all we have.'

All the more reason, Bansi thought, to be suspicious of Grandmother Bone's motives for sharing even a little.

She cut a slice of bread and a slice of cheese for each of them and hastily put the knife down, feeling the skin of her palm crawling horrifically.

Shuddering, trying to control her feelings of revulsion at the memory of the eye's touch, she placed the food on a couple of badly cleaned wooden plates.

As she crossed the room, her attention was caught by a sound from the top of the bookcase: the raven clearing its throat. She looked up at it; the bird was twitching oddly as if trying to shake its head without being noticed. Clearly it was trying to warn her of something.

Saying nothing, she handed the bread and cheese to Grandmother Bone and watched as the hag took a great bite.

'Eat!' Grandmother Bone commanded, chewing messily.

Bansi looked down at the meagre portion on the grubby wooden plate. 'I'm not hungry,' she said, and suddenly realized it was true.

'Hmmmph,' grunted the crone. 'Dreaming of escape? Of rescue, perhaps? Forget such thoughts. The house will never let you leave, and you know no one with the power to take you from me. You are mine for ever.'

Bansi felt the stirrings of fear – fear that Grandmother Bone might be right. 'You don't know that,' she said defiantly. 'I've been in more danger than this before now. I've been rescued from worse places.'

A rattling, mirthless laugh escaped the hag's bread-flecked lips. 'Any rescuer I cannot overcome, I can outrun!' she cackled. 'Without moving from this chair, without uttering a word, I can command my home to leap and run and wade and climb faster than any pursuer! There is none who can steal you from me! You are mine, girl; your fate is entirely in my hands. What say you, Paddock?'

In the globe, the toad stirred under its violet sky. Its eyes opened; closed again, as if it were concentrating on something; and opened once more. Then it spoke:

'The race is swift that must be run;
The girl, the prize that shall be won.'

Fixing its gaze on Bansi, the toad paused. It stared at her intensely, its dewlap pulsating, and said nothing, until at last Grandmother Bone broke in impatiently, 'But who shall the victor be? Who shall win the girl once and for all, and decide her fate? It shall be me, shall it not, running this race so swiftly from the comfort of my chair! Say on, Paddock; say on!'

The toad's head inclined towards her. Its throat pulsed slowly once more before it continued:

'The victor is the aged crone
Who, seated as upon a throne
Speeds more swiftly than the rushing wind has ever blown.
Faster than an eagle flies, and than the deer more fleet
She races to her victory, yet never leaves her seat.'

'Ha!' the hag barked triumphantly. 'You see, child? The aged crone who, without ever leaving her seat, races faster than the wind! You are mine, girl!'

'You don't know that!' Bansi said coldly. 'Just because your toad says so—'

'Paddock never lies to me, child, and he is never wrong!' Grandmother Bone said gleefully. 'If he says I am the victor, then so shall it be! Swifter than the wind, my house can run at my command, faster than the eagle, more fleet than the deer. None can catch us. You are mine. Now – eat your supper!'

There was something hungry in the way she regarded Bansi just at that moment.

Bansi looked at the meagre portion of bread and cheese she had cut for herself, and glanced at the raven. Again it twitched its head as if to say 'No'.

She deliberately didn't look at the wooden trunk; didn't see the lid lifting by just a few millimetres, or the pair of deep brown eyes that peered out at her.

'Pogo!' hissed Flooter. 'What're ye doing? She'll catch you and . . . and . . . and make you tidy her houshe, sho she will!'

'I don't care,' Pogo whispered back fiercely. 'I'm not letting Bansi eat anything that old witch gives her! I'll give myself away sooner than let it get anywhere near her mouth!'

The hag took another bite of her own bread and cheese. 'Eat, girl!' she commanded, her voice muffled by the sound of her own chewing. 'Eat!'

Bansi felt anger – fuelled by a sense of hopelessness, a fear that the toad's prophecy was true, and a certainty that Grandmother Bone was tricking her somehow – rise inside her. 'No,' she said defiantly. 'How do I know it's not poisoned? How do I know it's not enchanted?' And then, wanting to taunt the witch somehow, she added sarcastically, 'What say you, Paddock?'

Grandmother Bone's wrinkled mouth curled scornfully. But a second later the sneer died on her lips; for just at that moment, the toad spoke.

'If you eat what you are offered
in the country of the fae,
You will never see your home again.
In Tir na n'Óg you'll stay.'

Bansi stared at Paddock in surprise; but

Grandmother Bone's expression was one of utter disbelief. 'What tricks are you playing?' she demanded, rising from her chair like a snake uncoiling. 'What game is this?'

'What?' protested Bansi, confused and angered. 'I'm not! *You're* the one who's keeping *me* prisoner! *You're* the one who's just tried to trap me here for ever! I'm not the one who's playing tricks!'

'You commanded Paddock!' the crone spat. 'You come in the guise of a mere child, and yet you commanded Paddock! *And he spoke you the truth!*' She drew in a deep and rasping breath. 'How can this be? Where came a mortal by such power?'

Bansi stared at the hag, unsure of what to say. She hadn't expected the toad to answer; when it did, she had assumed it would answer anyone. But from Grandmother Bone's reaction, it seemed she had done something marvellous and magical without meaning to.

'Answer me!' Grandmother Bone snapped, stepping forward. As she did so, she trod on something amidst the clutter. There was a sudden small flaring of flame beneath her heavy boot. It burned for no more than an instant – but the hag's sharp eyes saw the flash, and her long hooked nose caught the scent.

She stepped back to see a long thin ribbon of smoke curling from the tip of a spent match.

Chapter Thirty-Two

Grandmother Bone picked up the match and, regarding Bansi warily, held it close to her crooked nose.

'Hmmmph!' she grunted, sniffing. 'Mortal-made.' She sniffed again, almost delicately. 'Hah! So – you lit the fire not by magic, but by trickery.'

Heart pounding, Bansi moved, putting herself between the raven and their captor; but Grandmother Bone's thoughts were far from her next meal.

'How now, girl?' she murmured thoughtfully. 'You take the wolf's form; you draw truth from Paddock – and yet, you cannot so much as summon a flame in the hearth. Speak, child! Whence comes your power? Why does it flicker so? Speak true! Unravel for me this mystery!'

Bansi glared at her captor, but said nothing.

'Good girl,' muttered Pogo, watching unseen from the wooden trunk. 'Don't tell her anything you don't have to.'

'Hah!' the hag snarled. 'Be silent, then. What say

you, Paddock? How can the girl perform such mighty magic at one moment, and fail the simplest of tasks the next?'

Again, the toad stirred wearily in its glass bubble:

'The ancient prophecy fulfilled,' it said,
'Forespoke great power; and such it brought
When on the ground her blood was spilled,
But yet the girl remains untaught.
Her magic being uncontrolled,
How strongly it shall manifest
May neither be foreknown nor told
If she be threatened, tried, or pressed.'

There was silence in the room when Paddock finished.

Grandmother Bone stared at Bansi thoughtfully, as if looking at her for the first time. 'I begin to see,' she said at last. 'But what to do?' Seizing Bansi's face suddenly in her cold, bony hand, palm roughly cupping her chin, she examined her closely. 'What brings you here, child? You have not the look of a patient victim, sent into my forest to die. What, then? You are on a quest? Seeking some talisman, perhaps – or something stolen?' Bansi, thinking at once of her mother, said nothing; but Grandmother Bone continued as if she had been answered. 'And a quest may mean enemies. Have you enemies, girl? Nay, look not at me so; I am not your enemy. I am neither foe, nor friend; I merely am.' Releasing Bansi, she stepped back, still fixing her with that enquiring stare. 'Paddock's warning now I understand. Were I to put you to the knife, your panic might release your power in some magic of great destruction. But might it not be almost as dangerous to let you live, if still your power be uncontrolled? So: what to do?'

Bansi folded her arms defiantly. 'Why don't you just let me go?' she said.

'Any servant is hard to come by, here in the forest,' Grandmother Bone retorted, 'but a servant with power such as yours may be a rare prize indeed. I will not let you go.'

Silence fell again. Grandmother Bone continued to stare at Bansi.

'We shall strike a bargain, you and I,' she said eventually. 'I shall teach you to use your magic; and one day, perhaps, I shall let you continue your quest, and with all that I have taught you, you will strike your enemies down. You in turn shall serve me and do me no harm. Will you so swear?'

Bansi shook her head. 'I'm not promising you anything,' she said firmly.

'That's the way,' Pogo murmured. 'Don't trust her. We'll get you out of this.'

'Are you going to reshcue her shoon, Pogo?' Flooter whispered from the darkness beside him. 'Only, I'm powerful thirshty, sho I am.'

'Is that all you can think about?' Pogo hissed. 'Away you go and find yourself a drink, then!'

'Ah, no, Pogo,' whispered Flooter. 'Sure, I'm here to reshcue Banshi with you, aren't I? And when we do, I'll get my bottle of whishkey. Jusht like you promished, eh?'

'*Your* bottle of whishkey?' came an outraged voice from behind them. 'That'sh *my* bottle of whishkey you're shpeaking about, you . . . you . . . you whishkey-thief!'

Pogo froze. The voice had carried across the room; the hag's head snapped round to look straight at their hiding place. 'Flooter,' he muttered as softly as he could, 'if this is your idea of a joke—'

'A joke?' roared the voice. 'Sho you think it'sh funny, do you? Promishing my whishkey to a whishkey-thief, ye whishkey-thief! Well, take that!'

Next second the whole trunk rocked as Flooter, hit by an unseen fist, slammed hard into Pogo, winding him.

'Ha!' the voice said, sounding very pleased with itself. 'That'll teach ye! Nobody takesh Hooligan'sh whishkey! Put 'em up! I'll pulverize ye!'

'Ah, now, hold on!' Flooter protested; and then grunted as he was picked up and hurled across the trunk. It rocked wildly as Hooligan threw himself in pursuit.

The lid was flung open. Two bony, claw-like hands reached in and scooped up all three little men, lifting them high to stare into the hideous face of Grandmother Bone.

'Ha!' the crone said, and Pogo recoiled as her foul breath washed over him. 'What have we here? Three little mannikins, ready for the pot – and two already steeped in marinade!' She chuckled ironically at her own joke. 'What do you here, mannikins?'

Pogo gave no answer, but struggled vainly against her grip. Flooter hiccupped and put on what was meant to be a winning smile. But Hooligan stuck out his chin pugnaciously, pointed at Bansi, and said defiantly, 'That one there owesh me a bottle o' whishkey, sho she doesh.'

'Oho!' Grandmother Bone said, with a glance at Bansi. 'Friends of yours, eh? Your brave rescuers? Now, perhaps, they shall rescue me from my hunger!'

Bansi's mind whirled. She had no idea who the second cluricaun was, but she was not about to see either him or her two friends served up for the hag's supper. But before she could find words to speak,

Hooligan opened his mouth and bit Grandmother Bone on the hand. The hag screeched in fury, and squeezed, but seconds later Hooligan was simply no longer there.

'What?' Grandmother Bone growled. 'How—'

'Ah,' put in Flooter. 'Nobody knowsh how the cluricaun travel.' He hiccupped again, and waved his fingers at her. 'Not even the cluricaun.'

And then he was gone, too, leaving only Pogo struggling in Grandmother Bone's clutches.

'And then there was one,' said the crone coldly. 'Your sort I know, little brown elf; and you have no vanishing magic. How will you taste, I wonder? Girl!' she commanded, turning to Bansi. 'Bring me the knife!'

Pogo vainly redoubled his struggling. But Bansi said, 'No. You want to make a bargain with me? Then leave my friend alone.'

The hag's face took on a look of cunning. 'Aha,' she said. 'Very well, child. Then let us bargain now. I shall swear to do no harm to the elf, or to any of your kith or kin, unless first they mean harm to me. I shall teach you to use the magic within you. And in return, you will do me no harm; you shall never turn your power against me; and whilst you are under my roof you will serve me well. Are we agreed?'

Pogo's eyes bulged wide in warning. The raven

fluttered anxiously on its high shelf.

Bansi thought carefully. She could see no reason not to agree, but she deeply mistrusted Grandmother Bone. Her eyes darted across the room in search of inspiration, and her gaze fell again upon the glass ball.

The toad's eyes were open, and it was staring straight at her.

'*Should* I agree?' she found herself saying. 'What say you, Paddock?'

This time there was no pause before the creature spoke:

'To save your mother from her snare
Unto this bargain you must swear.
But heed, lest you should be accursed,
My warning: let the hag swear first.'

Bansi glanced at her captor, expecting an outburst of temper; and was surprised at what she saw. Grandmother Bone was looking at her with an expression of amused respect.

'Very well,' the hag said. 'I shall swear first. You, dark elf, I shall set to work. There is plenty here to keep busy such a one as you.' She released her iron grip on Pogo, and set him down; he shuddered as he looked again at the filthy chaos of the room. 'Now, girl: let us swear our oaths, one to another; and then we shall begin our lessons.'

She spoke almost kindly; but her smile was greedy, and she licked her lips with her blood-red tongue.

Chapter Thirty-Three

'It's still awful dark, isn't it?' Granny said. 'It feels like it should've been morning hours ago.'

'If not days,' Mrs Mullarkey agreed, peering through the windscreen. 'That's the thing about Tir na n'Óg, though, Eileen: time works differently here. All the old stories agree. You could be here for days, and only gone for a few minutes in our world. Or here for a few hours, and yet when you return home you find a hundred years have passed.'

'Well, let's hope that doesn't happen,' said Granny. 'I haven't cancelled the milk. I wouldn't be able to get in the house for bottles. And it'd all have gone off, too. Just imagine the smell.'

'Bear left,' said the sat-nav.

'If this thing turns out to be leading us on a wild-goose chase . . .' Mrs Mullarkey muttered threateningly.

'To chase the nearest wild geese, make a U-turn when possible,' the sat-nav said. *'To find Bansi, bear left and drive seventy-eight point one kilometres to the next turning.'*

'Cheeky wee so-and-so,' Mrs Mullarkey said.

'*Battleaxe,*' the sat-nav replied agreeably.

'I wonder how it is it can do that,' said Granny. 'Work out where Bansi is, and come up with such an accurate character assessment of you, and so on.'

Mrs Mullarkey harrumphed. 'Accurate, indeed. Calling me a battleaxe when I'm as meek and mild as anything. As for everything else: it'll be magic, of course. Which is why I don't trust it.'

'Aye, but where does the magic come from? I mean, did the brownies put a spell on the car or something?'

Mrs Mullarkey shook her head disdainfully. 'Really, Eileen, do you know nothing about the wee folk? Brownies putting spells on things, indeed. They've no magic of their own, or very little of it at least.'

'Well, what do you think it is, then, if you're so clever, Mrs Expert-on-the-brownies-even-though-she-didn't-believe-in-them-six-months-ago?'

'I think it's something to do with the power of Tir na n'Óg, Mrs Never-believed-in-any-of-it-at-all-and-spent-her-life-scoffing-at-those-of-us-who-did-until-the-Good-People-came-along-and-kidnapped-her-granddaughter. I think the land of the Good People itself has brought it to life somehow. And mended all the cracks in the windscreen while it was at it.'

'Really?' said Granny in feigned surprise. 'So that's not just my imagination like you said it was, then?'

'Don't be ridiculous, Eileen. I never said any such thing.'

'You did too, and you know it. Anyway, if it's the power of Tir na n'Óg that's doing it, how come it didn't fix the car all by itself last time?'

'Because the prophecy hadn't been fulfilled then, of course. Why do you think?'

'Ah.' Granny nodded proudly. 'So it's my wee Bansi's doing, really.'

'Honestly, Eileen, sometimes you—'

'*Turn right*,' said the sat-nav.

'Ah, there, I told you this thing didn't know what it was doing,' Mrs Mullarkey said impatiently.

'*Turn right*,' the sat-nav insisted.

'You said it was seventy-eight kilometres till the next turning!' Mrs Mullarkey told it.

'*Turn right!*' the sat-nav said, and now there was an urgency in its computerized voice.

Sighing, Mrs Mullarkey checked the screen display and swung hard right as the arrow indicated.

A huge tree loomed in the headlights.

'Nora, look out!' Granny screamed; but Mrs Mullarkey had already jammed on the brakes, yanking hard at the wheel. The car slewed right round, missing the thick solid trunk by inches, and, facing backwards, slid to a graceless halt in a dense growth of bushes in the centre of a tangled woody thicket.

'Now, what the—' Mrs Mullarkey began.

'*Shut off the engine,*' interrupted the sat-nav.

'Now listen, you useless wee box of—'

'***Shut off the engine,***' the sat-nav insisted. '*And the lights. And cover me up,*' it added, though Granny could see that it was somehow dimming its own light even as it spoke.

'Whatever for?'

'*Shut off the engine, turn off the lights and cover me up,*' the sat-nav repeated.

'This had better not be some Good People trickery,' Mrs Mullarkey muttered threateningly, but turning off both lights and ignition.

'What now?' Granny asked, taking off her cardigan and draping it over the screen.

'*Wait,*' the sat-nav said. '*Silently.*'

They waited.

Once, Mrs Mullarkey broke the silence to mutter, 'What are we waiting *for*, for goodness' sakes?' but the sat-nav only replied, '*Shhhh.*'

And then they heard it. A pounding sound, one with which they had become all too familiar. The drumming of hooves, riding fast and hard and coming closer and closer.

Sheltered in the copse, they were surrounded by overgrown bushes and hidden in the shadow of the trees whose branches and leaves grew thickly overhead. But the meadowland they had crossed was lit with a ghostly brightness by the unnaturally large moon of Tir na n'Óg. So it was that they saw three cloaked figures on horseback appear, cresting the brow of a hill directly ahead of them, and gallop down straight for the car. The horses shone white in the moonlight, except for their ears, which – although all colour was stolen by the night – both women knew would be red, like the clothes of their ferocious riders.

Without speaking, without taking their eyes off the riders for an instant, Granny and Mrs Mullarkey took out their catapults and silently armed them.

But the little horsemen drew their mounts to a halt before they reached the concealing thicket, and sat as if impatiently waiting for something.

Before long there came more hoofbeats, and the riders turned their horses to the left – the direction in which Granny and Mrs Mullarkey had been travelling. The hoofbeats grew louder, and the little men were joined by three more riders, who spoke to them in voices that did not carry as far as the hidden car. The two old women sat silently, catapults in hands, and made no sound.

Eventually the little men seemed to come to a consensus. The first three turned to face the direction from which the car had come and spurred their horses on, the second three following immediately.

Granny and Mrs Mullarkey waited in the darkness, listening to the hoofbeats dying away.

'Well,' said Granny, breathing out loudly as the silence of the night returned, 'it's a good job we didn't just keep going, or we'd have run straight into that second lot, wouldn't we? Do you think it's us they were after?'

Mrs Mullarkey shook her head thoughtfully. 'It's them – or three more just like them – that stranded us here, Eileen. They knew where we were then, and they just left us there and went off.'

'Aye,' Granny agreed, 'to get Bansi. So do you think they're still looking for her?'

'If they are,' said a computerized voice, *'they should make a U-turn when possible.'*

Granny lifted her cardigan, and the glow of the sat-nav's screen lit up her wrinkled face. 'Thank you for the warning,' she said to it, patting it as one might pat a friendly little dog.

'You're welcome,' the sat-nav said.

'Huh,' Mrs Mullarkey muttered under her breath. 'Luck, most likely.'

'Oh, don't be such an old crosspatch, Nora,' said Granny amenably. 'Shall we get going?'

'Turn right,' said the sat-nav; *'then drive for seventy-two point three kilometres.'*

'It was seventy-eight kilometres just a minute ago!' Granny exclaimed. 'Nora, just how fast are you driving?'

'You do not want to know,' said the sat-nav helpfully.

Mrs Mullarkey fired up the engine and turned on the lights. 'So it's safe now, is it?' she said. 'Better get going, then, before those wee hallions notice the tyre-tracks.'

Granny glanced at the speedometer as the car shot out of the thicket and executed a sharp right turn. Within seconds its needle had shot up to a point a little over the maximum speed indicated on the clock, where it remained, bouncing around as though wanting to go much, much higher.

'We're coming, Bansi, darling,' she said under her breath, gripping her walking stick rather more tightly than usual. 'Hold on, sweetheart. We're coming.'

Asha O'Hara lay, utterly exhausted and panting for breath, against the foot of a steep rocky cliff that gleamed greyly in the moonlight. Confused, terrified, and under an enchantment that was growing ever stronger, her mind was hardly her own any more. She scarcely remembered anything of her life before this evening's endless flight into the never-ending night of this strange land. She felt as if she had been running for ever from shadows and shades, from dangerous night-beasts, from unknown terrors and unseen creatures and wild howlings in the darkness.

As her breathing calmed, and cool peace flowed slowly back into her burning lungs, a sense of self began gradually to return. The animal state of her terrified and hunted thoughts began to fall away from her. At last, for the moment at least, she was safe. At her back rose a great wall of granite; all around her stretched a desolate plain of rough stone. There were no creatures here; no form of life would choose to make its dwelling on this barren moonscape. In every direction, as far as the eye could see, lay nothing but lifeless rocks. She could rest.

A movement caught her eye. Instantly alert, she sat up and stared into the darkness; but there was nothing there. Nothing but a great round boulder which cast a long dark shadow in the moon's light, and a scattering of smaller stones, fragments from some long-ago rock fall. She lay back again, so weary she did not care how hard the cliff pressed against her spine.

Another movement. Her heart beat out a rhythm

of alarm as her head snapped round; but again there was nothing but rocks. Had she been more aware, less under a spell, she might have wondered if she was imagining things, or if some small terrified lizard was scuttling from stone to stone; as it was, her mind was still dulled and her nerves primed for danger. She scrambled to her feet, terror flooding back into her brain. And as she did so, she caught sight of another twitch of motion, and another, and with horror she realized what was happening.

The rocks were beginning to move.

All around her, from the largest boulders to the smallest pebbles, they were one by one shifting slightly – as if breathing, or stirring in their sleep. Asha O'Hara watched in wordless panic as the sinister movements rippled out across the plain, until every stone she could see was slowly pulsing as if it had somehow been brought to life, or half wakened from a deep and ancient slumber.

And then one round boulder uncurled. Like some sinister lump of clay reshaping itself, it stretched out, rough limbs extending from its shell-like bulk. A head appeared, like that of some monstrous turtle; it clambered clumsily to its feet, and turned.

It was hideous. Its face was a twisted, asymmetric mockery of human features, with dead flinty eyes and a distorted mouth crammed with jagged grey teeth. Its expression registered no emotion as it looked at her, but it uttered a single guttural rumbling grunt.

The effect was immediate. All around the plain, other rocks and stones and boulders began to uncurl, stretching out into grotesque parodies of humans and apes and bears and unidentifiable, frightful things that walk on two legs. Hooting and grunting and baying, they began to shuffle – haltingly, stumblingly, but unstoppably – towards her.

Asha O'Hara screamed. Long and loud, and born of unthinking terror, the sound echoed from the rocky cliff and the stone plain, carrying uselessly across the desolate craggy wilderness from where no help could possibly come.

The creatures paused. One let out a grunting breath, a gravelly 'huh' sound; another followed suit; and then the plain resounded with the noise, each of the stone monsters joining in with its own variation of the sound.

It sounded like laughter. A huge, mocking, cruel wave of laughter from the throats of gargoyles.

And then the shuffling began again, one step at a time as the creatures dragged their rocky bulks slowly, slowly towards Asha O'Hara. The sharpness of the cliff pressed into her back. She had nowhere to run.

Beneath the shuffling came another sound: a distant thundering, a drumming, a pounding against the rock beneath them. It began quietly but grew like a hurricane, reverberating through the ground under her feet.

The stone creatures paused, listening; one or two squatted, pressing their hands against the ground. The drumming grew louder and louder, echoing across the rocky plain.

'Hurrr,' one of the stone beasts breathed, and again the sound was taken up by the others until it ebbed and flowed like a tide. Their ugly heads swivelled, turning slowly from side to side, as if to locate the source of the sound.

Asha O'Hara, her mind wrapped in terror, her back pushing vainly and painfully into the cliff, shrank away from them, not knowing if the noise meant salvation or doom.

Then, gradually, each grotesque head ceased its turning, each looking in the same direction. Asha O'Hara, trembling, turned her own gaze to follow theirs.

Across the vast plain of stone, a horseman was coming. His immense steed was pale and ghostly in the moonlight; his armour shone like rubies in the grey blue of the night; his dark cloak streamed out behind him. As he came, he drew his great sword; it blazed in his hand, as though the sun itself was held prisoner within it. He was fearsome to behold, and the ground shuddered beneath him.

The Dread Cruach was coming to claim his bride.

The stone beasts moaned, a great ululation of fear. One by one they sank to the ground, curling in on themselves, hiding their heads and arms and legs. Before the Dread Cruach had reached them, they were nothing but rock, lying still and lifeless in the moonlight.

An unthinking, unnatural joy filled Asha O'Hara, sweeping away both the horrors of the last minutes, and all traces of memory. Her husband and daughter utterly forgotten, she ran to meet her grim rescuer.

Chapter Thirty-Four

It was hard to concentrate with Grandmother Bone hovering over her. The hag was showing surprising patience, but Bansi was all too aware of how violently her captor's mood could change; and the principles she was explaining were hard to grasp.

From what she could gather, the verses which Grandmother Bone spoke to cast her magic held no power of their own. It was the rhythm of the words and the feelings they created that concentrated the mind; any rhyme would do, as long as it helped her to focus on her task. And right now, the task was to set light to the small pile of firewood in the hearth.

'Do not think too hard, girl,' the hag coaxed. ''Tis not from your head that the power comes. Let your mind's eye see the flames dancing; let your heart feel their blazing heat; let your spirit find the words that speak the fire into being.' She closed her eyes, and settled back in her chair. 'I shall sleep now. Be sure you have succeeded by the time I awake.'

A movement caught Bansi's eye: Pogo, emerging

from Grandmother Bone's bedroom with a ragged cloth in his hand. Her heart sank as she saw once more how glazed and dead his eyes looked; it was as if the task of cleaning the hut had bewitched him somehow, and the hopelessness of it had taken his spirit. One more reason, she thought, to escape from here as soon as she could – and so, one more reason to learn to use the magic that apparently now lay within her. She turned her attention back to the firewood.

Just as Grandmother Bone had been instructing her, she let her thoughts drift, opening herself to the task before her. Flames flickered in her imagination; fires burned; wood became trees, and trees became a blaze that swept across her mind. A rhyme came to her: just four lines she remembered from a display-board at school. The class had been copying a famous picture of a tiger; the poem had been added by the teacher as an accompaniment to the work. It had felt wrong to Bansi, because the image it conjured up in her mind was nothing like the paintings she and her classmates had produced. It was darker, and more real. For her, the words had created in her mind a picture of a beast of living flame, stalking half hidden from her sight through the dense darkness of a night-forest much blacker than the one outside the hut of Grandmother Bone. She opened her eyes, stared into the heap of dry wood upon the hearth, and murmured the words:

'Tyger, tyger, burning bright
In the forests of the night,
What immortal hand or eye
Could frame thy fearful symmetry?'

She wasn't sure that she had remembered the words correctly – should it be *forests* or *forest*, *could* or *can*? She shook her head; pushed those thoughts away. What was important was not words that *were* right, but words that *felt* right. She tried again:

'Tyger, tyger, burning bright
In the forests of the night,
What immortal hand or eye
Could frame thy fearful symmetry?'

She felt it, then: a wave of . . . of what she could only describe afterwards as a cool warmth, lapping at her toes like the gentle tide at the beach, almost flowing into her – but then pulling away at the last moment as the picture faded. The last two lines were wrong somehow: the immortal hand and eye, the fearful symmetry and the frame – these told a different story, and the half-rhyme jarred. It was the brightly burning tiger she needed to picture, moving like untamed flame through the night of its dark forests. Again she spoke, letting the words flow through her, drawing the power of Tir na n'Óg in through the pictures in her imagination and the need in her heart:

'Tyger, tyger, burning bright
In the forests of the night . . .'

In her mind she could see the orange flames now, flickering in the darkness of the forest. She spoke again:

'Tyger, tyger, burning bright
In the forests of the night . . .
Tyger, tyger, burning bright
In the forests of the night . . .'

She repeated the words again and again, almost forgetting where she was. The firewood she was staring at became for her the shadowy trees of those forests of the night, their tindery dryness threatened by the blazing beast that stalked among them, burning brightly and fiercely and—

Bansi jumped, shocked from her reverie as the dry firewood suddenly and ferociously burst into flame.

'Blimey!' squawked the raven.

'Hah!' croaked Grandmother Bone triumphantly, sitting up.

Open-mouthed, too amazed to speak, Bansi stared into the fire, feeling its heat on her face. It was burning incredibly fiercely, consuming the firewood with a great hunger. Even as she watched, the blackened wood was withering away to nothing.

'Feed it, girl!' Grandmother Bone screeched suddenly. 'Before it dies!'

Bansi grabbed some more firewood – but too late. The last flame flickered and vanished.

Grandmother Bone leaped from her chair and dealt Bansi a stinging slap across the cheek.

'Ow!' Bansi protested. 'What—'

'Lighting the fire so well, girl,' Grandmother Bone snarled, 'gives no excuse to let it out so soon! Your studies are not your only duties! Build the fire again!' As Bansi bent to stack the wood, she added sharply, 'But do not light it yet. First, attend to your other chores. Only when they are done must you light the fire – and this time, be sure to keep it burning!' She snatched up her strange stone paddle and made for the door. 'Do not forget!' she snapped. 'If the fire is not ablaze when I return, you will be punished!'

The door slammed behind her.

'Blimey,' muttered the raven. 'And it was all going so well.'

Chapter Thirty-Five

'Turn left,' said the sat-nav suddenly.

'You're off your head!' Mrs Mullarkey exclaimed, braking. 'That'll take us straight into a tree!'

'Turn left,' the sat-nav repeated. *'It is not possible for me to be off my head.'*

'Oh, isn't it?' said Mrs Mullarkey scathingly. 'How do you make that one out?'

'I do not have a head,' the sat-nav said. *'To be off one's head, one first needs a head off which one can be. Now turn left.'*

'Better do as it says, Nora,' Granny said. 'It's been right so far. We haven't had a crash yet – which with you driving is nothing short of a miracle.'

'A fat lot you know about it, Eileen,' Mrs Mullarkey muttered. 'All right, then – I'll give it a go. But I'll go carefully.'

'That'll be a first,' said Granny as Mrs Mullarkey took off the handbrake and eased the car forward, steering to the left.

The forest they had been skirting seemed dark

and impenetrable, and Mrs Mullarkey's misgivings were entirely understandable: even at the edge the trees grew so close together that there scarcely seemed room for a person to slip between them, never mind a car. Yet to the surprise of both women, they found themselves looking down a long, wide corridor of trees, lit brightly by the broad beam of the car's headlights and the eerie moonlight of Tir na n'Óg.

'Well, now,' said Mrs Mullarkey, bringing the car to a halt for a second time. 'Who'd have thought it?'

'I would,' the sat-nav pointed out. *'Now drive straight ahead as fast as you can.'*

'As fast as I can?' Mrs Mullarkey squawked indignantly. 'Have you lost your senses? The speed this car's been going today, we'd be flattened against that big tree there in seconds!' She pointed to the end of the corridor; it was impossible, at this distance and at night, to tell whether it came to a dead end or turned to one side or the other, but what was clear was that there stood an enormous tree, with a trunk thicker than either of them had ever seen before. 'I'm not driving into that thing!'

'To reach Bansi, drive straight ahead as fast as you can,' the sat-nav insisted.

Mrs Mullarkey folded her arms. 'No,' she said. 'You'll just have to find a different route.'

The sat-nav binged thoughtfully. *'Recalculating,'* it said. Then there was a long pause, before it binged again. *'Unable to calculate route,'* it said.

'Hmmmph,' Mrs Mullarkey grunted. 'Try again.'

'Unable to calculate route,' the sat-nav repeated.

'Are you saying,' Granny demanded, 'that the only way to find my wee Bansi is to drive straight at that big tree as fast as we can?'

'Yes,' the sat-nav said.

'Well, then,' Granny said, turning to her friend, 'what are we waiting for?'

Mrs Mullarkey stared at her. 'Eileen O'Hara, are you out of your mind? What on earth makes you think this . . . this nattering excuse for a baby television isn't just part of some sneaky Good People trick to get us to smash our brains out against a tree?'

Granny sighed. 'Nora, talk sense. It's had dozens of chances to cause an accident if it wanted to – and not only that, it saved us from those wee red hallions on horseback. Anyway, it wouldn't be the first time you've driven straight at a big tree to save Bansi, now would it? It's got to be worth a try.'

'It is not worth a try, Eileen,' Mrs Mullarkey said firmly. 'I'm not doing it, and that's that.'

'Are you scared?' asked the sat-nav.

Mrs Mullarkey glared at it. 'What did you say?'

'I said,' the sat-nav repeated, *'are you scared?'*

'Scared? Me? Not a bit of it.'

'You are, aren't you?' the sat-nav said, its tone calm and measured. *'You're frightened. You're a big scaredy chicken.'*

'I am no such thing!' Mrs Mullarkey said indignantly.

'You are, too.'

'I am not!'

'Bawwwk buk buk bawwwwk,' said the sat-nav. *'Buk buk bawwwk.'*

'I am not a chicken!' Mrs Mullarkey insisted. 'Tell it, Eileen!'

'All right,' agreed Granny, turning to the sat-nav. 'You're right,' she said. 'She's nothing but a big fraidy chicken. Sure, the first time we came to Tir na n'Óg—'

'What!' Mrs Mullarkey said. 'Me, a chicken! Oh, I like that, Eileen! When I think of all those times you've sat in that seat screaming at me to slow down . . .'

'It's a bit different when you're driving at just any old tree without a magical talking box telling you it'll be all right!'

'Baawwwk buk buk baaawwwk,' said the sat-nav.

'I am not driving my car full speed at that tree,' said Mrs Mullarkey, 'and that's final!'

'Even if the wee talky box thing says it's the only way to find Bansi?'

Mrs Mullarkey pursed her lips. 'That's right,' she said.

'It is the only way to find Bansi,' the sat-nav said.

'I'm not doing it,' Mrs Mullarkey said.

'Fine,' said Granny, and released the handbrake. A sudden jab of her walking stick knocked her friend's legs away from the pedals and found the clutch; jamming the car into gear she stabbed at the accelerator and pressed down hard. The car launched itself towards the tree like a dark green missile.

'Eileen! Have you gone mad? What do you think you're doing?' Mrs Mullarkey screeched. She grabbed the wheel and tried to stamp on the brake, but the stick hampered her. She kicked out furiously and made a one-handed grab for it. 'Get your walking stick off!'

'No!' Granny yelled, fighting for control.

'Keep going,' the sat-nav said. *'Do not slow down.'*

'Will you be quiet!' Mrs Mullarkey roared. 'Eileen! You're going to kill us!'

'Baawwwk,' said the sat-nav.

Mrs Mullarkey and Granny wrestled madly. The car swerved and jerked from one side of the tree-lined corridor to the other, careering like a wild thing towards collision and destruction.

'Let go, I tell you!' Mrs Mullarkey yelled. With an enormous effort she pushed the walking stick down far enough to get her foot over it; kicked backwards, hard; freed the accelerator; stood on the brake. The car came to a screeching, shuddering halt.

Mrs Mullarkey put one wrinkled hand to her forehead. 'That, Eileen,' she said disapprovingly, 'was too close, so it was.'

'No, it wasn't,' Granny said firmly. 'Look.'

Mrs Mullarkey looked. The end of the tree-lined corridor seemed to be as distant as ever, as if the trees had somehow melted away before them. 'Well, I'll be— It must be some kind of optical illusion,' she said.

'Or maybe the trees saw you coming and got out of the way.'

'Don't be ridiculous, Eileen,' Mrs Mullarkey snapped. 'Trees moving out of the way, indeed. Sure, if that was the case . . .' The words died away on her lips as she turned to look behind them.

Granny followed her gaze. There was no sign behind them of any track or path. The trees of the forest appeared to have crowded round the rear of the vehicle as if to hem them in. Unnerved, she turned again to look ahead of the car – and her heart missed a beat as she saw that the corridor ahead of them had shrunk, sides and end closing in on them. 'Nora!' she said in alarm.

Mrs Mullarkey's head whipped round. 'Oh, no,' she said determinedly. 'Oh, no you don't.'

Next second, the old woman's right foot stamped down hard. The car roared like a tiger as it accelerated suddenly.

'Nora, what's going on?' Granny said.

'Drive straight ahead as fast as you can,' the sat-nav said. *'Do not stop again. Do not slow down.'*

'Don't look ahead too much,' Mrs Mullarkey answered, deliberately taking her eyes off the forest for a moment. 'It's when we're not looking at them that they move.'

'What – the trees? Didn't you just say that was ridiculous?'

Mrs Mullarkey tutted. 'I said no such thing, you daft old bat. No, there are ancient tales, right enough, in which the trees herd lost travellers wherever they want to lead them . . .'

'You mean they're herding us somewhere?'

'Not if I can help it, Eileen. I reckon they're bound by the same laws as the Good People – maybe some of them are even Good People in disguise, who knows – which means they won't want to be hit by a ton of steel going a couple of hundred miles an hour. They'll get out of the way, all right.'

'Drive straight ahead,' the sat-nav repeated. *'Do not turn to either side. Keep going, as fast as you can.'*

'All right, all right, no need to go on about it,' Mrs Mullarkey muttered.

'Drive straight ahead for twenty-four point three kilometres,' the sat-nav added.

'And then what?' Granny asked.

'Then arrive at your destination,' the sat-nav said.

It took a moment for this to sink in. 'What?' Granny said. 'You mean we're only twenty-four kilometres away from Bansi?'

The sat-nav binged softly. *'Twenty-three point eight,'* it said.

'Well, now,' Granny said, 'not before time! Keep going, Nora! Fast as you can!'

'Don't you start,' said Mrs Mullarkey. 'It's bad enough being ordered about by the wee talky box thing.'

Neither of the old women was aware of the ancient eyes watching them from above.

Travelling across the skies, Grandmother Bone had seen the strange roaring machine cutting a swathe through the woods, and she had scowled. The trees of her forest were used to herding prey towards her home, and dangers away; never before had she seen them being so cowed as to allow anything a straight path of its own choosing – and one that would lead directly to her hut, at that. Clearly this thing was a threat.

That being so, there was only one way to deal

with it. She swooped closer, her cumbersome paddle steering her swiftly through the cold night until she was riding the currents of air just above the outlandish machine.

Then she raised her heavy stone paddle high, ready to smash it down hard. Hard enough to shatter the windscreen; hard enough to stave in the roof.

Hard enough to kill anyone inside.

Chapter Thirty-Six

Even as Grandmother Bone raised her weapon, she became aware of a nagging, nauseous feeling of alarm. Her eyes widened with shock; she clutched her stomach, almost dropping the stone paddle as a spasm of cramp shot through her.

The pain passed moments later; she raised up the paddle again, but not, this time, to strike. She knew at once what had happened; she recognized the pain as the consequence of trying to break a magical bargain. Whatever was in this speeding container, it was kith or kin to her captive, and she was forbidden to harm it. Cursing, she began to paddle, beating the air furiously as she struck out for home.

Both Granny and Mrs Mullarkey ducked instinctively as something large swept close overhead, blocking out the moon.

'What on earth—' Granny began as the thing moved ahead of them and rose into the air.

'Now I've seen it all,' Mrs Mullarkey said grimly.

'That's . . .' She shook her grey head in disbelief. 'It can't be. It . . . Eileen, what does that look like to you?'

Granny looked. 'If I didn't know better,' she said, 'I'd say it was an old witch flying in a big cereal bowl and paddling away with an enormous skittle.'

'Or flying in a giant mortar and paddling with a giant pestle, perhaps?'

Granny shrugged. 'I suppose that's no dafter.'

'I was afraid you'd say that,' said Mrs Mullarkey. 'And going the same way as us, too.'

Granny put her hand to her mouth. 'That's where Bansi is!'

Mrs Mullarkey pressed her foot hard against the accelerator; but it was already as far down as it could go.

Bansi threw another log onto the fire and watched as the flames seized it. The second time of lighting the fire had been easier than the first, almost as if the tyger poem had become a part of her. Merely repeating those lines drew her deep into her imagination and released the tyger of fire into the dry wood.

The door burst open and Grandmother Bone stormed in. Bansi leaped to her feet; but the hag ignored both her and the blazing fire and, casting her giant pestle aside, hurried to the comfort of her chair.

As she sat, the room lurched suddenly. Bansi looked up in alarm to see a blur of darkness and flickering moonlight outside the window, like the view from a night train. There was a moment of confusion; the house seemed to be swaying rapidly, and bouncing gently but firmly as if on strong steel springs.

She realized that they were moving. The garden, and the flickering lights of the skulls' eyes, had been left behind, and the hut was rushing through the forest, bounding along at tremendous speed on its grotesque legs.

Quizzically she looked towards the hag, who was leaning back in her chair, her expression hidden in the dancing shadows cast by the candles.

'*Recalculating,*' the sat-nav said. '*Bear left.*'

'You said straight on would take us to Bansi!' said Granny.

'*Bear left,*' the sat-nav repeated.

'I hate to admit it, but it's been right so far,' Mrs Mullarkey said, turning the wheel.

'*Bear left,*' the device repeated a moment later.

'I just did,' Mrs Mullarkey pointed out.

'*Do it again, you silly old trout, and stop arguing,*' the sat-nav told her.

'Cheeky wee— Hang on, are you telling me Bansi's *moving* now?' Mrs Mullarkey said.

'Recalculating,' the sat-nav said again. *'Yes. Bear right . . . Bear left . . . Bear left . . . now turn left, quickly, and follow the track.'*

'What track . . . ?' Granny began anxiously, bracing herself as Mrs Mullarkey yanked on the wheel; but instead of the impact both of them half expected, the two old women found themselves racing through a long, thin clearing. At the far end, they caught a flash of movement as something large disappeared from view around a bend.

'Follow the track,' the sat-nav repeated. *'Do not slow down.'*

The Morris Minor Traveller tore up the earth as it raced to the curve and threw itself round it; and there, ahead of them, they saw for a moment the most extraordinary sight.

'Nora,' Granny said in disbelief, 'am I dreaming, or are we chasing a house that's running along on bird-legs?'

'Chicken-legs, to be precise, Eileen.' Mrs Mullarkey shook her head wonderingly. 'Who'd ever have thought those things'd turn out to be real? Or,' she added, 'able to go so fast?'

'Is that what we're after?' Granny asked. 'Is Bansi in there?'

The sat-nav gave out a soft beep. *'Yes,'* it said. *'Arrive at the hut, and you will find Bansi.'*

'If we can catch it, that is,' Mrs Mullarkey said, half to herself.

'We'd better, Nora,' Granny said. 'We'd just better.'

'Someone's after us, aren't they?' Bansi said.

'Silence, child,' snarled Grandmother Bone from her chair. 'Remember that Paddock is never wrong. Your fate is sealed; you are mine. Yes, we are running a race; but I shall win, and the prize belongs to me already. My house is taking us where our pursuers cannot follow.'

'Look out!' Granny shrieked as the hut leaped high into the air. An enormous boulder lay there, completely blocking the track.

Mrs Mullarkey jerked on the wheel; the car skidded, skittering towards a thick wooden trunk. There was a confused blurring, and then they were round the obstruction. Granny looked back; the tree they had been about to hit was no longer where it had been.

'I'd feel a lot safer if the trees back home got out of your way like that,' Granny remarked. 'Here! Talking of trees – where've they gone?'

In the instant at which she had looked round, the car had emerged from the forest onto a grassy moon-lit slope that ran down into a little valley.

'We'll catch up with it now!' she said, for the hut's pace seemed to have slowed a little as it picked its way downhill, whilst the thundering, bumping car was gathering speed.

'We'd better,' Mrs Mullarkey said grimly, 'before we get to the bottom.'

'Why's that?' Granny asked, peering into the darkness; and then she let out a little moan as she saw it.

At the bottom of the valley, growing rapidly nearer, lay a wide, deep, dry river bed; above that, on the other side, rose a hill whose slope was not a smooth incline but a series of ledges, like giant grassy steps cut roughly into the hillside. The hut, on its giant legs, would certainly be able to climb down into the river bed and up the hill; the car would have no chance.

'What do we do if we can't catch it in time?' Granny said anxiously.

The sat-nav binged quietly. *'Unable to calculate route,'* it said.

Now they were definitely gaining on the hut, but it was nearing the bottom of the slope. The grass was levelling out beneath it; it was picking up speed, its long legs striding out as it made for the steep bank of the dry river bed. Mrs Mullarkey pressed down her foot again, but fruitlessly, for there was nowhere for it to go.

'Come *on*,' she hissed.

As if in answer, the car's engine thrummed louder. But just at that moment the hut reached the bank and, without breaking stride, leaped down the sharp incline onto the river bed. Towards the far bank and safety it ran.

'Nora!' gasped Granny in dismay as the sudden slope of the near bank loomed.

'Hang onto your hat, Eileen,' Mrs Mullarkey said. 'It's not over yet!' She tugged the wheel; aimed the car like a missile at their quarry.

'Nora!' Granny screamed.

The ground beneath them dropped abruptly away.

Chapter Thirty-Seven

The sudden impact shook the hut with a juddering, jarring crash. The room tilted insanely; the raven squawked with alarm and flapped into the air; the tall bookcase toppled to the floor, spilling and scattering its contents as it fell.

There was a shriek from Grandmother Bone as her chair threw her off and went skittering and tumbling down the suddenly sloping floor. The air filled with a rain of arcane objects hurtling hard and fast. Almost by accident – stumbling, falling – Bansi caught Paddock's glass globe as it rolled off its low shelf; seconds later she hit the ground, sprawling. The knife with the eye in its handle quivered harshly as it buried the point of its blade in the floor, too close to her outstretched hand. A jar filled with something unspeakable struck her hard on the shoulder; another smashed against the door.

The hut rolled and crashed and spun; the room overturned wildly and madly; all was chaos. Bansi was thrown and tossed, slammed, rattled and battered like an egg shaken in a shoe box, whirled like a feather in a hurricane, like unwilling washing in some insane spin-dryer, until the frenzied wheeling chugged and jolted reluctantly to the end of its cycle and the hut bumped and shuddered and ground and struggled to a grudging halt.

All was suddenly silent.

Bansi felt a thousand fresh bruises blossom across her body, sending their signals of pain through her weary arms and legs and torso to her aching head. She groaned softly and heard Grandmother Bone do the same. From somewhere nearby came a ragged, black-feathered flapping.

The room swam back into focus, its clutter-strewn floor tilting gently uphill towards the door. Close by, Grandmother Bone slumped against the upturned table; she pressed her hands against her face and opened her eyes, glaring at Bansi from between bony fingers. She grunted, and seemed about to speak; but then, loud against the quiet, came a noise that made her snap her head round in disbelieving anger.

Someone – or something – was trying the handle of the locked door.

The hag's eyes widened furiously; her scowl deepened and twisted into a snarl, the black points of her teeth showing sharp against her blood-red lips. 'You prophesied, Paddock!' she spat, sitting up sharply and casting her gaze around the room. 'You foretold the race was mine to win!'

Bansi felt a stirring in her hand; realizing she was still clutching the cool glass globe, she looked down. The toad's eyes were open, and it was looking at her.

From outside, the handle was jiggled more fiercely. Beside it, the little lock bared its shiny brass teeth.

The jiggling stopped. A loud and threatening growl came from the lock – but moments later, there was a hard thud. The lock emitted a gasping, choking sound; it coughed, once, and a small metal ball fell from the little brass mouth and rolled noisily across the floor. The handle turned once more.

'No!' Grandmother Bone cried out in fear and fury. 'This cannot be! The prize is mine! You prophesied, Paddock!' Her harsh voice rose to a shriek as the door slowly swung open. 'You *prophesied*! The prize goes to the aged crone who races faster than the wind without ever leaving her seat!'

'Ah, now,' came a warm and welcomely familiar voice from the darkness outside. 'An old crone who goes faster than the wind without leaving her seat? That'll be you, so it will, Nora.'

'You watch who you're calling an old crone, Eileen O'Hara!' Mrs Mullarkey snapped, bustling into the room like a little old conquering hero in cardigan and driving shoes, catapult in her hand and handbag dangling from the crook of her elbow. 'If anyone's an old crone it'll be you!'

'Not a bit of it,' Granny said equably, following her friend into the room. 'I'm hardly a croney at all, considering my age; but there's nobody cronier than you in all of Ballyfey, and that's a fact.' Then, before any retort could be made, her eyes lit upon her granddaughter and Bansi found herself clasped in a wonderfully loving embrace. 'Bansi, sweetheart! Are you all right, love?'

'I'm fine,' Bansi managed to say through a mouthful of cardigan. 'I'm OK, Granny. But how—'

'Aha!' Mrs Mullarkey exclaimed suddenly, catching sight of Bansi's captor. 'What have we here? A kidnapper of wee girls, I'll be bound, and more besides! How now, you secret, black, and midnight hag!' She took a step towards Grandmother Bone, her expression fierce.

The hag hissed angrily and leaped to her feet; her hand went up, as if to ward off danger – or cast a spell. Instantly she found herself staring into a loaded catapult, its sling drawn back and ready to fire.

'Careful!' Bansi exclaimed. 'She can't hurt you unless you try to hurt her.'

'Is that so?' Mrs Mullarkey said, not for a moment taking her eyes from Grandmother Bone's face.

Bansi nodded. 'She swore a magical oath,' she said. 'She can't hurt my kith or kin; not unless they try to hurt her first.'

Lowering the catapult, Mrs Mullarkey looked at her. 'Hmmm,' she said shrewdly. 'I dare say you've a story or two to tell us about that, then; but that'll do for later. Let's get going.'

'Here! What about me?' came an indignant squawk; and the raven, with an unnecessary amount of fluttering and fuss, struggled out from under the upturned chair. 'Not going to just drive off and leave me here, are you?' it demanded, flapping up to perch once more on Bansi's shoulder and keeping one wary eye on Grandmother Bone.

An expression crept over Mrs Mullarkey's face which could have been amusement, but which could equally well have been relief or pleasure. 'Well, now,' she said. 'So this is where you got to, is it?'

Granny glared at Grandmother Bone. 'Have you kidnapped anyone else we should know about?' she enquired icily.

The hag ignored her. She had just caught sight of the glass globe still held in Bansi's hand. 'Paddock!' she hissed angrily, rising with sudden speed. 'Treacherous toad! On you at least may I take vengeance!' She reached out, but Bansi had already stepped back. Grandmother Bone narrowed her eyes.

'No claim have you on Paddock, child,' she said. 'He is rightfully mine; and, ill as he has served me, so shall I serve him worse!' Her eyes glittered with malice as she took another step forward.

Immediately Granny was there, blocking her way. 'You'll not touch my grandchild,' she said firmly. 'Nor take anything from her, neither.'

'I shall take what's mine,' the hag said, her voice cold.

As the two glowered at one another, Bansi felt a stirring in her hand. She raised it to eye-level. The toad squatted in its transparent orb, beneath its violet star-spattered sky, and looked at her, starlight reflected in its dark eyes, as if waiting for permission to speak. Hardly realizing she was doing so, she found herself whispering, 'What say you, Paddock?'

And the toad, its dewlap pulsing, answered:

'It was by Right of Conquest of a master true and brave
That first her claim upon my life was spoken.
And as by Right of Conquest she now claims me as her slave
By Right of Conquest may that claim be broken.'

Granny's eyebrows lifted. 'Is that so? Well, now, missus: it seems to me that my friend and I just kicked your bottom good and proper. So if Right of Conquest is what it takes, then I claim Froggy here by Right of Conquest and you can just go boil your head!'

Grandmother Bone's face contorted into a mask of pure rage. She uttered an angry howl of frustration and raised her sharp-taloned fingers as if to rake at Granny's face, but made no move towards her.

'A bit old for temper tantrums, aren't you?' Granny said.

'You can howl all you like,' added Mrs Mullarkey, 'but don't expect us to stay here and listen to it. Shall we go, Eileen?'

'We shall, Nora,' Granny agreed. 'And we'll take Bansi and the wee froggy thing with us, too.' She nodded imperiously at Grandmother Bone.

With a cry of fury, Grandmother Bone hurled herself past Granny. There was a metallic flash; somehow, the knife was in her hand, its point aimed lethally at Bansi's throat.

Before Bansi had time to react there was a blur of leather and steel, and with a sickening thud Mrs Mullarkey's handbag connected with the hag's head. Knocked sideways, Grandmother Bone spun dizzily and crumpled to the floor like a rag doll.

'Some people,' said Granny, looking down at where the hag lay unmoving, breath rasping and wheezing in her throat, 'are just sore losers. Nora,' she added, 'what *are* you doing?'

Mrs Mullarkey had bent down and carefully peeled back the unconscious hag's upper lip. She examined the sharp black teeth for a moment, before straightening up and clapping her hands together triumphantly as if dusting them off. 'I thought so,' she said. 'They're not iron at all. Just in need of a good clean.'

'What *are* you talking about?' Granny asked in bewilderment.

Mrs Mullarkey nodded at Grandmother Bone. 'Her teeth. According to the old stories, her kind has iron teeth; but that's just a load of old nonsense, isn't it? Probably made up to stop the Russian peasants working out how to beat them, I shouldn't wonder,' she went on. 'Right – have we got everybody? Me, you, Bansi, raven, wee froggy paperweight thing. Let's go, then.'

'Hang on,' said Bansi, looking round. 'Where's Pogo?'

'What?' Granny said in astonishment. '*Our* Pogo? The brownie?'

Mrs Mullarkey raised her eyebrows and folded her arms. 'Well!' she said. 'Some kind of reunion, is it? Should we expect that goaty fellow and the Dark Lord both to turn up any minute? Not to mention Fido the wolf-boy?'

'And talking of Fido,' Granny added, stepping over Grandmother Bone and picking up something rough and hairy, 'isn't this his cloak?'

'Not any more,' Mrs Mullarkey reminded her with a look of some satisfaction. 'It's Bansi's now. By Right of Conquest,' she added sardonically with a scornful look down at the motionless Grandmother Bone.

Bansi stood, hands on hips, and looked around. 'Pogo!' she called. '*Pogo!* You can come out now. We can go.'

There was no answer.

'Maybe he's frightened to come out with Grandma Boney still here,' the raven suggested. 'Or maybe he banged his head with all that rolling around.'

'*Pogo!*' Bansi said again. 'Come on! We've got to go!'

'Maybe he's left already,' said Granny. 'You know what these wee folk are like.'

'Oh, like *you're* a big expert in the wee folk all of a sudden, Eileen,' Mrs Mullarkey muttered. 'Six months ago you didn't even believe in the Good People.'

'Aye, well, you didn't believe in brownies, did you?' Granny retorted. 'Which is what we're talking about, after all.'

'Pogo, *please*,' Bansi pleaded into the room, and then added, 'We're not leaving without you, you know.'

There was a pause, during which the only sound was the wheezing of the unconscious Grandmother Bone's breath. And then, slowly, a jumbled heap of books in the corner of the room slid apart and Pogo stood there; but a more melancholy Pogo than any of them had ever seen before. His arms hung limply; his expression was almost dead; his eyes stared at them helplessly.

'You've got to,' he said.

'What?' said Bansi, not understanding.

'Go without me,' said Pogo. 'You have to leave me here.'

'No!' Bansi said, just as Granny exclaimed, 'What *are* you talking about, wee man?'

Pogo stared at them helplessly. His hands lifted at his sides, palms raised in a weak gesture that took in the complete chaos all around them. 'Look!' he said, his voice heavy. 'Look at this mess! How could any brownie leave a place in this state? It was bad enough before you two old biddies knocked it over,' he added bitterly, 'but now? I can't leave it. I just *can't*.'

Bansi and her granny stared at him, lost for words.

But Mrs Mullarkey laughed, a dry ironic bark of

amusement. 'Hah!' she said. 'Call this a mess?' She rolled her eyes scornfully.

Dull puzzlement crept across Pogo's expression. ''Course I do,' he said. 'It's a dreadful mess, and no mistake. I've never seen a worse one.'

Mrs Mullarkey raised her eyebrows. 'Never? I could show you one right now, if you like.'

A sort of life seemed to be coming back into Pogo's eyes. 'What d'you mean?' he said, with a glimmer of curiosity. 'Where?'

'My car,' Mrs Mullarkey told him. 'It's just outside, all tangled up in this wee hut's great big chicken-legs where we tripped it up, battered and scraped beyond all recognition and with all manner of stuff spilled all over the inside. Don't know how we're ever even going to get in. Oh, but I forgot . . . we're to leave you here, aren't we? Can't take you away from this tiny wee bit of tidying.'

Pogo glanced around the room again. 'Messier than this?' he said. 'Really?'

'Just come and see for yourself,' said Mrs Mullarkey.

'Well . . .' said Pogo hesitantly. 'I suppose it would do no harm just to go and have a look . . .'

Mrs Mullarkey looked down at him. Something almost like a smile twitched in the corner of her mouth. 'If you must,' she said.

Chapter Thirty-Eight

The hut sprawled, awkward and unmoving, on the dry river bed beneath the eerie brightness of the huge moon of Tir na n'Óg. Its small porch was propped unevenly on the roof of the Morris Minor Traveller; its huge legs splayed out clumsily in front, giving evidence of how the car had slammed into them and knocked them out from underneath.

If any creature was watching as the door creaked open, spilling light out into the darkness, it gave no sign and made no movement. All was still and quiet as, one by one, a girl, a raven, a hesitant brownie and two old ladies emerged and clambered down.

It was as if Pogo had been under an enchantment, which fell away as they left Grandmother Bone's home. By the time they had opened the car doors, he was already almost himself again.

'Call this a mess?' he grumbled as he climbed over the rear seats into the boot-space of the car. 'Hah! It'll take me no time at all to sort this out! "Don't know how we're ever even going to get in", indeed!'

'And would you rather be back in there, tidying up after thon old black-toothed hag?' Mrs Mullarkey enquired reasonably, settling herself into the driver's seat.

Pogo scowled. 'Aye, well,' he muttered; and then, under his breath, something that could possibly have been, 'Thanks, missus.'

'Oh, you're welcome, I'm sure,' Mrs Mullarkey said, equally quietly and looking straight ahead, just the hint of a smile on her lips.

'Right,' Granny said, getting into the car as Bansi settled herself in the back seat. 'Now all we have to do is work out how to get us all home.'

Bansi felt her stomach drop away within her. Enslaved by Grandmother Bone, her focus had been on survival; her mother's plight had been constantly with her, but pushed to the back of her mind. Now the urgency of the need to find her bore in upon Bansi. For the moment, all the questions she wanted to ask her grandmother – how she and Mrs Mullarkey had found her, how they had got to Tir na n'Óg in the first place – had to be set aside.

'No,' she said. 'We can't go home yet. We've got to find Mum.'

Granny and Mrs Mullarkey turned in their seats and stared at her.

'What?' Granny asked. 'Are you saying Asha's here? In Tir na n'Óg?'

'Are you sure?' Mrs Mullarkey asked as Bansi nodded.

'I'm sure,' Bansi said. 'As sure as I can be. I mean, I saw her, and I followed her, and then we were here, and—' She stopped as she felt her jaw trembling. The horror of her captivity, the relief of rescue and of having her grandmother there, her fears for her mother, all the things that had happened to her since the day before – if it *was* only the day before; she felt as if she had been in Tir na n'Óg for ever – all these things crowded in upon her suddenly and she realized she was about to break down and cry. *There'll be time for tears later*, she told herself firmly; and she breathed in deeply and tried to calm herself.

'Just take your time, love,' Granny said gently.

'Only be quick about it,' put in Mrs Mullarkey. 'If your mother's here in Tir na n'Óg, we ought to find her as soon as we can.'

'Aye, but how do you propose we do that?' put in Pogo, climbing over the seat-back and settling himself next to Bansi. 'Tir na n'Óg's a big place, and getting bigger as the magic returns to it. And we've no idea where to even start looking.'

'Ach, that'll be no problem,' Mrs Mullarkey said

smugly. 'I've got a sit-nav.' She indicated the glowing box on the dashboard.

Pogo gaped. 'Are you daft?' he said. 'How's that ever going to work here?'

'I'm not a bit daft—' Mrs Mullarkey began, her voice filled with righteous and knowing indignation.

'Yes, you are,' the sat-nav interrupted her in a measured tone. *'Please enter destination.'*

'We need to find Bansi's mother – Asha O'Hara,' Mrs Mullarkey told it calmly, enjoying the stunned disbelief of Bansi, Pogo and the raven. 'And I am *not* daft, you cheeky wee pile of transistors.'

The sat-nav binged softly. *'Drive for forty-three point seven kilometres,'* it said. *'Then bear left out of river bed and drive one hundred and seventy-four point four kilometres to your destination. And transistors are* so *last century.'*

'Well, now,' said Granny. 'That doesn't sound too far. We'll be there in no time, judging by the speed Nora's been going tonight.'

'And there'll be just time,' Mrs Mullarkey added, 'for you to tell us exactly what's been going on, young Bansi.'

About two hundred and eighteen kilometres away, between crisp linen sheets, in a luxuriously soft four-poster bed in a gorgeously splendid bedchamber, Asha O'Hara was slowly waking up.

Not that she remembered that she was Asha O'Hara; or that she had a family; or indeed anything very much about who she was. In fact, as she slowly and contentedly emerged into a dreamy consciousness, she remembered only one thing:

Today was her wedding day.

'You did *what*???' Granny screeched.

'I put on the cloak,' Bansi repeated, 'and then I . . . well . . . I turned into a wolf.'

'Bansi, darling, do you not think that sounds awfully dangerous?'

'Talk some sense, Eileen!' Mrs Mullarkey snapped. 'She was in a house that'd been magicked so none of the doors led where they should've done; her mother was under a spell and in danger from some kind of cross between Casanova and Count Dracula; there was a big fearsome beastie trying to break into her room and get her; and the only way out was to jump out of a first-floor window on top of a crowd of Good People who were all baying for her blood. It doesn't sound like she had much choice, if you ask me.'

'Nobody *did* ask you, Nora,' Granny huffed. 'Maybe it was the best thing to do at the time, sweetheart; but promise me you won't make a habit of it.'

'I won't,' Bansi began.

'She's only done it once since,' the raven chipped in.

'What?' Granny yelped. 'You did it again? Why? When?'

'Let her tell the story her own way, for goodness' sake,' Mrs Mullarkey said impatiently, 'or we'll never get to the end of it.'

'All right, all right,' Granny muttered, pulling an apple from her pocket. Giving it a polish on her cardigan, she raised it to her mouth.

'So, girl,' Mrs Mullarkey said, 'what happened th— *Eileen!*'

Next second, Granny felt herself being thrown forward violently as the car jerked to a halt. The apple was slapped away from her mouth so hard that her hand stung; black feathers beat wildly against her face; in the darkness of the car, someone small and brown and wiry blurred in the corner of her vision.

The apple hit the door with a thud and fell to the floor.

'Well!' said Granny, aggrieved. 'If the rest of you wanted a bite, all you had to do was ask!'

But the car was filled with a clamour of voices.

'Eileen O'Hara, of all the stupid things to do!' Nora Mullarkey was yelling; the raven was cawing, 'That was close! Blimey, that was close!' as it flapped agitatedly in the confined space of the car; Pogo was growling, 'Typical ignorant mortal – for goodness' sakes, do you know *nothing*?'

'Would youse all stop making such a fuss and tell me what is going on?' Granny yelled.

'Granny,' Bansi said, understanding suddenly, her voice loud and clear enough to cut through the others, 'where did you get that apple?'

The others quietened and glared at Eileen O'Hara accusingly.

'Why . . . off a tree,' Granny said. 'We stopped by this campfire, you see, to ask directions, and . . .'

'Here?' Bansi asked. 'In Tir na n'Óg?'

'It was, aye,' Granny said uncertainly, uncomfortably fixed by four pairs of eyes.

'Only . . .' Bansi said hesitantly over the exasperated sighs and tuttings of Pogo and Mrs Mullarkey, 'if you eat the food of Tir na n'Óg, you have to stay here for ever.'

'What?' Granny exclaimed. 'Who says so?'

'It's the nature of things,' Pogo said harshly. 'It's the way it's always been. As you'd know, if you paid any attention at all to the old tales.'

'Well . . . but . . . oh, my goodness!' Granny said. 'I didn't know . . .'

'Well, you know now, you barmy old haddock,' Mrs Mullarkey said gruffly.

Bansi's eyes widened with horrified realization.

'But Mum doesn't,' she said, anxiety filling her.

Granny gasped, her hand raised to her mouth.

'Right,' Mrs Mullarkey said grimly, jamming the car into gear. 'All the more reason to hurry.'

The dress was the most magnificent she had ever seen – glamorously, gloriously elegant, every stitch perfect. No queen could have hoped for a more beautiful garment; no mortal seamstress could have created one so flawless and exquisite. It was so white it almost shone. She stared into the wardrobe, lost in wonder.

The chamber door opened behind her.

'Is the dress to your liking, my lady?' asked Hob Under-the-Hill, sweeping his shimmering top hat low in a courtly bow.

She turned, lost for words. 'It's . . . it's . . . yes, it's beautiful.' Holding her hands to her cheeks, she laughed with disbelieving joy. 'Is it really for me?'

'Of course, lady,' Hob replied, his smile roguish and cunning. 'A perfect dress for a perfect wedding. And when it pleases you to put it on, your wedding-day breakfast will be served.'

Chapter Thirty-Nine

When Bansi had finally finished her story, there was silence inside the car.

'So,' Mrs Mullarkey said slowly, 'you actually lit a fire by magic?'

'Well,' Bansi said tentatively, 'I suppose—'

'What do you mean, you *suppose*?' cut in Pogo curtly. 'You did, and you know you did!'

'Now, that just might come in handy!' Granny said proudly. 'I wonder what else you can do!'

Mrs Mullarkey grunted. 'Just you be careful, young Bansi. I dare say no good can come of *their* magic.'

'What nonsense, Nora!' Granny bridled. 'As if my Bansi would ever do anything but good!'

'Aye, well,' Mrs Mullarkey grunted, but said no more, for just at that moment the sat-nav announced:

'Drive for one kilometre; then arrive at your destination.'

They peered into the darkness, and ahead of them they could make out what looked like lights faintly glowing through high windows set within a vast many-turreted shadow of blackness.

Mrs Mullarkey switched off the headlights, slipped into neutral, and cut the engine. The shadow grew in the windscreen as they coasted silently towards it.

'*Arriving at your destination,*' the sat-nav said.

'Right, then,' Granny said. 'Here we are.' She put her hand on the door.

'Just hold your horses a minute, Eileen,' said Mrs Mullarkey. 'We can't just march up to the door and say, "Excuse me, you've kidnapped someone and we'd like her back," can we? I dare say this place is a bit more fortified than the hut with the chicken-legs.'

'So do you have a plan, then, if you're so clever?'

'Well . . .' Mrs Mullarkey began, rubbing her chin. 'Well . . . We need to find Asha, of course.'

'Yes, but *how*?' Granny asked. 'It's not as if we've got a map of this . . . this Dread Crook's castle, is it?'

'We've got the sat-nav,' Bansi said, reaching forward between the seats and pulling it carefully off the windscreen.

'Can it find its way about indoors, do you think?' Granny asked.

'You can, can't you?' Bansi asked it anxiously. 'And you can find a way in for us as well?'

'*Yes,*' the sat-nav said matter-of-factly.

'Well, then,' Granny said. 'What are we waiting for?'

'Hang on,' Bansi said. 'We don't know how many people there are in there . . .'

'If you can call them "people",' Mrs Mullarkey muttered.

'Shouldn't we try to create some kind of distraction?' Bansi went on. 'Something to get as many as possible of them out of the way?'

'Aye,' Mrs Mullarkey said. 'If someone were to just raise some kind of a commotion . . .'

'Aye,' Granny said. 'If someone could do that . . .'

'Just the thing,' said Pogo. 'I wonder who would be the right person for that job?'

'Oh, no,' said the raven, suddenly aware of being fixed by four pairs of eyes. 'No way. I've been in enough trouble for one night.'

'Oh, come on,' Bansi said. 'Please.'

'You'd be good at it, so you would,' Granny put in flatteringly.

'It's not like you'll be in any danger,' said Mrs Mullarkey. 'You can fly away if anyone sees you.'

'Which none of us can,' Pogo said. 'We'll be the ones in real danger, going in there.'

'If you don't do it, who will?' added Bansi.

'Exhactly what I was goin' to shay,' said a voice

from the back of the car. 'Um . . . what ish it that needsh doin', anyhow?'

Pogo leaped up and looked over the back seat. 'Flooter!' he growled. 'I'd just tidied that up! What d'you think you're doing?'

Flooter's cheery face popped up on the other side of the seat-back. 'Ah, jusht lookin' for me whishkey,' he said.

'*Your* whishkey, ish it?' came an outraged voice from behind him. 'That'sh *my* whishkey, ye whishkey-thief!'

There was scarcely time for a look of alarm to cross Flooter's face before he disappeared behind the seat again, as if jerked backwards with great force.

'Take thish!' Hooligan's voice went on, punctuated by a series of thumps. 'And thish! And thish! And— Whoopsh!'

'Right!' roared Pogo, and leaped over the seat-back himself. A moment later he reappeared, bundling an irate Hooligan over with him.

Bansi shifted sideways to make room for the furiously squirming heap of brownie and cluricaun. As she did so, she became aware of something small and slightly uncomfortable under her leg; she had obviously been almost sitting on it for the entire journey. She drew it out and examined it; it was a small cardboard box, very crushed and battered, containing a couple of blister-packs of what had once been tablets but were now nothing but dark powder.

'Right!' Pogo fumed again, straddling Hooligan and holding him down. 'I've just about had it with you! First you give us away and get me caught by the old hag; now you come here and start a fight—'

'When you should be starting it in *there*,' Mrs Mullarkey broke in.

Pogo stared at her. 'What?' he demanded.

'That big castley place,' Mrs Mullarkey said. 'If there's any whiskey round here, that's where it'll be.'

'D'you think sho?' Flooter asked merrily, peering over the seat-back; and a moment later he wasn't there.

'Here!' Hooligan protested angrily from beneath Pogo. 'If anyone'sh getting that whishkey, it'll be me!'

Pogo suddenly found he was sitting on empty air.

'Well, now,' Mrs Mullarkey said. 'I reckon in just a minute or two we'll have all the distraction we need. Shall we go?'

Bansi examined the box for a moment longer, paying particular attention to the safety warning on the back. Then she slipped one of the blister-packs into the pocket of her fleece, where Paddock's globe nestled, and scooped up the wolf-skin cloak.

'Hang on,' croaked the raven, hopping onto her shoulder. 'You're not leaving me all on my own.'

* * *

Hob Under-the-Hill was waiting for her, in a beautiful room with a great table set for one.

'My lady,' he called her again as she entered, and it did not seem strange to her. Nor did it seem strange that she had no name; or that, if she did, she did not know it. 'Come and sit, and be served.'

She smiled radiantly, shaking her head in wonder; she felt as though the world were filling her up with an enchanted joyfulness. 'I'm too excited,' she said; 'too happy to eat. I don't think I can.'

'Oh,' said he, 'but you must, my lady.' She did not see the cunning behind his own smile as he repeated, 'You must.'

Obediently she sat.

Chapter Forty

Getting into the castle was easy. Locked doors are no obstacle to a brownie, and finding one which was small and unattended was no problem for the sat-nav.

'It's quiet in here, isn't it?' Granny whispered as they slipped inside and found themselves in a small, round, undecorated vestibule from which led three doors.

'It would be if you'd shut up with all your whispering, Eileen!' muttered Mrs Mullarkey.

'If the pair of you would just stop your squabbling,' Pogo said, 'maybe we could get on and do what we came for.'

'Shhh!' the raven hissed nervously, making itself as small as possible and pressing against Bansi's neck for comfort.

The sat-nav, carried carefully in Bansi's hand, binged softly, almost inaudibly, and said, '*Go straight ahead, through the middle door.*'

Bansi was there straight away. 'Ready?' she asked, her other hand on the handle.

Granny and Mrs Mullarkey stood on either side of her, catapults primed, and nodded. She turned the handle, and pushed.

The door opened onto a narrow corridor. Like advance troops Granny and Mrs Mullarkey stepped quickly out, eyes sweeping the corridor, catapults ready. No one was there.

'Phew!' the raven muttered.

'Turn right,' the sat-nav said, *'and walk four hundred metres. Then turn left.'*

Even between the two old ladies – Mrs Mullarkey taking the lead, Granny keeping guard at the rear – Bansi felt terribly exposed, walking along this long stone passageway with nowhere to hide. No doors led off this section of corridor; there were no recesses or curtains. It was stark and bare and deserted.

'Turn left,' the sat-nav advised, its voice quietened but, Bansi felt, still much too loud in this silence. Mrs Mullarkey sidled up to the corner, peered round it, and then swivelled on her left foot, bringing the catapult to bear on the turning.

Granny rolled her eyes. 'I think you've been watching too many old cop films, Nora,' she muttered.

'Take the third door on the right,' the sat-nav said.

Bansi hurried to the door, readied herself and, at a nod from Mrs Mullarkey, pushed it open. Once more the two old ladies went first, catapults at the ready; Bansi followed, the raven on her shoulder and Pogo close by her side.

They found themselves in a small stone kitchen. A large tray lay on the table, bearing a silver platter temptingly laden with good things to eat and a golden goblet of some rich-red, sweet-smelling drink.

'Don't even think about it, Eileen!' Mrs Mullarkey snapped, seeing her friend glance at the tray.

'As if I would, Nora!' Granny retorted, reddening. 'I was just wondering if . . . if all this might be meant for Asha.'

'If it is,' Mrs Mullarkey said determinedly, 'we may still be in time. No one's touched this food yet.'

Bansi looked at the tray, and her hand went to her pocket.

'Which way now?' Pogo said.

The sat-nav binged quietly. *'Recalculating,'* it said.

Mrs Mullarkey cast it a suspicious look. 'Not lost, I hope?' she muttered.

'Turn left,' the device said. *'Then go through the door.'*

'Right,' Granny said, turning the handle and pulling. Mrs Mullarkey stood ready to let a ball bearing fly, but again there was no one on the other side of the door. 'Come on, Bansi, love,' Granny said urgently. 'What's keeping you?'

'I was just—'

'Shhh!' Mrs Mullarkey hissed.

They all fell silent and listened.

'Are they coming this way, do you think?' Granny asked anxiously after a moment; for now that they were listening, they could all hear the sound of voices – indistinct, but loud and urgent.

They strained to hear, but could make out no clear words; nor could they tell from which direction the voices were coming.

It was Pogo who said, 'Nothing to worry about. It's those daft cluricauns fighting with each other, that's all.'

'Are you sure?' Granny asked.

''Course I'm sure! And if you didn't have the dull ears of all your kind, you'd be sure, too. I just heard one of them say, "Whoopsh!"'

'Aye, well,' Mrs Mullarkey said, 'maybe that's why we haven't bumped into anyone yet. A castle this size, you'd think it'd be full of people. Perhaps our distraction's working.'

'*Recalculating*,' said the sat-nav. '*Turn right*.'

'My pardon, my lady,' Hob had said. 'There is one small matter to which I must attend, and then breakfast will be served.'

He had left the room quickly, and she had neither

seen the dark look upon his face, nor heard the distant sounds of drunken arguing.

Now she sat, and patiently waited, not knowing how long he had been gone, nor thinking to wonder. He would return, and she would eat, and then she would be married.

'Stop,' the sat-nav said suddenly.

Bansi and her companions halted where they were, pressed against the cold grey stone wall of another unlit corridor, the third or fourth such that they had passed through. Ahead of them stood a junction with yet another corridor, this one dimly lit by torchlight. From where they stood, they could see that a door a little way down the other corridor was slowly opening.

'Do not move,' the sat-nav said, its voice almost muted.

They stayed as still as statues, watching, hardly daring to breathe as a figure emerged: a figure in a long, elegant coat and top hat that shimmered sea-green and peacock-blue. Without looking round, he set off hurriedly down the corridor in the opposite direction.

Nobody spoke, until at last the sat-nav said, *'Move straight ahead. Then turn right. Then go through the door. Then arrive at your destination.'*

Bansi's heart leaped to think they were so close to their goal at last. As fast as she dared, the rest of her party close behind, she hurried to the door and flung it open.

Crossing the threshold, she found herself in a small room containing a shabby and crudely made little bed, an upright piece of wood fastened to each corner in poor imitation of a four-poster. On a wooden box in the corner lay, neatly folded, a pair of jeans and a lilac sweater that she recognized as her mother's.

No other door led from the room. And Asha O'Hara was not there.

Chapter Forty-One

Hob Under-the-Hill stalked angrily along the passageway, the harsh clipped sound of his footsteps echoing behind him.

At the top of the stairwell, he paused and listened. The voices were clearer from here, the sound amplified as it echoed up the stairs. The intruders were evidently in the cellar. He stepped down, following the curve of the staircase for a few paces; and now he could make out what they were saying.

'Water!' came one voice, shrill and angry. 'It'sh jusht water! What kind of a fool takesh a good wine bottle and putsh water in it?'

'Ah,' came the second, in a tone that suggested the speaker thought he was being wise, 'I exhpect shomebody jusht made a wee mishtake. There'sh prob'ly wine in thish one.' There was the sound of a cork being pulled, and then a loud gulping, followed almost immediately by a disgusted spitting noise. 'Eeeeuuch! Water! Shome idiot'sh put water in thish bottle!'

'Here!' said the first voice suspiciously. 'Are you jusht pretending? Are you trying to fool me sho you get all the wine for yourshelf? Give me that!' There was a sound like a little fist hitting a little face, and another noise like a small bottom sitting down suddenly on a stone floor, and then another glugging sound, before the first voice continued: 'Faughhh! Water! Shomebody'sh put water in thish bottle!'

'Ish that right?' the second voice asked, with apparently genuine curiosity. 'What short of eejit'd do a thing like that?' There was a clinking sound. 'Hey! Look! Thish looksh like a good 'un!' Another cork popped; another spitting noise. 'Eeeeuch! Here! You'll never believe it, Hooligan, but shomebody'sh taken out the wine and put water in it inshtead!'

'Water! That'sh outrageoush! You jusht tell me who'sh done a thing like that an' . . . an' I'll pulverize 'em, sho I will! Here! What'sh that you're drinkin'?' Once more, the sound of a punch; a glug; a retch; the sound of a bottle smashing. 'Faughhhh! Water!'

Hob stayed to hear no more. Certainly it was a nuisance to have cluricauns in the cellar, today of all days; but if it was nothing more serious than that, it could wait. They could do little damage down there. Meanwhile, he had a most important breakfast to serve – one which should not be delayed any longer.

* * *

'What kind of a wild-goose chase is this you're leading us on?' Granny demanded. 'You're supposed to be finding my daughter-in-law, not just her clothes!'

'Recalculating,' the sat-nav told her.

'What do you mean, *recalculating?'* snapped Mrs Mullarkey. 'That's the third time in as many doors that you've said that! You're just guessing, aren't you?'

'Recalculating,' the device repeated.

'Ah, go and recalculate all you want,' Mrs Mullarkey said irritably. 'First thing we have to do is go back through this door, in any case, for there's no other way to go.' She turned and, easing it open, peered through the gap; and then she gasped in surprise. 'What kind of tomfoolery is this?' she hissed, so urgently that Bansi, Granny and Pogo all rushed to see.

The door, which had led from a cold grey stone corridor, now opened into a great and magnificent hall whose walls were panelled with dark, glossy oak and whose great windows were draped with long velvet curtains of a deep and rich red. Intricate and wonderful tapestries hung on every side; the ceiling was painted with dazzling pictures of warriors and maidens and marvellous creatures so real they almost seemed to move. Three great banqueting tables stretched from one end of the hall almost to the other, where stood a fourth, clearly at the head. They were laid for a great feast, and the two chairs at the centre of the top table were like wooden thrones, their backs and arms ornately carved. Thick, tall candles stood along the length of each table, their bright steady flames lighting the whole room.

The hall was empty of people as they stepped cautiously out into it. Behind them, the door shut with a soft *click*.

'Aw, bloomin' 'eck,' muttered the raven to itself.

'What kind of trickery's going on here?' whispered Granny.

'Good People trickery, of course,' Mrs Mullarkey said. 'Wicked magic.'

'This is what happened at home,' Bansi said, her stomach turning as she remembered the nightmare of entrapment and how the topography of her own home had been twisted into a weapon and used against her. 'None of the doors led where they were supposed to. I think it was only by luck that I ever got back to my own room.'

'Maybe we'll have the same luck if we try a few doors, do you think?' Granny suggested doubtfully.

'In a castle this size?' said Pogo. 'I hardly think so.'

The raven trembled on Bansi's shoulder. 'That's it,' it said despairingly. 'We're done for now. We'll never get out.'

Bansi held the sat-nav up. 'Can you find Mum?' she said. 'Now that you know about the magic?'

The sat-nav made a sad little binging sound. *'Recalculating,'* it said; and then, after a pause, *'Unable to calculate route.'*

'Hmmph,' Mrs Mullarkey grunted. 'Well, Mr Pogo, it looks like it's up to you.'

'Me, is it?' Pogo said, folding his arms and looking at her. 'And why's that, then?'

Mrs Mullarkey raised an eyebrow. 'I'd have thought that was obvious. You're the expert on houses, after all.'

Pogo shook his head. 'This kind of enchantment's beyond any brownie. Getting into houses, or tidying them up: that's one thing. But finding your way around a house, let alone a castle that's been enchanted like this? Not a chance.'

The raven let out a little moan.

Bansi was suddenly aware of the weight in her pocket. 'What say you, Paddock?' she asked, taking the glass sphere and holding it up, brushing away a little dark powder from its surface as she did so.

The toad stirred beneath its violet sky, and looked at her.

'Magic which begets illusion,' it said,
'Plants deception, spreads confusion.

Magic which can pierce the lie
Will prove the stronger, by and by.'

'Well, what's that supposed to mean?' Mrs Mullarkey said; but the toad had closed its eyes. Its dewlap pulsed, once, and then it was still again. 'By and by, indeed,' she said. 'By and by's no good. We need something that'll help *now*. And where do we get this . . . this "magic to pierce the lie" from, in any case?'

'Well now, Nora; I'd have thought that would be obvious,' said Granny proudly.

Bansi tucked Paddock back inside the large front pocket of her fleece, and the sat-nav, too, and looked up to see all eyes upon her.

'What – me?' she said. 'But . . . I can't . . .'

'You can,' Pogo said intensely. 'You can, and it's time you accepted it. Bansi, you're the heir to Derga. You have his power, when Tir na n'Óg touches you; and for better or worse that evil old hag taught you how to begin to use it. And now it's time you did.

'Come on, now. For your mother. Gather your thoughts; focus on finding her. Show us the way.'

Chapter Forty-Two

Bansi pushed away the wave of doubt that tried to swamp her. Pogo was right, she told herself: she *could* do this, or at least she could try. She had become a wolf; she had lit a fire by magic. She had felt the power of Tir na n'Óg flow through her. And perhaps it hadn't just been luck that had saved her when her own home had been turned against her; hadn't she felt something guiding her, telling her which door to choose?

Aware of the eyes upon her, she closed her own and tried to think. She needed a rhyme, something on which to focus her thoughts and create a channel for the magic. But every song and every verse that ran through her head was about being lost, about seeking guidance rather than getting it, about not having found what she was looking for. The words she needed were words of joining, not separation; words to show the way through the enchanted maze of this grey castle; words that would light the darkness that separated her from her mother.

A stab of fear pierced her. What if she was already too late? What if she never found her mother? At that moment there might as well have been an ocean between them: although her mum was somewhere in this very castle, she felt no nearer than her dad was, and he was in another world.

Perhaps it was the thought of her dad, or the thought of her mum, or the thought of them both, separated from her by worlds and oceans; but that was when a song swam to the surface of her mind. It was one of her dad's favourites, one he would sing to her mum sometimes, larking around in the warmth of their kitchen; and to Bansi it was at once a song of great longing, and a song that meant her family, together and safe and happy.

Softly, almost without thinking, she began to sing:

'I wish I was
In Carrickfergus,
Only for nights
In Ballygran.'

Where Carrickfergus and Ballygran were, she did not know; but it was the longing for her parents, and for togetherness with them, that flowed out in the words and the melody. She felt the raven shift uncomfortably on her shoulder, but did not see its beak open to speak, nor the glares from Granny and Mrs Mullarkey that silenced it. She sang on, her voice quiet but growing in confidence:

'I would swim over
The deepest ocean,
The deepest ocean,
For my love to find.'

And then, as her voice soared with the melody, she felt her longing almost overpower her, and she rode it as a surfer rides a wave. Singing into her despair, she welcomed it, taking the strength of her sadness and her love for her parents, and feeding it into the song:

'But the sea is wide
And I can't swim over,
And neither have I
The wings to fly . . .'

She paused for a moment, feeling the magic begin to gather around her; and then, her voice almost a whisper in the quietness, emptied herself into the closing words of the verse:

'I wish I met me
A handsome boatman
To ferry me over
To my love, and die.'

At the word 'die' the raven shivered; but Granny and Mrs Mullarkey continued to fix their eyes on Bansi, willing her to succeed. Bansi herself was lost in the echo of the song, almost disappearing, behind her eyelids, into a warm deep trance as she began the verse again – or perhaps it began itself, and she merely let it come. There was the song; and the soft orange darkness behind her eyelids; and the longing for her parents; and a flowing feeling, moving gently upwards through her; and that was all. A second time she sang it through, and then a third, pouring all her longing into that wish for a handsome boatman to ferry her across the wide, wide ocean that separated her from her mother.

She barely heard Granny's muted gasp, or the approving grunt from Pogo; but slowly she became aware that the orange darkness of closed eyes had brightened into gold, and that her own voice had died away – though in her head the song continued, steady and strong.

She opened her eyes, and blinked at what she saw.

Hovering in the air before her was a dim,

flickering light. It was not a flame, and yet it was like the pictures that live in the heart of a fire. Its shape was somehow like a tiny boatman, standing upright on his boat and steering it with a long pole, leaving ripples of light in the air behind it as it began to move, slowly and steadily, towards a door in the far corner of the hall.

She followed, knowing without question that this was the right thing to do. On her shoulder the raven flapped its wings, once; beside her walked Pogo.

'I'm not at all sure about this, Eileen,' muttered Mrs Mullarkey, following on behind. 'No good can come of *their* magic, whoever's summoned it up.'

'Ach, listen to yourself, Nora,' Granny replied. 'Right now, finding Asha's the important thing.' Priming her catapult once more, she bustled ahead of her friend, ready to guard her granddaughter as she passed through the next door.

The song still singing itself in her head, the figure of light moving before her, her companions around her, Bansi made her way through door after door, from room to corridor to corridor to room. The faster she walked, the faster went the magical light; its path turned to left and right and back on itself; they crossed thresholds as if at the whim of some mad maze-maker. They passed through chambers and halls and along passageways – most of them stark and cold and grey, but an occasional few ornately and extravagantly decorated. Once they passed through the little kitchen again, and Bansi saw with a jolt that the tray was no longer there. The light flickered before her, as if distracted by her distraction, and she looked full at it and sang aloud to restore its strength.

On and on the light led them, until time in that strange castle seemed to have no more meaning than place.

'Is it just going to lead us round in circles for ever, I wonder?' Mrs Mullarkey grumbled; and although Granny shushed her, she too was beginning to wonder.

In another part of the castle, the door opened again and Hob Under-the-Hill stood there, a tray in his hands. She smiled as he crossed the room and, with a small bow, set it down on the table. 'Your breakfast, my lady.'

She looked at the silver platter as he took it from the tray and laid it before her. Never, it seemed to her, had she seen such a meal; yet it was not of food that she thought, but the excitement of her wedding day.

'I don't think I feel hungry,' she told him brightly.

'Oh, but you do, lady,' he replied, placing the golden goblet by her hand.

And suddenly she did.

With a fresh appetite she looked at the platter; a firm round pomegranate caught her eye. She reached for it; took a silvery knife; cut the fruit open. The seeds in their tempting fleshy cases lay glistening like dark-hearted rubies.

She took one daintily in her fingers and raised it to her lips.

Chapter Forty-Three

Now they were following the light down a long and winding flight of stairs. Almost every turning on the staircase revealed a new door or arch or passageway, but the little figure of light ignored these and moved resolutely onward, its form ever shifting and yet always somehow Bansi's ferryman, trailing ripples of light in its wake.

'I'm telling you, Eileen,' Mrs Mullarkey said quietly, 'if this thing knew where it was going we'd have got there by now.'

'Ah, hush, Nora,' Granny told her, more confidently than she felt. 'By and by, the wee froggy thing said. We'll get there by and by.'

Down they went, down and down, until the stairwell opened out onto another long corridor like so many they had seen in this castle.

'Hmmph,' grunted Mrs Mullarkey. 'Up and down the corridors again, is it? Here! Where's it off to now?'

For the light had suddenly moved off as if caught by a swiftly flowing current, accelerating away from

Bansi without waiting for her to follow. Faster and faster it sped, until it reached the door at the end of the passageway, and there it stopped. As Bansi ran to catch it, it flared up, brightening and brightening until the unlit shadows were swept away by the ferryman's light and she could almost make out features on its indistinct little face; and then it faded, and was gone.

'What the—' Mrs Mullarkey said; but Bansi understood immediately.

'She's through there!' she said, hurling herself at the door. 'We've found her!' And without waiting for the others, she flung it wide and dashed through.

Her eyes took it all in in a moment. There, in the centre of a large and splendid room, stood a table; and by the table stood Hob Under-the-Hill, craftiness and triumph gleaming in his eyes; and at the table, wearing a beautiful white dress, sat her mother.

Eating.

'Mum! Stop! Spit it out!' Bansi yelled; but her mother looked at her blankly, and swallowed.

She looked up when the door burst open, to see a strange, wild-eyed girl in a wolf-skin cloak who shouted something that she did not quite catch. A glance at her protector, the chatelain of her lord's court, told her there was no cause for concern, for he was smiling at the child; and so she smiled, too, and finished her dainty mouthful, and plucked another seed from the pomegranate.

'Mum! *No!*' Bansi cried again, and moved towards her; but in an instant Hob stood between them, blocking her way, smiling his merry, charming, infuriating smile.

'You've lost, child,' he said. 'Maybe the Lord of the Dark Sidhe couldn't defeat you; but the Dread Cruach is mightier by far, and in him you've met your match.'

'Mum!' Bansi pleaded again. Behind her the figures of Granny and Mrs Mullarkey filled the doorway, catapults at the ready; but Hob merely laughed.

'Welcome, old crones,' he said. 'Will you join us for the wedding feast?'

'You watch who you're calling an old crone!' Granny almost spat, stepping forward and taking aim; but Hob ignored her, and gestured to where Asha O'Hara, smiling like one in a dream, was slipping another pomegranate seed between her lips.

'Twelve such has she eaten,' he said triumphantly. 'Twelve pomegranate seeds from the orchards of Tir na n'Óg. So here she must stay. 'Tis nature; 'tis the law; 'tis the way it has always been.'

'We'll see about that!' Granny said, letting fly with

the catapult; but Hob snatched up the tray from the table and struck the little ball away.

'You may rage and you may fight, old one,' he said, that maddening smile still on his face, his eyes sparkling with merriment and exultation, 'but it changes nothing. She has eaten of the food of Tir na n'Óg, and nevermore may she return to the mortal realm.'

Granny was already arming the catapult again when she felt a hand on her arm. She turned to see Mrs Mullarkey looking at her in utter sorrow.

'He's right, Eileen,' her old friend said. 'Much as it pains me to admit it, all the old stories agree. Should a mortal eat of the food of the Other World, she's condemned to stay there for ever.'

'But—' Granny began. 'Asha . . .'

'I know,' Mrs Mullarkey said quietly. 'But there's nothing more we can do for her. We'd best be getting Bansi home safely, at least.'

Hob Under-the-Hill mocked her with his smile. 'Your friend speaks true, old crone. By rights, I should throw you all in the darkest dungeon of the Red Court for your insolence in entering my lord's castle uninvited. But today is the Dread Cruach's wedding day, and in his honour I shall let you go unhindered – if you but leave now.'

'Asha!' Granny said. 'Come on, Asha, it's me! It's

Eileen! And look – here's your wee Bansi! For her sake, if nothing else, snap out of it!'

'She does not know you,' Hob said, 'and never shall again. Now go, while you still may.'

Granny stared from one to another. Nora Mullarkey was looking at her with the deepest expression of sympathy she had ever seen; Hob Under-the-Hill was grinning like the cock of the walk, insufferably victorious. The raven had fluttered up to perch mournfully out of reach on a high chandelier. Pogo, in the way of his kind, was nowhere to be seen, though Granny was sure he was somewhere in the room.

And Bansi – her darling wee Bansi – was gazing at her mother with an expression which so combined hope and desolation that it made her heart break. She lowered her catapult and, moving to her grand-daughter, put her arm around the girl's slight shoulders.

'Come on, love,' she said. 'We're too late. There's nothing more we can do.'

Chapter Forty-Four

The woman who had once been Asha O'Hara looked at the strange girl and the two old ladies before her, and although their words seemed to make no sense to her she felt moved by the sadness on their faces. Now one of the old women was holding the girl, trying gently to persuade her to leave with them, but the girl would not go.

They should not be sad, she felt, on such a joyous day; and perhaps if they understood how happy the day was, their sadness would leave them. She looked again at the girl and, unfamiliar though she was, something about the child tugged at her heart.

She stood.

'Strangers,' she addressed them; 'honoured guests.'

The old women turned to stare, and the child continued to look at her as if captivated.

'Be not sad or downcast,' she continued, 'but of good cheer, for today I am to be wed, and I wish for all to share my joy!'

The two old women looked at one another as if in disbelief; but the child's eyes remained locked on hers.

'Hob!' she said. 'Bring wine, that our guests may drink to my happiness! And I in turn,' she went on, raising the golden goblet, 'shall drink to theirs. Good health, old women! Good health, child! And may your days bring you much joy!'

One of the old women started forward, as if in alarm, as she raised the goblet to her lips; but the child closed her eyes for a moment, as if in prayer or hope, and so it was to her most of all that she drank deeply.

The drink burned as it hit the back of her throat; burned like poison. She gasped; choked; retched. Then her stomach heaved agonizingly, and she screamed; and as she screamed her throat was flooded with bitter liquid and scalding pain that rushed upwards through her gullet, through her mouth, to spill out in a mess of stinking vomit across the fresh linen whiteness of the tablecloth.

She heaved once more; gasped; breathed in cool air; uttered a small whimper of distress as she raised her suddenly aching head and saw before her a face she knew.

'B-Bansi?' she murmured groggily.

Bansi was already halfway to her mother, a sound

escaping her that was at once sob of relief and joyous laughter.

'Well, now,' said Mrs Mullarkey, examining the foul puddle on the table. 'Twelve pomegranate seeds, you said, were what was keeping her here.' She turned to stare Hob defiantly in the face. 'Looks to me like all twelve have come back out again, and a lot more besides. So we'll be taking her home now.'

Hob's smile dropped away completely. 'How is this possible?' he demanded. 'By what magic have you done this?'

Bansi, crouching by her mother, looked at him, enjoying her own moment of victory. 'Not magic,' she said. 'Medicine. Mortal medicine.' She pulled the blister pack from her pocket and held it up. 'Two tablets: *iron* tablets, crushed into her drink.'

Hob's composure had completely gone now, his smile vanished, his expression one of angry bewilderment. 'But you came not near the goblet!'

Bansi stood, and looked him in the eye across the table. 'That's what you think,' she said, remembering how they had come across the tray in the kitchen; how they had guessed who it might be for; how she had, on an impulse, unnoticed by the others, popped two of the blisters and poured the crushed tablets into the drink – enough, she had hoped, to get some iron into her mum's body without poisoning her. 'There'll be no wedding today, Hob. The spell's broken. Your trick didn't work. And we're taking my mum home.'

'I think not,' Hob said savagely, taking one threatening step towards her. Instantly Eileen O'Hara was there, raising her catapult again and in one swift movement, firing. Enraged, he whirled, raised the tray, swiped the ball away, and bore down on Granny like a maddened tiger.

Before he reached her there was a *swoosh* as something hard and heavy cut through the air and connected with the side of his face like a wrecking ball. He was flung sideways, twisting limply to the ground like a puppet whose strings have been sliced through. There he fell, and lay still.

'Goodness,' said Granny admiringly. 'I have *got* to get me one of those handbags, Nora.'

'Aye, well,' Mrs Mullarkey said. 'Maybe I'll make you one for Christmas. Right, time to get out of here. How's Asha? Can she walk?'

'I think so,' Bansi said, helping her to her feet. 'Oof. Maybe not,' she added as her mother suddenly lurched and became a dead weight.

'Sorry,' Asha O'Hara mumbled faintly. 'Don't feel well.'

'Well, you let us see to that,' Granny said, slipping her arm around her son's wife. 'You just concentrate on finding us the way out of here before that there hallion wakes up again.'

'And not just out of the castle,' Mrs Mullarkey added, moving Bansi aside and taking Asha by the other arm, 'but all the way back home.'

Bansi closed her eyes. Somehow, she felt, Carrickfergus would not work now; in her mind, it was still tied to the search for her mother, the search that had brought them to this room. She needed a new song to lead them away from it: one that meant home, or the road that led there. And, as she thought, memories of another homeward journey came to her.

She and her mum and dad had been visiting friends in Bristol. It had been one of those perfect, happy days that every child should have, so perfect that nobody had wanted it to end; and so, instead of leaving after tea as planned, they'd gone with their hosts to a concert. Just being with their friends for a few more hours would have been pleasure enough, but the performer – a singer-songwriter named Jane Taylor – had enraptured them all. They'd bought her album and played it repeatedly all the way home, singing along bit by bit as they slowly learned the songs; and one song especially – the one that had closed the concert – Bansi had asked for over and over again.

Now the opening chord of that song sounded in her imagination, bringing back to her that sense of happiness and safety, and above all of the homeward journey; and she began to sing:

'Travelling this lonely road,
Just feeling my way,
Watching myself unfold
Day after day.'

And as she sang on, something began to unfold inside her. She felt the power of Tir na n'Óg flowing, more easily than before, almost as if it was part of her. Some of the lyrics, as they left her mouth, began to take on a new meaning, the magic changing them and remaking them according to her need.

'I don't need you to rescue me,
I'm not trying to be saved,
I'm not looking for sympathy,
I've got to find my own way.'

Confidence bloomed in her. She *could* do this, and without help. The promised power was hers, and she was learning to use it; and if she trusted it, and herself, she could get them safely away from here. An invisible choir swelled in her head as she sang on:

'There's something inside
That's guiding me
To somewhere I've got to be.'

The music soared in her mind, and although her own voice was singing loudly and strongly, the voice she was listening to was the one in her head, the one she knew so well from the album, singing with passion and honesty and belief.

The power, though, was her own. It was the power of Tir na n'Óg, the power promised to Derga's heir; and as the music in her imagination suddenly quietened, it flowed through every word:

'With a little hope
And a lot of faith,
A little love, and time . . .'

She paused; smiled at her granny; sang the last line of the chorus – the song's title – almost in a whisper:

'I will get there.'

In answer, a bright silver light appeared in her mind's eye. It swelled inside her like the sound of an unseen orchestra, until the world around her seemed to dim. Then it burst from her, so brightly that her companions had to cover their eyes.

And as it faded, a wide pathway of light appeared, unfolding with a shimmer like moonlight on waves, stretching out before them to lead the way.

'Well, now,' said Granny approvingly. 'You're getting good at this, aren't you, love?'

'Never mind the congratulations,' the raven muttered, fluttering down from its high perch to alight once more on Bansi's shoulder. 'Let's get out of here.'

'Oh, *now* you join in,' came a voice from under the table, and Pogo appeared from the shadows. 'Now it's safe.'

'I didn't see *you* doing much!' cawed the indignant bird.

'Oh, didn't you?' Pogo said sarcastically. 'Who do you think stirred up the drink at the last minute, so the wee bits of iron were all swirling around in it instead of sunk to the bottom? Would you have liked me to wave a wee flag while I was doing that, just so's you could see me doing my bit?'

'Aye, well, well done, Mr Pogo,' Granny said. 'Let's go, shall we?'

The way out of the castle was no more straightforward than the way in, and as they followed the silvery path they found themselves trailing once more through corridors and chambers, up and down staircases short and long, turning left and right and back on themselves. Once, they found themselves back in the bedchamber. Asha's clothes were still there folded on a wooden box, and Granny scooped them up in her free hand.

'She'll need to get out of this silly dress before she gets home,' she muttered.

And then, with a few more twists and turns, they were back in the little vestibule and Bansi was opening the door that led outside. The cool night air rushed in upon them.

'Isn't it ever morning in this place?' grumbled Mrs Mullarkey as she and Eileen O'Hara helped Bansi's drowsy mother into the car.

'Maybe that's why they call it the Nightlands, do you think?' Pogo enquired sarcastically.

'You get in the front, Bansi, love,' Granny said as she clambered in beside her daughter-in-law, who slumped into the seat, exhausted. 'I'll try and help your mother get changed.'

'I'll give you a hand,' Pogo offered.

Granny looked scandalized. 'You'll do no such thing! You may only be a foot tall, but you're still a man!'

Pogo rolled his eyes. 'I'm a *brownie*,' he said. 'It's

not the same thing.'

'Would you stop arguing and get in?' Mrs Mullarkey snapped.

The silvery path stretched out before them, glowing in the darkness, lighting their way homewards. Bansi was still singing the song silently in her head as she got in and closed the door . . .

. . . and the guiding path vanished. One second it was there, the next there was no trace of it.

'What the—' Mrs Mullarkey burst out. 'Bansi, can you make it come back?'

Bansi began to sing again, but something felt wrong. The power of Tir na n'Óg, with its strange cool warmth, was simply not there. It had ceased to flow through her. They were lost, in the Dread Cruach's lands, with pursuit likely to follow at any moment.

Chapter Forty-Five

'Just drive, Nora!' cried Granny, and Mrs Mullarkey slammed the car into gear and drove.

'Where did that blinking trail go?' the raven demanded.

'I don't know!' Bansi said. 'It was there, and then, just as I got into the car . . .' She groaned. 'The car! It's made of steel.'

'So your magic won't work when you're in it?' Granny finished for her. 'Well, that's a blow.' She paused, thinking. 'But then – how come the wee talky box thing worked in the car?'

'Talking of which!' Bansi said, pulling it from her overloaded pocket and fastening it back onto the windscreen. 'Can you find us the way home?'

The sat-nav binged. *'Unable to calculate route,'* it said.

'A fat lot of good you are, then,' Mrs Mullarkey said.

'Work it out yourself, if you're so clever, you grumpy old haddock,' the sat-nav answered.

'So how come it *does* work in the car?' Granny asked again.

'Different sorts of magic,' Pogo said after a moment. 'Iron works against the magic of Tir na n'Óg; but magic like the magic of the mortal world—'

'Magic of the mortal world!' Mrs Mullarkey burst out, steering resolutely onwards into the darkness. 'There's no such thing, you daft wee pixie!'

Pogo bristled. 'You think so? Do you not think there's something magical about just being alive? About the way your body heals itself when it's been wounded? It seems to me those are amongst the greatest magics of them all! And perhaps that kind of magic, whether the mortal world's or Tir na n'Óg's own version of it, can work in spite of iron.'

'Look,' the raven broke in, 'this is all very philosophical, but it ain't getting us home!'

'Well, what will?' Mrs Mullarkey demanded bad-temperedly. 'Have you any ideas yourself?'

'I do, as it happens!' the raven said proudly, turning to Pogo. 'You can get us home, can't you? You found your way to the mortal world and back again easy enough.'

Pogo scowled. 'There are different ways between the mortal world and here,' he said, 'and the only paths I know are small enough for the brownie folk, but too large for mortals. There's no way even Bansi could use them, never mind these two daft old biddies and their great big car.'

'Right,' Granny said. 'Anyone else got any ideas?'

Bansi did: a forlorn hope, she felt, but one worth trying. 'OK,' she said to the sat-nav, 'so you can't show us the way home. Can you take us to someone who can?'

The sat-nav binged. After what seemed like an interminably long time, it spoke again.

'Unable to calculate route,' it said.

Bansi let out a breath that she didn't know she had been holding.

'Well,' said Mrs Mullarkey heavily, 'that's it, then. Looks like we're well and truly lost.'

In the distance, a light flickered into existence.

'That's all we need,' Granny said, seeing it. 'One of them Wispy Willy fellas.'

'Oh, you know about them, then?' Pogo said. 'Best steer clear.'

'Recalculating,' said the sat-nav suddenly. *'Drive two point three kilometres. Then turn left.'*

Hope glimmered in Bansi's heart. 'You've found someone who can show us the way?' she asked. Then, gripped by a sudden suspicion, she added, 'It's not the will-o'-the-wisp, is it?'

The sat-nav made no answer. In the distance the flickering light went out.

* * *

The will-o'-the-wisp, a wrinkled little goblinesque creature in a tall wide-brimmed hat, lowered its lantern with a sigh. It knew – it just *knew* – that the mortals in the strange roaring machine had been lost; it had an unerring sense for such things. They had been the perfect prey for it; they should have leaped with joy at the sight of its lantern, and come in search of it, and then – it almost hugged itself at the deliciously wicked thought – it would have led them astray: into a bog, perhaps, or off a cliff, or simply into the darkness of the forest.

And yet, moments after it had shown them its lantern, it was as if they had simply stopped being lost. Suddenly and mysteriously they were so *un*lost that it could no longer so much as sense them. They had apparently gone in an instant from having not the first idea of which direction to take, to knowing exactly where they were going.

Sighing once more, it sat back against a tree and sank into a daydream of what might have been: a mouth-wateringly good fantasy, filled with lost travellers spurred to false hope by the sight of its lantern. A merry dance indeed it would lead them, for there was not a path or a trail it did not know, and their swings from despair to relief and back again would taste as sweet and as fresh as wild strawberries . . .

It closed his eyes and daydreamed, knowing that if any other lost traveller happened by, it would sense them; knowing that no one ever chanced upon this peaceful glade. Which is why it didn't notice the roaring sound until it was too late and the dark green Morris Minor Traveller hurtled from behind the trees into the clearing.

Panicked from its reverie, the will-o'-the-wisp leaped to its feet just as the car screeched past and a pair of hands reached out and hauled it inside.

'Right, then, you wee hallion,' someone said. It twisted in the grip of the girl who held it, to see an old woman sitting beside her, pulling on some kind of wheel. 'I know you think it's funny to lead people astray,' the old woman went on, 'but just this once you're going to show us the *right* way. Otherwise my friend might get upset.'

She gestured behind her, and it looked round to see another old woman. This one was holding a weapon, some kind of sling armed with a silvery ball made of iron, and she was pointing it right at its forehead. 'Pleased to meet you, Mr Willy,' she said. 'I do hope you're going to cooperate.'

It tried to speak, but all that came out was a feeble little noise that sounded like '*Myerp*'. So instead, it nodded frantically.

'Good,' the first old woman said. 'London, please. And no funny business.'

Eyes wide with fear, the will-o'-the-wisp pointed with a trembling finger.

The old woman nodded; turned the wheel; stamped one foot down, hard. The car leaped forward. And the will-o'-the-wisp suddenly understood what it meant to be truly terrified.

Far behind them, within the courtyard of the castle of the Dread Cruach, a horn blew a single, long, sinister note. The great drawbridge lowered; the fearsome portcullis was raised by unseen hands. And with a mighty pounding of hooves an immense horse, the colour of sun-bleached bones, thundered from the entrance and out into the night. It bore on its back a rider in blood-red armour that shone like tainted rubies. His face could not be seen beneath his hood of midnight blue but, if you had been there, you would have felt his anger and his thirst for revenge tearing through the air like furious waves across a stormy ocean; and you would have thought, perhaps, that his great horse reeked of death.

Chapter Forty-Six

'Drive for three kilometres,' the sat-nav suddenly announced. *'Then arrive at your destination.'*

Mrs Mullarkey brought the car to an abrupt halt, so that the will-o'-the-wisp almost banged its head on the windscreen. 'What – that's it? No hocus-pocus or anything like that? We just keep going for a couple of miles and we're there?'

The sat-nav binged. *'Yes,'* it said.

'So we don't need Wispy Willy any more?' Granny asked.

'No,' said the sat-nav.

'Right,' said Mrs Mullarkey, taking the will-o'-the-wisp by the scruff of the neck. 'I hope that's taught you a lesson. I'm not ever going to catch you leading people astray again, am I?'

'Myerp,' said the will-o'-the-wisp nervously, shaking its head as rapidly as it could.

'Good,' said Mrs Mullarkey, and dumped it out of the window. Hurriedly it picked itself up and scurried away before she could change her mind.

'Right, girl: let's get you and your mother home.'

'Flippin' 'eck,' said the raven as Mrs Mullarkey slammed the car into gear. 'I'm glad that's over. What a night, eh!'

'It's not over yet,' Pogo said tersely.

'Ah, cheer up,' the raven said. It seemed at last to be recovering its demeanour. 'We got away from Grandma Boney. We got Bansi's mum back from that Hob bloke without so much as seeing his boss. We'll be back in the mortal world in about a minute. What could possibly go wrong now?'

Pogo merely glared at the bird.

'How's Mum doing?' Bansi asked.

'Fine, love,' Granny reassured her. 'I think she's properly asleep now: none of this enchanted non-sense, just good, proper, honest-to-goodness sleep. She's exhausted, poor thing, and no wonder. I've got her back in her own clothes again, too.'

'Here we go!' said Mrs Mullarkey suddenly as the car entered a corridor of trees that bent together to form a sort of natural tunnel.

'*Drive one mile,*' the sat-nav confirmed. '*Then arrive at your destination.*'

The moonlight flickered strangely between the trees as they sped onwards. A silence fell inside the car; there was no noise except for the thrumming of the engine, and even that seemed to be coming from far away. Bansi strained to stare ahead, but the headlights caught nothing in their beams. It was as if they were nowhere, a place that did not exist. Time and space stretched out around them, losing their meaning. The car was climbing, or perhaps falling . . .

. . . through a noiseless, colourless nothingness . . .

. . . towards a light that blossomed like a white poppy . . .

And then all the colours and noises and smells and textures of the world slammed into Bansi's senses and she gasped as the car exploded from the mouth of the tube station and slid to a rubber-burning halt in the middle of the road outside. The sudden brightness stung her eyes, and she squeezed them shut for a moment.

'Well,' she heard Mrs Mullarkey say. 'It looks like we're not out of the woods yet.'

'Flippin' 'eck,' the raven groaned.

Bansi opened her eyes. They were home, but far from safe. For around them, lit only by the flickering of a hundred blazing torches, stood a great crowd of faery creatures in a vast circle that was already closing up behind them. Across the circle stood three white horses with red ears, their riders – dressed all in red – each whirling a sling threateningly.

'Ach, not this lot again!' muttered Granny, grabbing her catapult and squeezing out of the back after Mrs Mullarkey, who had stepped out of the car, her own catapult at the ready. 'Stay in the car, Bansi!' she began; but Bansi had already climbed out of the passenger door and was standing defiantly, arms folded, staring at the little men.

'You have something there,' the rider in the centre began, 'that belongs to a friend of ours.' His voice was high and reedy and filled with contemptuous mockery. Granny could not tell if he was the same little man who had first appeared at her door, however long ago it was.

'If it's the cloak you're referring to,' Mrs Mullarkey said coldly, 'I'd say that's ours by Right of Conquest, wouldn't you?'

A ripple of condescending laughter ran round the circle, rather as though Mrs Mullarkey was a toddler who had inadvertently said something clever. Bansi glanced around the spectators, trying to calculate how hostile they were. She guessed they were here to be entertained, as children gather at the promise of a playground fight.

'Ah, now, Mrs Mullarkey,' the little rider said. 'Right of Conquest, is it? Well, maybe I'd dispute that. And maybe we should settle it by Rite of Combat.' His sling began to whirl faster, in obvious menace.

He smiled unpleasantly as another mocking laugh

travelled around the circle. This, Bansi suspected, was what they were waiting for.

But before she or Granny or Mrs Mullarkey could give an answer, a great voice rang out, reverberating across the gathering like a roll of thunder:

'HOLD!'

Screams and cries came from the crowd behind Bansi; spectators jostled and pressed each other aside in desperate haste, pushing to make way before it was too late.

And from the mouth of the tube station, the horseman came. His armour shone like the blood of thousands. His steed was a giant among horses, its coat a deathly white. Into the circle he rode, and three times around it, and the crowd drew together in fear and was silent. The little men in red sat still, as if hoping not to be noticed, their slings now dangling limply from their hands.

The Dread Cruach gazed at them, and in a voice that could have made the skies tremble he said, *'I claim the Right of Challenge in precedence over all here. Will any deny me?'*

The little men in red shuffled uneasily.

'Lord,' the one who had spoken before said hesitantly, 'we accept your precedence. But we beg a favour. The cloak the girl wears – we claim it on behalf of another. When the battle is done . . .'

As the Dread Cruach turned towards them, the little man fell silent – perhaps not daring to imagine what terrible eyes might now be gazing upon him from beneath the hood.

'You may have what remains of the girl,' he said, *'when I have finished.'*

Not waiting for their reply, he turned to Bansi. Without a word, the little men in red nervously turned their horses and moved into the crowd.

'Now, child,' the Dread Cruach said. *'Let us do battle.'*

Chapter Forty-Seven

Bansi stared up at the Dread Cruach. He was much more horrifying than she had expected. Even his horse was fearsome: unnaturally huge, as if built from the bones of some prehistoric behemoth, with cold dead eyes and foam-flecked lips. It stamped beneath him, restless and angry.

'Well, child?' came the voice from the darkness beneath the cowl. *'I claim what is mine: I claim my bride. I challenge you to combat to prove my right. Do you accept?'*

Bansi found her voice. 'Don't be stupid!' she said angrily, and a murmur – half alarmed, half amused – went up from the watchers. She felt Granny and Mrs Mullarkey moving closer to her, standing shoulder to shoulder in defiance, and their presence gave her strength. 'She's not yours,' she went on. 'She doesn't belong to you. She'd never have gone to you if you hadn't put spells on her. Anyway, fighting doesn't prove anything except who's bigger.'

Someone in the crowd made a jeering sound, but

she ignored it and continued to stare defiantly at her enemy. The horse, snorting, stamped one great hoof.

The Dread Cruach looked down at her, and although she could not see his face she felt the coldness of his stare. '*Mortal ways are not the ways of Faery. Accept my challenge, or I shall cut you down and take the woman.*'

'I see,' Bansi said, matching coldness with coldness. 'If I accept your challenge, you'll kill me and take Mum, but if I don't, you'll kill me and take Mum anyway. Is that it?'

'Typical Good People nonsense!' she heard Mrs Mullarkey mutter.

The horse snorted and stamped again, eager for battle. '*Face me in combat,*' its rider said, '*and your companions shall live. Refuse, and they too shall be cut down.*'

Bansi felt despair begin to well up within her; but her rage grew faster. 'You don't have a right to my mum! And you never will!' She looked around the circle, hoping for help; but she could see the crowd wanted a fight and would be satisfied with nothing else. 'If you beat me, it still doesn't prove anything, but—'

A voice interrupted her: 'Let me be your champion!'

She looked down to see Pogo standing there. 'What?' she said.

He looked at her with an expression that was both sorrowful and resolute. 'Let me be your champion,' he repeated. 'I'll take the challenge. I'll face him in combat. I've let you down enough tonight, Bansi; but I'm not going to let him kill you. I swore once to protect you with my life, and I'll do it.'

Bansi knelt and looked into the brownie's eyes. 'You haven't let me down,' she said. 'Not at all. And I'm not going to let you be killed for me.'

'Quite right,' Mrs Mullarkey said. 'I'll do it. At least I'm armed.' She hefted her handbag in one hand, and her catapult in the other.

'You will not!' Granny declared. 'If anyone's going to be my wee Bansi's champion, it'll be me!'

'Don't be ridiculous, Eileen!' Mrs Mullarkey snapped back. 'Sure, it's only by luck you've ever hit anything with that catapult. Bansi'll want a champion who can shoot straight!'

'Well, I like that, Nora!' Granny shot back. 'I hit them wee red men more than you did, that's for sure, only you claimed all my hits as your own! But you won't be able to do that if—'

'I'll do it,' Bansi said firmly, standing between them. 'If any of you try, he'll kill you and then he'll take Mum. But if I do it . . .'

'Then he'll kill *you* and take your mother,' Mrs

Mullarkey butted in. 'Don't be as daft as your grandma, girl.'

'He *might* kill me,' Bansi said. 'But of all of us, I've got the best chance.' Even as she said it, she felt slightly foolish; but now that she was out of the car, she could feel the power of Tir na n'Óg again – not flowing up through her feet as before, but blowing like a warm breeze from the mouth of the tube station. 'Maybe I . . . maybe I can use magic.'

Mrs Mullarkey grunted. 'All you've done with it so far, child, is set light to some kindling and guide us through a maze. That's not the same thing as defeating this kind of brute in battle.'

'All the same,' Bansi insisted, 'it's my only chance.' Struck by a thought, she reached into her pocket. 'What say you, Paddock?' she asked, pulling the globe out.

The toad stirred and opened its eyes.

'Magic which begets illusion
Plants deception, spreads confusion,' it said.
'Magic which can pierce the lie
Will prove the stronger, by and by.'

'It said that before,' Granny said anxiously. 'Do you think it's broken?'

'It's no more use than the wee talky box thing, that's for sure,' Mrs Mullarkey harrumphed.

But the toad continued:

'The slumber of the grave is deep.
The creature summoned from its hold
Finds resurrected bones too cold
And longs for death's eternal sleep.'

'Now what's *that* supposed to mean?' Mrs Mullarkey said in exasperation. 'Can you not tell us something useful, like, I don't know, tickle him under the arms and his head'll fall off, or something?'

But the toad was silent, its eyes once more closed as if asleep.

'Is it saying this Dread Crook fellow's some kind of a zombie?' Granny asked. 'But what's all the non-sense about sleep? Does it expect you to sing him a lullaby or something?'

The crowd was growing restless now, beginning to jeer and catcall impatiently. The Dread Cruach, by contrast, had been standing as still as a statue; but now his horse stamped its foot, once, and the ground trembled. A hush fell as the Dread Cruach spoke again:

'An answer, girl! I challenge you, by laws long established, to single combat: to prove my right to my

bride, and to end for all time your interference in my affairs. Do you accept the challenge?'

Bansi O'Hara glared at her foe. 'Your claim is false,' she said. 'Fighting me will *not* prove it.' She took a deep breath, squeezing her grandmother's hand for comfort as she passed her Paddock's globe for safekeeping. 'But I accept your challenge.'

A great roar went up from the crowd. The circle began to stretch out along the street as the spectators edged back to make room for the combat, and – with great reluctance – Granny and Pogo and Mrs Mullarkey retreated to where the boundary did not quite touch the car. Granny peered in through the window: Asha was still, somehow, fast asleep. The raven was nowhere to be seen.

The Dread Cruach walked his horse arrogantly around the makeshift arena, forcing the perimeter yet further back and stretching the crowd thin. One more full circuit he made, and then stopped, like a knight at one end of the lists.

'I wouldn't take your victory lap just yet, mister,' Granny muttered darkly, glaring at him. Her gaze switched to her granddaughter, standing alone and brave at the other end of the ellipse. 'Come on, Bansi,' she said quietly. 'You can do it.'

The Dread Cruach drew his great sword. The crowd stilled. The weapon flashed in the light of the flames, blazing like a great fire itself. Then he spurred his steed to action.

The horse's immense hooves pounded the road, faster and faster, louder and louder, deadlier and deadlier, as it bore down on Bansi O'Hara.

Chapter Forty-Eight

Bansi walked forward, slowly but resolutely, as the galloping horse drew nearer. Although his sword was drawn, it seemed to her that the Dread Cruach intended to run her down. She hoped she was ready; she hoped her idea would work.

In the crowd, Granny gasped and clenched her fists. Across the arena she could see the little men in red, tall on their horses, their mouths already twisted in smiles of ugly triumph. 'What're you doing, Bansi, love?' she said under her breath as the horse drew closer. Her granddaughter appeared to be doing nothing more than walking to meet her doom, one hand raised to her chest.

As the horse filled her vision Bansi leaped backwards and to one side, throwing out her hand and flinging the dust of the remainder of the crushed iron tablets into the great beast's muzzle. The creature neighed in alarm, its voice a ghastly, ghostly parody of a horse's cry. Its hooves clattered and skidded on the road as it turned in panic; the muscles and bones beneath the skin rippled and fought distortedly, as if twisted into a shape they were never meant to hold.

As the Dread Cruach fought to regain control, Bansi leaped forward again to smear the last sweat-stuck residue of powder from her hand onto the horse's flank. She cried out as she touched it. The beast was cold: a waxy, clammy cold that sucked at her flesh and entered her bones as if to feed upon the life within. But the horse cried out again, too, and sprang away from her as if burned.

Gasping for breath, clutching her hand, Bansi retreated to her end of the lists. She wiped the last specks of powder onto her jeans, and felt the power of Tir na n'Óg blowing upon her; and her hand began to warm again, and to return to life. Yet the horror of that cold dead touch stayed with her. Paddock's prophecy came into her head, with its words about the sleep of death, and the coldness of resurrected bones, and she thought she began to understand.

'Bansi!'

A shout came from the crowd, and she half turned, keeping one eye on the Dread Cruach, to see Pogo nearby, signalling frantically. She strained to hear what he was saying, catching only fragments above the hubbub of the excited crowd.

'... understand now ... horse ... old bones ... enchanted ...'

Before she could piece it together, there was another roar and she realized the Dread Cruach was once more on the attack. His horse was far from calm, but it was under control again and galloping furiously towards her. She had no iron powder left.

The blazing torchlight lining the lists caught her eye, and she remembered her second idea. Without meaning to, she fell into the rhythm of the pounding hoofbeats as she focused all her mind on the nearest flame and began to chant:

'Tyger, tyger, burning bright,
In the forests of the night,'

and this time she did not stop there, but continued:

'What immortal hand or eye
Could frame thy fearful symmetry?'

The hoofbeats again grew louder and closer and faster, and without thinking she kept pace as she repeated the rhyme:

'Tyger, tyger, burning bright, in the forests of the night
What immortal hand or eye could frame thy fearful symmetry?

Tyger, tyger, burning bright, in the forests of the night,
What immortal hand or eye could frame thy fearful symmetry?
Tyger, tyger, burning bright, in the forests . . .'

The Dread Cruach rushed onwards, closer and closer, but she felt the power of Tir na n'Óg flow through her; saw in her mind's eye that immortal hand shaping the lithe and deadly night-stalking predator; and suddenly a current of power ran through her body so strongly it made her tremble. An admiring murmur went up from the crowd as the flame erupted into the form of a great cat born of black shadow and orange fire. It leaped from the torch's blaze into her enemy's path, blocking his way, bringing the great ghostly horse up short to rear and kick in terror and fear. The firetiger crouched, sprang; the horse reared; the Dread Cruach slashed and parried, was driven back, forward, back again. Away from Bansi the firetiger harried her foe, pushing him further back up the lists, but each slash, each kick, tore flame from its body and threw it into the night, and Bansi could see now that it was fading, dwindling away. She had to think of something else.

Pogo was still yelling urgently at her, trying to get her to understand something. 'The horse,' she heard again, and something that sounded like, 'doesn't know it's dead . . . never really alive . . . just a heap of bones and magic . . .'

Understanding crept over her. Piecing it all together – Pogo's words, Paddock's prophecy, the shudderingly deathlike, vampiric feel of the horse's cold skin – she could picture the Dread Cruach animating a collection of ancient skeletal remains, enchanting them, maybe even drawing some poor dead animal-spirit from the underworld and pressing it into service as his steed. And as she thought this, some corner of her felt sorry for it.

She looked down the lists to where the last remains of her firetiger were still harassing the Dread Cruach and his monstrous, pitiful, tragic collection of bones and magic, and she thought of Paddock's words about the creature summoned from the grave who longs for death's eternal sleep, and of her granny's sarcastic suggestion – *Does it expect you to sing him a lullaby or something?* – and she thought, *Why not?*

Now the tiger was nothing but a few dancing flames, and the poor, ghastly, maddened horse was stamping them into the ground in an insane fury, with its rider coldly calming it and readying it for another attack.

As the Dread Cruach wheeled the horse round,

radiating palpable waves of hatred and anger and raising his sword high, Bansi was already walking steadily up the lists towards him, eyes fixed on the horse, singing the song with which her father had so often sung her to sleep:

'Hush, little baby, don't say a word,
Daddy's going to buy you a mockingbird.'

There were a few jeers from the crowd at this; but many of the onlookers were looking on with interest, having seen now that this would not be the easy victory they were expecting. Bansi sang on:

'If that mockingbird won't sing,
Daddy's going to buy you a diamond ring.
If that diamond ring is brass,
Daddy's going to buy you a looking glass.
If that looking glass gets broke,
Daddy's going to buy you a billy-goat.'

Waves of power washed from her as she sang. She walked on towards the horse, only half aware that the Dread Cruach was spurring it on towards her; not at all aware that its hooves were somehow less thunderous, its galloping less frantic and slowing by the second.

'If that billy-goat won't pull,
Daddy's going to buy you a cart and bull.
If that cart and bull falls over,
Daddy's going to buy you a dog named Rover.'

The beast was almost upon her now, but it had slowed to a walk, and then, as if hypnotized, to a standstill. Its head drooped, as if it were fighting sleep. The Dread Cruach kicked it viciously, commanding, *'On! On!'* in a voice that made the earth tremble and drowned out the sound of Bansi's singing, but she hardly noticed. She was aware only of the horse shaking its head suddenly and wildly and stamping the ground with one restless foot; and she felt its tiredness, and was sorry for it.

'If that dog named Rover won't bark,
Daddy's going to buy you a horse and cart.
And if that horse and cart falls down,
You'll still be the best little babe in town.'

The horse suddenly neighed with outrage, struggling against its crushing weariness. The Dread Cruach spurred it on. It shook his head again and leaped heavily forward, ready to ride Bansi down and grind her into the road. In the crowd, Granny let out a shriek and covered her eyes. The little men in red leaned forward eagerly, eyes bright and savage. A wave of murderous anticipation ran through the crowd, a barbaric murmur rising to a bloodthirsty roar.

But Bansi, almost in a trance herself, simply smiled and repeated the last couplet, slowing, as her father always did, to bring the song to a peaceful ending:

'If that horse and cart falls down,
You'll still be the best
little babe
in
town . . .'

Then the horse hit her.

Chapter Forty-Nine

There was no impact, no noise but a gentle *whoomph* of rushing air as the great horse struck her and, softly and almost silently, exploded.

All around her, gigantic bones whirled and wheeled, spinning upwards and outwards, and then downwards to rain on the road with a dull and musical clattering. None hit her. It was as if she was caught in a protective bubble of warmth, and drowsiness, and sympathy, and the firm, gentle unravelling of enchantment.

She turned to see the Dread Cruach, unseated, tumbling through the air with the last of the great bones. He fell loud and hard, with a discordant crash of armour against tarmac.

A hush descended.

The Dread Cruach rose slowly to his feet. His sword, still in his hand, blazed like fire.

An uneasy murmur ran through the crowd. The midnight-blue hood had been ripped from his head as he landed, and now all could see what was underneath. It was a mask: a horrifying mask, blood-red like his armour, with dark, sinister slits for eyes. It was smooth and plain like the helm of a medieval knight but, as the torchlight caught it, faces could be seen within: terrible, tortured faces that screamed without sound, that appeared and disappeared one after another as the flames flickered upon it. It was a mask that spoke of cruelty, and torment, and agonizing punishment, and promised that the face that lay beneath would be more dreadful yet.

The cruel dark slits of the Dread Cruach's mask turned towards Bansi, and he roared: a single, violent, deafening cry of overpowering rage that rattled the still, dead bones on the road around him.

'Now, child,' he snarled, in a voice that chilled all who heard it, *'you will feel the wrath of the Dread Cruach!'*

He raised his sword, and the light within it burned brighter until it seemed almost to be made of flame; and the flame danced on his blood-red armour until he became a dark ruby fire in the shape of a man.

And the flame grew. As if the very air around him was catching alight, the ruby blaze became brighter and bigger and stronger, swelling up until the Dread Cruach loomed over the street, a giant made of fire, towering over everything; and still he grew. His mask now was a mosaic of flames, and in each flame the face of a tormented soul wailed wordlessly, screamed without sound. His cloak was a great midnight-blue shadow that rippled out behind him and blotted out the stars. His immense sword flickered and flashed as he brandished it, and he swept it down towards Bansi, his voice echoing off the buildings as he hissed, *'Yield!'*

Bansi stepped back but, alone amongst all those there, she did not tremble. Paddock's repeated prophecy was in her head: the words about magic of illusion, and magic that pierced lies. And a feeling was growing within her, or flowing through her, that did not believe all she was seeing. It made no sense that this furious vengeful flaming giant should demand her surrender, when with one stamp of his enormous foot he could put an end to her for ever – if he was real; if he was all he seemed.

Unbidden, words swam up from some dark animal part of her mind, and they were the right words, and without hesitation, without stopping to think how she knew them or where she had heard them, she looked up into the great and terrible mask far above and said, quietly but firmly:

'Cast aside this dark disguise,
Let truest nature to my eyes
By no enchantment be concealed

Nor hid by any magic shield.'

The Dread Cruach's colossal sword trailed fire as he raised it to strike.

In the jostling crowd, Granny raised her catapult.

'Don't be daft, Eileen!' Mrs Mullarkey snapped. 'Look at the size of him! He won't even notice!'

'I've got to do something!' Granny retorted, taking aim. 'Bansi's just standing there! He'll kill her!'

Sparks flew as the fiery blade struck the ground, missing Bansi by a hand's-breadth. She did not flinch. Feeling the power flow through her like a warm stream, she focused it upon the Dread Cruach and repeated:

'Cast aside this dark disguise,
Let truest nature to my eyes
By no enchantment be concealed
Nor hid by any magic shield.'

Again the sword lifted, and this time the Dread Cruach looked set to bring it smashing down through Bansi's head. But she did not falter; the words flowed from her lips, over and over, and the power poured from her, and the flames flickered, halting and hesitating.

As if a tap had been turned or a switch tripped, the gigantic flaming figure vanished. Before her stood the Dread Cruach, terrible in his armour but no taller than a man. A rumble of approval ran through the crowd, but Bansi hardly noticed. She was caught in the magic's flow, swept along in its current, feeling it pour from her as she spoke on:

'Cast aside this dark disguise,
Let truest nature to my eyes
By no enchantment be concealed
Nor hid by any magic shield.'

The Dread Cruach hefted his sword menacingly and stepped towards her, but even as he did the air around him seemed to tremble. His cloak dissolved; his gleaming blood-red armour dulled and tarnished and turned from red to blue; his sword melted into mist; his mask faded and disappeared; and then it was no longer the Dread Cruach who stood there, but Hob Under-the-Hill in his iridescent coat of blue and green, staring in dismay.

The crowd rumbled discontentedly, caught between admiration for Bansi and anger at having been cowed by such a trick.

'Well!' Granny said. 'Who'd have thought it was him all the time?'

'What have I always told you, Eileen?' Mrs Mullarkey said imperiously. 'You can't trust them! Not a one!'

But Bansi had not finished yet. Still caught up in the flow of the magic, she pointed at Hob, the same words tumbling from her mouth:

'Cast aside this dark disguise,
Let truest nature to my eyes
By no enchantment be concealed
Nor hid by any magic shield.'

And now the last layers of disguise peeled away. The shimmers of peacock-blue and sea-green faded and dulled into a matt, grubby brown, holed and patched and frayed; Hob's tall, elegant frame shrank and hunched; his hair receded to nothing; his healthy complexion sallowed and dirtied; his forehead thickened and his eyelids retreated; and Hob Under-the-Hill stood revealed as nothing more than a skinny, cowering hobgoblin, scarcely taller than Bansi herself.

Bansi felt the stream of magic run its course, and she let it trickle from her.

'Now,' she said, stepping towards him. '*You* yield.'

Chapter Fifty

As Bansi advanced, Hob tried to scuttle away, tried to melt into the crowd; but the crowd wanted blood. They closed ranks against him to stop his escape, refusing to let him past, until he had no choice but to cringe on the ground before her and beg for mercy.

'Now could you do it, child,' a voice whispered in her ear, and she looked up to see, standing at the front of the pressing throng, a gaunt old woman with hollow cheeks and glittering eyes who leaned towards her conspiratorially. 'As you stripped away all his deceits and illusions, so too could you strip away his life.'

''Tis your right,' added a matronly, apple-cheeked woman nearby, grinning at her jovially. 'He challenged you; you conquered him. No one'd blame you for finishing the job.'

'You could stop his heart,' said a beautiful girl who stood between the other two and smiled a perfect, clear-skinned, film-star smile. 'I could teach you a pretty song to still its beating, and another to tear it from his chest.'

Bansi ignored them. 'Give in?' she asked. She folded her arms and stood over the cowering figure on the ground.

Bloodshot eyes unnaturally wide, Hob nodded his misshapen head frantically. 'I yield! I yield!' he whimpered, in a squeaky, grating voice quite unlike the sepulchral tones of the Dread Cruach. 'Have mercy!'

Bansi crouched down. 'You don't deserve mercy!' she said. 'You stole my mum! You made her forget who she is! You tried to trap her in Tir na n'Óg! *And* you tried to run me over with your horse!'

'Mercy!' Hob whimpered weakly, curling up small as if trying to hide himself from her.

'Promise,' Bansi said, leaning over him, 'never to come to the mortal world again. Promise never to kidnap, or threaten, or . . . or even *bother* any human being. Or any brownie, for that matter, or . . . well, or *anyone*. Promise!'

'I swear!' Hob squealed. 'I swear! Only have mercy!'

Bansi stood up; stepped back. 'Go on, then,' she said. 'Get out of here. And don't come back.'

There were dark mutterings from the crowd nearby; few of them were satisfied with Hob's humiliation. Remembering how his illusory form had terrified them, they wanted to see him suffer more than this, and many wanted blood. But Bansi, still aware of the power of Tir na n'Óg flowing around her, had their measure.

'I'm letting him go,' she said in a voice that carried, strong and clear, across the crowd. 'I beat him, fair and square, and now I'm letting him go. Does anyone have anything to say about that?'

She gazed around. None of the grumbling spectators would meet her eye. Slowly the crowd began to break up, returning only half-heartedly to the revelling that had clearly been interrupted earlier. And when she looked down, Hob had slipped away.

'Oh, now, what about you wee red fellows, eh?' Granny called out across the street, bustling over to rejoin Bansi. 'One of you wanted to be next, didn't you? Which one of you said you'd fight my wee Bansi for your old hearth rug?'

'Aye,' Mrs Mullarkey agreed. 'Rite of Combat, you said. Come on: who's first?'

From the further pavement, the little men glared at them in cold silence. At length one of them spoke, his voice hard and bitter.

'We renounce our claim to the cloak of Conn,' he said as though the words were being forced from him.

'But its rightful owner will not!' spat another after a moment. 'And when he comes to reclaim it, girl,' he added, glowering at Bansi, yet not quite meeting her eye, 'you will wish you had surrendered it to us.'

'We will leave now,' the third added frostily. 'But do not think you have heard the last of this.'

They wheeled their horses angrily and, spurring them through the crowd, galloped away into the mouth of the tube station and disappeared from view.

'Well!' Granny said. 'I've said it before, and I'll say it again: some people are just sore losers!'

'Aye, well,' grunted Mrs Mullarkey. 'I hope for their sakes it's the last we've seen of them; but I wouldn't put it past them wee hallions to come and have another go. Nor that Hob fellow, either. You'd better keep a close eye on your mother from now on, Bansi.'

Bansi felt her heart sink at the thought, but before she could answer, she realized that Pogo had scuttled up to perch on her shoulder.

'There'll be no worries on that score, missus,' he said. 'He challenged Bansi, to prove his claim by Rite of Combat, and he lost. He couldn't come back to bother Mrs O'Hara now even if he wanted to.'

Granny nodded. 'That's a mercy, at least,' she began; but she got no further before an anxious voice interrupted her.

'Bansi? What's . . . what are we doing out here so late? And who are all these . . . these . . . *people*?'

Bansi spun round. Her mother was standing with a look of frightened bewilderment on her face, gazing in utter incomprehension at the crowds of faery folk milling around her. She turned her gaze back towards her daughter, and the worry and puzzlement in her expression deepened. 'Eileen? What are you doing here? Shouldn't you be at home in Ballyfey? And Mrs Mullarkey? What was I . . . was that your car I was in? Why is there a bird hiding under one of the seats? I thought I heard it say something! And . . . and . . . *Bansi!* What on earth is that creature on your shoulder?'

Bansi's mind went blank. How could she possibly give an explanation that would make any sense to her mother? *Remember your friend Bob, Mum? He was really a wicked faery who wanted to marry you, so he hypnotized you by magic so you forgot who you were, and then he kidnapped you, and we rescued you but then he came after us disguised as a mighty and powerful faery lord and I had to fight him, and it's all got to do with people stretching Hallowe'en out for weeks till it leaks at the edges . . .*

Her mother would think she'd gone mad – or that one of them had, anyway. 'Mum . . .' she began, not having the first idea what she was going to say next;

but before she could think of anything, a great bell rang out. It was like the chime of a clock, yet unlike any clock Bansi had ever heard before; nor did she have any idea where the sound was coming from. Again it pealed, and again, and again. A stirring ran through the milling crowds and, as one, they turned and began to flow into the tube station.

'What's that?' she asked anxiously.

'Midnight,' Pogo said, and Bansi's mum stared to hear him speak. 'The land of Tir na n'Óg is calling its people back as Hallowe'en ends, before the morning of All Saints' Day dawns.'

Granny and Mrs Mullarkey looked at each other in puzzlement and alarm as Bansi exclaimed, 'Hallowe'en *ends*? But Hallowe'en's not for *weeks* yet . . . Pogo!' she said as understanding dawned. 'How long have we *been* in Tir na n'Óg?'

Bansi's mother looked in baffled worry from one face to another. 'We've been *where*?' she asked.

Bansi paled as another thought hit her. 'I'll explain, Mum,' she said, wondering how she ever would, 'but right now we've got to get home. Dad'll be worried sick!'

Chapter Fifty-One

'Worried sick' did not describe Fintan O'Hara's response when his wife and daughter, missing since he had returned from his conference, came back just after midnight on Hallowe'en night.

The moment the door opened he had leaped up from his lonely seat in the kitchen, red-eyed from sorrow and sleepless nights, and come running – not, as Bansi had expected, to clutch them both in relief, but to launch into the biggest and most frightening argument Bansi had ever witnessed between her parents.

'What do you mean, you didn't write it?' he was yelling, waving a piece of paper in her face. 'Do you not think I know my own wife's handwriting? And what are you doing back here, if this is the way you feel? *I haven't been happy for years,*' he read furiously. '*I'm leaving you . . . don't try to find me* . . . And who's this "someone else", answer me that!'

'There *isn't* anyone else!' Bansi's mum protested in tearful outrage. 'How can you even *think* that?'

'I can think it because you wrote it!'

Bansi stood as if paralysed, caught in the middle, wanting to help, knowing the truth but knowing it would not be believed. After all she had been through to rescue her mother and to bring her parents back together, it seemed so unfair that it should end like this; yet she could see no way out. Her dad was so enraged he could see nothing but the hurt that had been done to him; he was hardly even aware that his own mother was in the room instead of hundreds of miles away, or that his daughter was wearing the skin of a wolf and carrying a raven on her shoulder. Her mum, convinced of her own innocence and in utter confusion over the events that had led to this, was now almost as furious. Bansi had never seen either of them like this; she was sure neither of them had ever *been* like this; and now, having fought so hard to reunite her family, she was forced to stand helplessly and watch it fall apart.

She was dimly conscious of her granny's arm around her; had vaguely heard her say, 'Bansi, love, can you not *do* something?' – but what could she do? How could she ever convince either of them of what had happened?

And then, slowly, she became aware that Mrs Mullarkey's hand was on her shoulder, and that the old woman was saying something – *had* been saying something, quietly but clearly, for some minutes: the same words, over and over again; and though Bansi had never heard them before, they were slowly sinking into her mind, taking on a growing familiarity. Hesitantly at first, but more confident with each repetition, she joined in:

'If these shadows have offended,
Think but this, and all is mended,
That you have but slumbered here
While these visions did appear.'

Again she spoke the words, and again, and again, feeling herself grow calmer, feeling the power of Tir na n'Óg – fading as the dawn of All Saints' Day approached, but still strong enough to cast a gentle spell upon two mortal minds – flow through her. A longing for peace, and for sleep, and for all to be as it should between her parents, poured out in those words. And as she spoke, their shouting grew less furious, and, perhaps without knowing it, they moved to the kitchen table, and sat, and yawned, and gently laid down their heads upon their arms upon the hard wooden surface. And then they slept.

Bansi breathed deeply, a great sigh of effort and relief.

'Blimey!' the raven said. 'That was a bit of a row, and no mistake.'

'Do you think it'll be all right?' Granny asked. She laid a troubled hand on her son's curly head and stroked it tenderly, as if he were still a child. Then she took the offending note gently from his hand and hid it in her handbag.

''Course it will,' Pogo said gruffly as he emerged from hiding. 'I'm proud of you, Bansi O'Hara. There's none could've done better than you've done, this long night in Tir na n'Óg. You held strong; you rescued your mother; you've begun to learn to use your inheritance, and to use it well and wisely. And when I came to rescue you – well, it seems you rescued me instead. Once more, I'm in your debt.'

Mrs Mullarkey cleared her throat meaningfully and fixed her gaze on him.

'Oh, aye,' he muttered. 'I suppose you two daft old bats helped as well.'

'I'm sure we did,' said Granny archly. 'And thank you very much for noticing. But you're right, Mr Pogo: where we'd be without my wee Bansi, who knows.'

'Aye, well,' Mrs Mullarkey said. 'This is all well and good, but we'd better be out of here before Asha and Fintan wake up, or we'll have a devil of a time convincing them we just took it into our heads to cross the Irish Sea and pop in on them in the middle of the night. I suppose you'd like a lift, would you?' she added in the raven's direction.

The bird shuffled awkwardly from side to side on Bansi's shoulder. 'Um, yeah, great,' it said. 'Unless . . . maybe . . .' It hopped down onto the table and looked up. 'I don't suppose that, um, that rhyme about dark disguises and all might . . . you know . . . work on me?'

Bansi suddenly felt all eyes on her again. She smiled. 'I'll try,' she said.

And she did; for more than twenty minutes, feeling the power of Tir na n'Óg – weaker now, and growing weaker still – flow through her as she spoke. Yet the more she tried, the weaker the flow became – not just because the power was fading, but because, it seemed to her, some force was acting against her. Still she tried, until it became clear that her attempts were in vain, and she had to admit defeat.

In a dark chamber, somewhere in Tir na n'Óg, the faery who had once been Lord of the Dark Sidhe scowled to himself. For the second time since that mortal child had thwarted him, someone had challenged his power; and this time it had taken much greater force of will to repulse their efforts.

No matter. He had a feeling he knew exactly who

had dared to provoke him in this way. One day, sooner or later, he would have his revenge.

And then it was time to part. The goodbyes were long and – on the part of Bansi and her granny, at least – tearful, before Eileen O'Hara and Nora Mullarkey buckled themselves in and Bansi, with one last wave, closed the door.

'Well, Nora,' Granny said as her friend started the engine, 'I suppose we've a long old drive to get home, have we?'

The sat-nav binged. *'Turn right,'* it said. *'Drive nought point five kilometres. Then enter tube station.'*

'Enter the tube station?' Mrs Mullarkey protested. 'Do you think we can drive this car onto a train? Or is it back to Tir na n'Óg you're taking us?'

'Neither,' the sat-nav retorted.

'Ah, do as it says, Nora,' Granny said cheerfully. 'It's not been wrong yet, and maybe it knows a short-cut.'

'Exactly,' the sat-nav added; and had you been there, you might have been forgiven for imagining a note of smugness in its electronic voice. *'Drive nought point five kilometres, and enter tube station, to proceed to Ballyfey via the Knoll of Aphrodite.'*

'Well, now,' said Granny approvingly; 'that'll cut a good bit off the journey, and no mistake!'

'Might get me back to my tree before sunrise,' the raven added.

'And then I get my bottle of whishkey!' said another voice, from the back of the car. 'Wey-*hey*!'

Granny and Mrs Mullarkey barely had time to exchange a weary, eye-rolling glance before a second voice put in: '*Your* bottle o' whishkey, ish it? It'sh *my* bottle o' whishkey, ye . . . ye . . . ye . . . ye whishkey-thief, ye!'

Mrs Mullarkey shook her grey head wearily. 'Maybe it won't *take* so long to get home . . .' she said, over the sound of clumsy little punches and cries of 'Whoopsh!'

'But it's going to *feel* like days,' Granny agreed, just before the tube station swallowed them up and the dark green Morris Minor Traveller disappeared.

Back in her room, Bansi O'Hara tucked herself into bed.

'Pogo,' she said sleepily.

'Aye?' the little brownie answered.

'Will you still be here in the morning?'

Pogo shrugged. 'If I can. The ways to Tir na n'Óg are closing up now, and I must be gone before they do; but I'll stay with you until the last minute.'

'And when they do close . . . now that

Hallowe'en's been and gone, it'll be a while before the next time, won't it?'

Pogo paused uncomfortably. 'I'd like to say so,' he said at last. 'I'd like to say it'll be a good long time. But the truth is: just as mortal folk have stretched out the edges of Hallowe'en far beyond where they should be . . . well, I'd guess that tomorrow there'll be shops putting up their displays for Christmas.' He shook his shaggy head despondently. 'At this rate, there'll come a day when one border time bleeds into another, and that one into the next, and the good folk of Tir na n'Óg'll just be able to wander into the mortal world whenever they feel like it.' He sighed deeply. 'I don't suppose you wanted to hear that, did you?'

But Bansi O'Hara had not heard it, for – overcome by weariness – she was fast asleep. Pogo sighed once more, and reached out one small brown hand to stroke her hair gently.

'Goodnight, Bansi,' he whispered. 'Sleep well.'

Then, turning the light down low, he set to work tidying the room. The wolf-skin cloak he tucked away in its hiding place under the floorboards. The toad, in its glass globe, he set on Bansi's desk as if it were only a paperweight. And once the tidying was done, he turned the light off and sat in the darkness, watching over the sleeping girl.

In a few hours' time, Bansi's parents would

awaken. They would smile embarrassedly, wondering how they had come to fall asleep at the table, and each remembering fragments of a strange and disturbing dream. Then they would tiptoe together into Bansi's room and, unaware of the watchful brownie, kiss their sleeping daughter before stealing away to their own bed for the rest of the night.

And, for the rest of the night at least, the O'Hara household would be at peace.